The Christmas Inn

The Christmas Inn

A Novel

PAMELA KELLEY

ST. MARTIN'S
GRIFFIN
NEW YORK

First published in the United States by St. Martin's Griffin, an imprint of St. Martin's Publishing Group

THE CHRISTMAS INN. Copyright © 2024 by Pamela Kelley. All rights reserved. Printed in the United States of America. For information, address St. Martin's Publishing Group, 120 Broadway, New York, NY 10271.

www.stmartins.com

Design by Meryl Sussman Levavi

The Library of Congress Cataloging-in-Publication Data is available upon request.

ISBN 978-1-250-86163-4 (trade paperback)
ISBN 978-1-250-28361-0 (hardcover)
ISBN 978-1-250-28362-7 (ebook)

Our books may be purchased in bulk for promotional, educational, or business use. Please contact your local bookseller or the Macmillan Corporate and Premium Sales Department at 1-800-221-7945, extension 5442, or by email at MacmillanSpecialMarkets@macmillan.com.

First Edition: 2024

10 9 8 7 6 5 4 3 2 1

To Judith Campbell and Chris Stokes, the best neighbors ever.
Thank you for your friendship and support.
You both inspire me.

The Christmas Inn

CHAPTER ONE

Riley Sanders sipped a caramel latte as she walked back to her office. It was a little past three and all around her fat snowflakes swirled and danced on their way to the ground. The first snowfall of the year always gave her a thrill. It made her want to go home, curl up on the sofa, and watch a Hallmark Christmas movie.

But she couldn't do that tonight. She and Jack had dinner plans. They were going to their favorite neighborhood Italian restaurant, which was a good thing, because it was close to home. There was barely a dusting on the ground now, but it might get messy later.

Riley turned onto Madison Avenue and walked half a block to her building. She said hello to Gerry, at the security desk, and took the elevator to the fourth floor.

"Boost Marketing, please hold." Marissa, the normally bubbly front desk receptionist, paused when she saw Riley. "They're all in the conference room. Hank said to tell you to join them as soon as you returned." She looked serious, worried even.

Riley dropped her purse on her desk, then went to the conference room where the entire content team of eight people was gathered. In January, she had been promoted to a senior content manager role, which came with a nice raise. She'd loved the role so far, as her responsibilities were still writing related—and included writing content for their website, social media, email, and print. They were also expanded to managing a small team and working more directly with several of their top clients. Hank looked up and nodded when he saw her. He wasn't smiling. Hank normally always smiled. He was the director of the group and was one of the most upbeat managers Riley had ever worked for.

"Riley, come on in. You haven't missed anything." Hank cleared his throat. "Well, I'll just come right out and say it. I'm afraid I don't have good news. We're laying the content team off, effective immediately. Myself included."

The room was silent. Riley was in shock. She glanced around, and everyone looked equally confused. Finally Sheila, the most senior-level person on the team, spoke. "I don't understand. I thought the company was doing so well. We just landed two big accounts."

"The company is doing better than ever. But apparently we are replaceable," Hank said shortly.

Sheila's jaw dropped. "AI?"

Hank nodded. "Yes. Half of the copywriting team is being laid off as well. Those who remain will oversee all content work done by the AI tools."

"Terrible timing, so close to Christmas," someone else said. It was barely December and normally it was Riley's favorite time of year. This put a huge damper on things.

"Please feel free to use me as a reference," Hank said. "I'm hopeful that we'll all easily find new jobs. I don't think every company is embracing AI the same way. We still have plenty of value to offer."

They all went back to their desks and started packing up their belongings. Riley was just about done when her phone rang and she breathed a sigh of relief when she saw who it was. "Hi, Jack."

She was looking forward to their dinner even more now. After such unexpected news, she welcomed the chance to get out and vent about it.

"Hey, Riley, I can't talk long. I need to cancel for tonight. This case is a killer. I won't get out of here until nine or ten." Jack was a senior associate on the partner track at a big law firm. He was smart and very successful, but he worked long hours. It wasn't unusual for him to cancel last minute like this. Riley understood, though it was a disappointment.

"No worries. Another night." She didn't want to talk about the layoff over the phone, especially since her cubicle was in an open area where others could overhear. Even though she knew they'd be sympathetic, she valued her privacy.

"Definitely. How's tomorrow? I'll be out early and we can have a nice long dinner, anywhere you like."

Riley smiled. "Sounds good. I'll see you then."

All of her personal belongings fit easily into the cardboard box that had appeared on all their desks while they were in the conference room. Marissa nodded sadly as Riley said goodbye as she walked past the reception desk on her way out.

She sighed as she stepped into the elevator and pushed the button for the ground level. It didn't seem real yet. Thankfully, she had enough savings to tide her over until she landed something new. Riley wondered how easy it would actually be to find another job. She enjoyed her work, which was mostly writing company blogs, newsletters, white papers, website content, and social media posts. She hoped that Hank was right and there would be plenty of companies that would still hire people to do the work.

Her one-bedroom apartment was a fifteen-minute walk

from the office and she didn't even mind that it was cold and snowflakes kept falling on her face. Riley walked along in a daze. It didn't seem real that they'd all lost their jobs. It was just starting to sink in by the time she reached her apartment. She let herself in and dropped the box onto the kitchen table, hung her coat up, and rubbed her hands together to warm them.

"Meow!" Lily, her beautiful silver-and-brown Maine coon cat, hopped down from her favorite perch by the window that overlooked the busy street below and ambled over to say hello. She rubbed against Riley's leg, purring loudly. Riley bent down and scratched her behind her ears. Lily then threw herself onto the floor and rolled around so Riley could scratch her back and pet her belly. This was their daily routine. When Lily'd had enough, Riley fed her, then stared blankly at her empty refrigerator, wondering what to make herself for dinner.

She hadn't planned anything because she'd thought she was going out to eat. She found a can of pea soup in a cupboard, and while it heated on the stove, she toasted an English muffin and buttered it liberally. She ate in her small dining area and searched on her laptop for her resume. It had been five years since she'd last updated it. Riley sighed, dreading the start of a new job search. She felt numb with the shock and disappointment of the layoff. She'd finally earned her dream job only to have it snatched away too soon.

She stared at the old resume, which needed a major rewrite. She didn't have the energy to do that yet. She closed her laptop, and decided to deal with it all tomorrow. Tonight she was going to pretend that all was well and get lost in a cheerful Christmas movie.

She changed into comfy pajamas, made herself a cup of cinnamon tea, and settled on the sofa. Lily jumped up next to her and Riley picked up the remote as her cell phone rang. It was her sister. Which was odd, Amy almost never called Riley in the evening. They usually spoke in the morning, though it had been a few days since they'd talked.

"Hey, Amy, is everything okay?"

"It's Mom." Amy sounded stressed and a bit shaken. Not at all like her usual calm and annoyingly organized sister. "She broke her leg a few days ago. Is there any chance you could come home for a week or two? She won't ask you—but she really needs some help."

"What happened?"

"She fell off a ladder. She was trying to change the lightbulb in the foyer and lost her balance."

"Oh no. She's okay, though, otherwise?"

"She is. But she can't put any weight on it for at least a month. So, she's going to need help at the inn. I can help a little for a few days, but it's really impossible to do more than that with the girls—they need me at the same time Mom does."

Riley thought for a moment. "Lily and I can drive home tomorrow and stay for at least a few weeks, maybe longer."

"That's great. You can take that much time off work?"

Riley chuckled. "I can now." She told her sister about the layoff.

Amy sounded furious on her behalf. "That's just awful. Can they actually do that? It doesn't seem right."

"There's no law against it. I'm sure I'll be able to find something else. As Mom always says, everything happens for a reason."

"Well, I'm sorry it happened, but I'm so glad you can take the time to come home. It will be nice to hang out. It has been way too long." Riley had only made it home twice in the past year—at Christmas and for a long weekend over the Fourth of July. She'd meant to get back again but the weeks seemed to fly by.

"It really has. I can't wait to see the girls, too." Amy had twin girls that were four years old. Bethany and Emily were adorable and Riley looked forward to a reading session. The girls loved when Auntie Riley read to them. They'd snuggle together on the sofa, a girl on each side, and Riley would read book after book until the girls fell asleep.

She looked forward to seeing her sister in person, too. Amy was four years younger and they'd always been close. Though with Riley living in Manhattan and Amy and her family in Chatham, they didn't see each other often enough. And of course, Riley looked forward to seeing her mother, too. Her parents had divorced years ago, when Riley was twelve, and her father remarried a year later to someone less than half his age. Her father lived in Maine, and they didn't seem him often, maybe once a year, if that.

But they had a much closer relationship with their mother. After the divorce, it had felt like the three of them against the world. Her father hadn't worked steadily back then because of a back injury, so child support was minimal. Her mother had worked for two different restaurants, waitressing the lunch shift and often the dinner shift, too, to make enough to pay the mounting bills. She always managed, but there wasn't much left over.

When her grandparents on her mother's side passed, they left everything to her. It wasn't a fortune but it was enough that her mother was able to pay off her mortgage and buy a bed-and-breakfast that was walking distance to her home. That was about five years ago and her mother finally seemed happy and more relaxed.

Not that running the Chatham Coastal Inn was a relaxing job—it definitely had its stresses—but it was a different kind of stress. Her mother had explained that it was exciting to own the business and do everything her way. She'd always loved taking care of people and the guests enjoyed the extra attention to detail. There were only ten rooms, so it wasn't overwhelming. And she had help now to do the cleaning. She'd done it all herself at the beginning and that was definitely too much.

Riley called home as soon as she hung up with her sister. Her mother didn't mention the broken leg right away and Riley didn't want it to seem like Amy had called to ask her to go home. She wanted to have it come up in conversation so she could just offer to and her mother wouldn't feel that she'd been forced into it. Her mother always worried about being a burden, which was the furthest thing from the truth. So, instead Riley shared her news about the layoff.

"Oh, Riley, honey, I'm so sorry. I know how much you loved that job. And right before Christmas, too." Her mother sounded as disappointed as Riley felt and her supportive sympathy made Riley's eyes unexpectedly well up.

Riley took a deep breath. "The timing isn't the best," she agreed. "But I'm sure I'll find something else easily enough. I haven't taken any time off in ages, so I'm looking forward to a little break. I thought I might come and visit, if it's a good time?"

"Of course! It's always a good time to see my girls. Actually, I had a bit of an accident the other day." She told Riley about the fall and the broken leg.

"Oh no! Are you able to get around at all?"

"I'm on crutches. I can still get things done, I'm just slower. At least I have help for the cleaning. And Amy has popped over with the girls to visit. She's manned the front desk while I read to the girls. We're managing."

Riley smiled. Her mother always looked on the bright side even when things were challenging. "Well, I can help, too. I'll be looking for things to do to keep busy. I thought I'd head home tomorrow, if that works for you?"

"That's perfect. I'll see you then, honey."

Beth felt pensive as she ended the call with Riley. She was relieved that she hadn't had to ask Riley to help—she hated to do that as it wasn't like her daughter lived nearby. She didn't want to have her use vacation time to help out. She was excited to see her but also worried to hear about the layoff, especially at this time of year.

As she glanced at the clock, there was a knock at the door. It was exactly seven. She hollered for her best friend, Donna, to let herself in. Donna entered the room holding a big bag of takeout from their favorite Thai restaurant and a bottle of Pinot Noir.

"You didn't have to bring wine, too," Beth said as Donna set the bag on the counter and fished around in a drawer for a wine opener.

"We don't usually drink Pinot, but the guy at the wine shop said it goes well with Thai if you prefer red. So let's see." She poured them each a glass and Beth went to get up to help her with the food, but Donna shot her a look.

"Don't be silly. I've got this. I know where the paper plates are."

Beth laughed and sat back down as Donna handed her a glass of wine. She took a sip. It was smooth and light and a bit peppery. Donna returned a moment later with paper plates, napkins, and utensils and she put all the boxes of Thai food on the coffee table, within easy reach for Beth. They loaded their plates with pad Thai, spring rolls, and Massaman curry with rice. As they ate, Beth told her that Riley was coming the next day. Donna looked thrilled to hear it.

"That's awful about the layoff. But great timing. I'm glad she's able to come and stay for a while. We don't see enough of Riley these days."

That was true. Riley was busy with her job and boyfriend in Manhattan and made it home just a few times a year and usually just for a long weekend. It would be nice to have her around a bit longer.

"She doesn't seem worried about finding a new job, but it seems like a tough time of year for that," Beth said.

"If she's not worried, I wouldn't be. Riley is good at what she does. She'll find something soon enough. And it will be nice for you to have company this time of year especially."

Beth nodded. Donna was right about that. She was one of the few people that knew that Beth suffered from mild depression, mostly around the holidays. Every year, ever since her marriage ended a week before Christmas, Beth had struggled with the blues at what should be one of the happiest times of the year. She hid it well and forced herself to go all out for the holidays. It kept her busy and she'd created some wonderful memories with Riley and Amy.

Beth had always tried to make sure that the girls never had any idea that this was a tough time of year for her. The heaviness usually lifted a few weeks after the New Year. And over time, it seemed to lessen some. But it was still there. When she broke her leg so suddenly, it was all she could do not to give in to the self-pity and wallow in it for a few days. But of course, she couldn't do that.

"How's Bill?" she asked. Donna's husband was traveling for work this week. Donna was an attorney and had a thriving practice right on Main Street. Many years ago, Bill had been one of her clients and they'd been attracted instantly. Once her work was finished for him, he asked her out to dinner and that was it for them. They married six months later. Beth liked Bill. He was fun to be around and she often went out to dinner with the two of them.

"He's good. He's not crazy about the food in Louisiana, though. At least not the fried alligator. Says it does not taste like chicken!"

Beth laughed. "At least he tried it."

"True. Speaking of trying things—have you given any thought to putting a profile up and trying online dating? Don't you want someone fun like Bill to do things with?"

"I do. I'd love that," Beth said. "But I don't think I'm ready for online dating. I'm not sure I ever will be."

Donna sighed. "Well, I'm keeping an eye out for you as I always do. But you know all of our friends. I ask Bill all the time if he knows anyone but he says they are all married or people he wouldn't want his friend dating."

Beth smiled. "I appreciate that. I'm not even thinking about any of that right now . . . might be a little difficult to date at the moment anyway." She glanced at her leg, which was propped up on the ottoman. The cast was heavy and it itched occasionally. She couldn't wait to get it off. But until then, she knew she had to be careful so she didn't reinjure herself.

"True. It will be fun for you having Riley around at least. Do you two have anything planned?"

"Just the usual holiday things. It will be a huge help just having her with me at the inn during the day."

"And next weekend with the Christmas Stroll, I'm sure you'll be extra busy," Donna said.

Beth took a sip of her wine. "This is actually very good with the Thai food. We'll have to remember that." She took a bite of a spring roll. "I'm actually not as busy as I was last year at this time. I'm hoping Riley might have some marketing ideas for me."

Donna frowned. "You're not sold out for next weekend?"

"No. Not yet."

"Hmm. Well, hopefully you fill up at the last minute with people that couldn't get to the Nantucket Stroll the night before."

"Maybe. We'll see."

Donna looked at her quietly for a moment, then smiled and lifted her glass, tapping it lightly against Beth's. "Well, cheers to a happier holiday season than usual."

Beth grinned. She was looking forward to spending more time with her girls this year. "Cheers to that."

Riley got up early the next day and packed her biggest suitcase with a wide assortment of clothes—lots of layers as it was the time of year when the temperature in New England could be all over the place. She'd rented a car the night before. After breakfast she'd scoot back to her apartment, and as soon as her rental arrived, she'd grab her suitcase and Lily, and head to the Cape.

She met Jack at seven thirty sharp at their favorite bagel shop. She'd texted him the evening before to share the news about her mother and her trip to the Cape and suggested they meet for a quick breakfast before she left. He was there already when she walked in, which didn't surprise her. Jack was always early. He smiled, and she saw that he'd already ordered for both of them.

"Tall, black, no sugar, and an everything bagel toasted with chive cream cheese. How'd I do?" The flash of annoyance that he hadn't waited to see what she wanted faded when she realized that it was exactly what she would have ordered.

"Perfect, thanks."

"So, you're heading to the Cape today? The agency didn't mind a last-minute day off?" Jack asked.

Riley sighed and told him about the layoff.

His eyes radiated sympathy as she finished recounting the events of the day before. She noticed as usual that not one of his hairs was out of place. Jack was always dressed and groomed impeccably. Today's suit was black with pinstripes, a crisp white shirt, a charcoal-gray tie, and his thick, wavy black hair had just enough gel to give it a polished look and keep the waves under control.

"That's rough. It's not entirely surprising, though. We expect to see more of this now that AI can be used in so many ways. Have you thought about shifting gears a little and doing something slightly different, maybe more analytical or strategic? Something the AI can't easily take over?"

Riley nodded. "You're probably right. I thought I'd take some time to mull that over and see what other skills I have that might be a good complement to the writing. I'm looking forward to not thinking about it at all for a week or two and just helping out my mom and relaxing on the Cape."

Jack frowned. "Don't take too long. The sooner you get back out there the easier it will be to find something new. You know companies hate gaps on resumes." Riley knew he was right. She also knew Jack had never had a gap to worry about.

She smiled. "Of course. This tends to be a slow time of year for hiring. Lots of hires are put on hold until after the holidays. It always picks up in January."

Jack didn't look convinced. "It's still a good idea to get the ball rolling."

Riley felt a rush of annoyance. She hated when he lectured her—especially when she knew he was probably right. "I need to update my resume. That's the first step."

Jack checked his watch as it beeped with a new text message.

"I need to run. I have a client call in fifteen minutes. That was just my reminder alert. Text me when you get to the Cape safely."

Riley stood. "I will. Good luck with your case." She gave him a quick kiss goodbye and they walked out together, then turned in opposite directions as she headed back to her apartment.

Her rental car was delivered at ten, so she could avoid rush hour traffic. She quickly brought her suitcase and tote bag with cat food and her laptop down first and put it in the back of the small Honda SUV. Then she ran back upstairs for her purse and for Lily in her soft pink cat carrier. Lily was already not happy about the situation and was meowing in protest as Riley carried her downstairs and settled her onto the passenger seat. Riley climbed in, and turned on the ignition.

Riley's stress about the layoff eased up some as she stepped on the gas. In a few hours she'd be crossing the bridge to the Cape Cod Canal and that always brought a sense of peace, knowing that she was almost home. She was looking forward to relaxing and spending time with her mother and not thinking about her job search for at least a few days.

"Okay, Lily, we're off."

CHAPTER TWO

Riley crossed the bridge at the Cape Cod Canal a few minutes past four. She'd hit the beginning of rush hour traffic when she came through Providence, but it wasn't too bad. She relaxed as she glanced out the window at the ocean below and a barge making its way through the canal. She was almost there.

Forty minutes later she made it to Chatham and drove down Main Street. Chatham was one of those quaint small towns that looked like it belonged in a Hallmark movie. She drove by the renovated movie theater and cute shops, including her favorite bookshop. She passed by the Chatham Squire, a casual restaurant and bar where she'd spent many fun nights. She drove a little farther, turned to the left, and into the driveway of her childhood home. Her mother's car was in the driveway.

Riley parked and walked to the front door, holding Lily's carrier. She knocked lightly and her mother called for her to come on in.

She stepped inside and smiled when she saw her mother sitting in her favorite recliner with her leg up on an ottoman. She moved to get up.

"Stay where you are, Mom. Don't get up." Riley set Lily's carrier down and unlocked the door. Lily bolted out and stopped short when she didn't recognize her surroundings. "I'll get you some water in a minute, Lily."

Riley walked over to her mother and gave her a hug. She glanced at her mother's leg, which had a cast on it. "Does it hurt?"

Her mother shook her head. "Not anymore. It just itches now and then." She grinned. "I can handle that. It's so good to see you, honey. Thank you for coming."

"Of course! Lily and I would have just been moping around the apartment, looking at job listings. I'd much rather be here. What did the doctor say? How long will you have to wear the cast?"

"He said it's a clean break, so it should heal quickly as long as I don't overdo it. I'm supposed to keep my weight off it for at least a month, then he'll take another X-ray and maybe it can come off."

"What have you been doing about the inn?" Riley wondered how she'd been getting to and fro and how she was managing.

"I've had help, and your sister has done what she can. She's been great about driving me if I need to go somewhere. And filling in at the inn. But of course, I'm limited and can't do much more than sit at the front desk. Thankfully, Ethel has been in charge of cleaning the rooms since I took over the inn. I don't know what I'd do without her. She assured me that I won't have to worry about housekeeping."

"Oh, that's a relief." Riley could pitch in and help with the cleaning if she had to, but she'd never liked doing it.

"We're not too busy at the moment either. It's actually been slower than usual for the past six months or so. Two of the rooms need some repairs that I haven't rushed to do yet since we haven't been full in a while." That was surprising to hear.

Riley just nodded. "How are you managing with breakfast?" The inn was a bed-and-breakfast, and every morning her mother set out coffee, juice, an assortment of pastries, bagels and breads, cereals, and usually a hot dish of some kind, scrambled eggs or a quiche.

"That's been a little trickier to navigate. Ethel has helped me carry the coffee and food out from the inn's kitchen. And I've just heated up some store-bought quiches. Your sister did the grocery shopping for me." Her mother winced a little as she shifted position and looked exhausted just thinking about it all.

"Well, I can take over and help with all of that." Riley smiled. "I'm going to get Lily settled and then we can catch up."

"Perfect. I thought we could have a pizza delivered for supper, if that works for you? And there's a cold bottle of Chardonnay in the refrigerator. Your sister picked it up when she went shopping yesterday."

"That sounds good to me." Riley went to the kitchen and got two bowls out and filled one with cold water for Lily and put some of her favorite dry food in the other and set the bowls in a corner of the kitchen. Lily came running and ate as though she hadn't seen food in days. Riley found the wine, opened it, and poured two glasses while her mother ordered the pizza.

"So how did you manage to fall off a ladder?" Riley asked, once she was settled in a comfy leather armchair facing her mother. Her mother was in good health and in her mid-fifties. It wasn't like she was too old to use a ladder.

"I was startled by a knock at the door and lost my balance. It was just the mailman and he heard me scream when I fell. He called 911 and felt terrible thinking he'd caused me to fall. I told him it wasn't his fault, but it sort of was. Though, I should have been more focused."

"How's everything else going? You said business has been slow?"

Her mother nodded. "It's been off this past year. We're almost never full and if I'm more than half booked that's a good week. That's why I haven't rushed to make the repairs in those two rooms."

"Any idea why the slowdown?" Riley asked.

"There are two other bed-and-breakfasts that opened in the past few years. It was gradual at first, just a few off weeks here and there, but then it stayed steadily lower. I had to start cutting some expenses like the advertising I was doing. It dropped even more after that unfortunately. Though I suppose that's not too surprising. I used to wonder if the ads were worth it, but I guess they do help. I can't afford to turn them back on yet."

"You need things to pick up first."

"Yes. I'm watching what I spend very closely."

Riley sipped her wine and thought for a moment. "Paid ads are great, but it's not the only way to generate traffic. I can help you with some free stuff, like social media and blogging."

Her mother looked grateful but also a little confused. "I don't have a blog. Just a website."

"I can add the blog. I'll start posting a few times a week. Little articles that match things people might search for, like Chatham bed-and-breakfasts or inns. I can do some fun ones, too, like where to stay to see sharks in Chatham."

Her mother laughed. "You really think people search for that?"

"I do. You'd be surprised."

"The shark tours have become popular. Some of the guests have asked me about them," her mother said.

A few minutes later, the pizza was delivered and Riley got paper plates and napkins and put a few slices on a plate for her mother. It was their favorite, pepperoni with pineapple.

While they ate, Riley asked about Amy. "I can't wait to see

her and the girls. Do you really think she won't go back to work? I assumed she would once the girls were in school, but she said she likes being a stay-at-home mother. Said they ran the numbers and with twins, the math didn't make sense once they paid for daycare, not until they are in school full-time."

"Daycare is expensive. And Rob's job pays well enough that they can get by on one income."

"I suppose. But I would think she'd want to get out of the house and be around adults again. I couldn't imagine not working. Amy used to love her job and she was good at it," Riley said. Her sister had worked in finance. Riley never understood what she did but knew it had something to do with numbers.

"People's priorities change when they have a family," her mother said.

"Hmm." Riley got up for another slice of pizza and handed one to her mother as well.

"How are things with you and Jack?" her mother asked.

Riley smiled. "Good. I have fun when I see him. We were supposed to have dinner last night, but he had to cancel because of work. That happens a lot," she admitted.

"He's on the partner track at his law firm? How much longer will he have to work these long hours?" Her mother lifted her wineglass and took a sip. Riley could see the concern in her eyes. She knew her mother would like Jack as much as she did once she met him. But he hadn't been able to come to Chatham yet. Something had always come up.

"Not for a while," Riley said. "He still has a few more years before it will be his turn for partner consideration and the long hours will continue for a few more years after that. It's all about billable hours and profitability at the firm."

"That sounds exhausting," her mother said.

Riley agreed. It sounded horrible to her, too. "Jack loves

the work, though. I don't think he minds the hours because he knows it's working toward a goal and for the most part, he enjoys it."

Her mother nodded. "I suppose that does make sense. When I was waitressing all those double shifts I was just going through the motions. But once I opened the inn, the hours would sometimes be even longer, but I have never minded, because it's my business. And I love it."

"It's perfect for you, Mom." Riley had been thrilled when her mother bought the inn. It was hard work for sure, but she'd never seen her mother so happy. "I'll get started on the web marketing and that blog tomorrow. We'll see what we can do to get the inn fully booked again."

"Thanks, honey. Oh, I have a bit of news. Remember Aidan Shaw? He and his son are staying at the inn probably through the holidays."

Aidan Shaw?! "Why is Aidan staying there?" Even though it had been many years since she'd dated Aidan, her heart still fluttered a little at the mention of his name. Aidan had been her first love, and she'd written *Mrs. Aidan Shaw* over and over in her notebook. They'd started dating in tenth grade and during the summer before they both went away to college they had talked about getting engaged someday.

And that's where it all fell apart. Aidan had his future planned out. He was going to college at UMass Dartmouth, getting his CPA, and then he'd be moving back to Chatham and joining his father in his accounting business. He was excited about working with his father and someday taking over the business. And he loved working with numbers. He assumed that Riley would be part of that plan, too.

But, like many of her classmates, Riley was eager to cross the bridge and leave the Cape behind. Employment opportunities for college graduates were limited on Cape Cod, unless one had a family business or worked in the hospitality industry. Riley had always dreamed of living in the city, either Boston or New York, and doing something with writing and business. She didn't want to move home to Chatham after graduating.

So, sadly, they decided to break up then, before heading off to college. She'd run into Aidan a few times over the years and heard updates from friends. She wasn't entirely surprised when he married a local girl a year after getting his CPA. They had a child a year later, a boy. Riley guessed that he must be nine by now. She knew that Aidan's wife passed unexpectedly a few years ago, a tragic car accident. She'd thought about him now and then over the years and wondered how he was doing. They'd lost touch when she ended things and moved away from Chatham.

"How is he?" she asked.

"You know Aidan, he's always upbeat. His son, Luke, is adorable, looks like a mini-Aidan. He's a serious little thing. Always has his head in a book. I do feel for them both, though. I'm sure the holidays are bad enough without Nicole. This is only their third Christmas without her. But now they're stuck in a hotel during the holidays."

"Why are they here?" Riley asked.

"The two of them went away for the weekend and the hot water heater burst while they were gone. Flooded the whole first floor and it has to be completely cleaned out and renovated."

"Ugh. That sounds awful."

"It was a disaster. And those types of projects always take longer than anticipated. Aidan was hoping to be home by Christmas but it looks like it will be after the New Year now."

"That has to be hard for them. Maybe they can get a small tree in their room? You probably have them in the Johnson suite?" The Johnson suite was their biggest room—it was two bedrooms and a sitting area in the middle.

"They are, and I suggested that. There's definitely room for a tree. But Aidan won't hear of it. He said they are basically skipping Christmas this year. It surprised me because he's usually so cheery."

"Skipping Christmas!" That sounded extreme to Riley. "What about Luke?"

"He said Luke will still have plenty of Christmas presents, but he's not partaking in all the fuss. He told me that since Nicole passed, he has felt more Scrooge-like this time of year. He just wants it over with. I feel for him."

"I do, too." Riley loved all things Christmas. She couldn't imagine the amount of pain Aidan must be in to feel that way about the holiday. She smiled as an idea came to her. "We'll have to get an extra big tree in the inn's living room. Really go all-out this year with the decorations. If Aidan won't get a tree, then we will just bring one to him that everyone can enjoy."

Her mother's eyes lit up. "I like that idea, honey. Let's do it."

CHAPTER THREE

Riley and Lily slept soundly in Riley's old room. Her mother's house was a classic Cape Cod–style with gray wooden shingles along the side of the house. Riley's bedroom was on the top floor and had slanted ceilings and a small window that looked out over Main Street and in the distance, the ocean. It was a cozy room and it always felt good to be home.

She made her way downstairs, fed Lily, and made a pot of coffee. She'd just taken her first sip when her mother slowly came into the kitchen, on her crutches. Her hair was still damp from the shower. Riley got her a coffee and they sat at the kitchen table and split a blueberry muffin.

Her mother had two bites, and said she didn't want more. She'd never been a big eater at breakfast. Riley always woke up starving. She finished the muffin, refilled her mother's coffee mug, and took a quick shower while her mother read the paper.

"Do we need to cook anything?" Riley asked as they drove the short distance to the inn.

"No, your sister stocked the kitchen yesterday for us. We don't have to go grocery shopping for a few days. There's a quiche defrosting in the refrigerator. It's fully cooked, we just need to heat it up in the oven and set it on a hot plate to keep warm."

It was seven thirty when they pulled into the driveway and made their way inside. Breakfast service started at eight and went until ten. The inn was silent as they walked through the living room to the kitchen. The living room was lovely. Her mother had all the rooms painted when she bought it. It had a big gas fireplace and creamy white ceiling moldings. The walls were a deep cranberry shade and the rich color popped against the moldings. With the fire glowing merrily, it already felt ready for the holidays. All it needed was a green Christmas tree in the corner and a few other holiday decorations.

The kitchen was small but efficient and after insisting that her mother sit and prop her leg up on a stool, Riley got to work. She put the quiche in the oven to warm up and made two pots of coffee, one regular and one decaf, and put both in thermoses to stay warm. She also filled an electric teakettle so if anyone wanted hot water, it would be ready in a minute or two.

Breakfast was served in the adjoining dining room and Riley brought everything out to an antique wooden side table. In addition to the coffee and teakettle, she filled several carafes with milk, cream, and orange and cranberry juice, and set them in a tray of ice to keep cool. She cut up fresh cantaloupe and sliced strawberries and added them to a platter with blueberries. She brought out an assortment of cold cereals, bagels, and bread, as well as butter and cream cheese. There were also blueberry muffins. Her mother liked guests to have a choice of something healthy or more of a treat like the muffin. And she also liked to always have one hot item.

As soon as the quiche was ready, Riley put it on the heated warmer in the dining room. Her mother sat at the kitchen table, writing out checks and paying bills. She smiled when Riley returned to the kitchen.

"That's the last of them. Would you mind popping these in the mailbox so they go out with today's mail?" She handed

Riley a stack of stamped envelopes and she went to drop them in the mailbox at the door. On her way back to the kitchen, she paused at the sight of a familiar face coming down the stairs. It was Aidan, followed by a young boy that she assumed must be his son, Luke. Aidan stopped short when he saw her. Aidan had once been everything to her. It was surreal to see him again after so long. He looked the same and yet very different.

"Riley. This is a surprise. It's good to see you," he said warmly. He still had the same dark brown hair, brown eyes, and easy smile. Riley glanced at the boy beside him. He really was like a mini-Aidan.

"This must be Luke?"

"Yes!" Aidan turned to his son. "Luke, this is Riley. She's . . . an old friend. We went to school together."

"Cool. Dad, can I have a muffin?"

"Sure, buddy, help yourself." Luke ran ahead of them into the dining room.

Riley's mother had relocated to the dining room and was sitting at a corner table with her coffee and a slice of quiche. She looked pleased to see Riley and Aidan walk in together. Aidan said hello to her.

"You're welcome to join us," her mother invited. "The quiche is excellent. It's ham and cheese, from a local bakery."

"That sounds good to me." Aidan headed over to help himself to a slice and Riley did the same. Luke sat next to Riley's mother and the two of them were deep in conversation when Riley and Aidan joined them. Her mother always liked to eat her breakfast with the guests. They liked the attention and she enjoyed meeting everyone.

"My mother told me about the water heater breaking. I'm so sorry," Riley said.

Aidan cut into his quiche. "Thanks. The timing is pretty bad. Though I don't suppose there is a good time for this sort of thing. Hopefully they will get it resolved and cleaned up soon."

"How are your parents doing?" Riley wondered why Aidan and Luke didn't stay with them.

"They're good. They're in Arizona now. They moved there two years ago when my mother's arthritis got really bad. The warm, dry air is better for her."

"Did your father retire already?" Riley guessed he was only in his late fifties or maybe early sixties.

Aidan shook his head. "No. I'm taking over more of the business here, but he still works with his clients remotely. I miss having them around, but they still get back for a few weeks every summer. They sold their house and just stay with us now."

So, there was no house here for them to go to. Now it made sense why they'd chosen to stay at the inn. In the summer months, there were plenty of short-term rentals, but not in the winter.

"It definitely is warmer there. I bet they appreciate it this time of year," Riley said. There was a damp chill in the air that promised snow soon. It was in the forecast for later that day.

Aidan smiled. "They are liking it, though of course they miss seeing us as often. What brings you back here? Are you just visiting?" He glanced at Riley's mother's leg in its cast.

"I'm just back for a few weeks to help out and to enjoy the holidays. I also just got laid off unexpectedly," she admitted. "But the silver lining is that I don't have to rush back."

He frowned. "I'm sorry to hear that. Layoffs are rough anytime, but especially just before the holidays. I don't know why companies do that."

"I don't either. But if it was going to happen anyway, at least the timing worked out. I'm sure I'll find something after the holidays," she said cheerfully. She'd checked online and it seemed like there were plenty of job opportunities. She planned to update her resume over the next few days and start applying for positions. She knew hiring typically slowed this time of year, but she could still get the ball rolling and hopefully get something lined up for early January. She was looking forward to relaxing a bit and helping out her mother, but she was also anxious to get settled into a new job and back to her life in the city.

"Are you still in New York City?" Aidan asked.

"Yes. I live right in Manhattan."

There was a long moment of quiet before Aidan simply said, "Just like you always wanted." There was no edge to his tone, but Riley still felt a twinge of sadness.

"Where are you two off to today?" her mother asked.

"We're heading over to the house to check on progress and after that we're off to Hyannis to run some errands," Aidan said.

"Do you think you might be back later this afternoon? If so, I could use your help."

"Sure, we'll be back early afternoon. What do you need?"

"Would you mind giving us a hand getting a tree in here? Riley and I both have small cars and your truck would be perfect. If it's not too much trouble?"

Aidan didn't hesitate. "Of course. Just let me know where and when."

"Why don't you and Luke meet us at the tree lot at four? It's about a mile from here, in the church parking lot."

"I know the one you mean. We'll see you there."

"Dad, can we get a tree, too?" Luke asked hopefully.

But Aidan shook his head. "We don't have room, buddy. We'll have to enjoy the one in the lobby."

"You can hang a stocking by the fire here, honey," Riley's mother said.

Luke stared at the fireplace. "Okay. I wish we were going to be in our own house for Christmas. With our own tree!" He looked miserable and Riley didn't blame him. It couldn't be fun to be a kid stuck in a bed-and-breakfast over the holidays.

"You and me both," Aidan said. "We'll just have to make the best of it." He grinned. "Santa will still be able to find you."

That made Luke laugh. "Very funny, Dad. Are you ready to go?" Luke stood by his seat hopping from one leg to the other, anxious to get going.

Riley smiled. At nine, Luke clearly knew the truth about Santa. He was at that age where he wanted to be a grown-up but was still very much a kid.

Aidan took his last bite of quiche and swallowed the rest of his coffee in one sip. "Okay, let's go." He glanced at Riley and her mother. "I'll see you two at the tree lot at four."

Once Aidan and Luke left, the room felt oddly quiet. Riley took the empty dishes to the kitchen, rinsed them, and put them in the dishwasher. Once that was done, she topped off her coffee and her mother's as well.

"So, what did you think of Aidan? It's been a long time since you've seen him," Beth asked. Riley was unusually quiet and she wondered what was going through her daughter's mind.

Riley smiled. "He looked good and Luke is his spitting image. It was a little strange seeing him. I've run into him a few times over the years, but not in a long time. He looks exactly the same. Almost like time has stopped."

"Except for the wife and child," Beth said.

Riley laughed. "Right. It is so sad about his wife. How long has it been now?"

"Three years, I think. Luke seems to be doing well, though. I'm sure the holidays are hard for both of them. We'll have to make it as festive as possible. It might be good for both of them to be around people."

"It might be, actually. I imagine it must be lonely this time of year with just the two of them left in the house."

Beth thought the same. "Aidan doesn't seem very into the holiday but Luke, like all kids his age, is excited about it. I thought that asking for their help with the tree might be good for both of them."

Riley laughed. "I wondered about that request. I probably could have managed getting it onto the top of my car, using bungee cords or something."

"I wouldn't want to risk you scratching your rental. This will be easier. I suspect Luke might enjoy helping us decorate the tree. Can you get the decorations out of the basement before we leave?"

"Of course. I'll bring them right into the living room, so we are ready to go when the tree arrives. And we can make hot chocolate for after."

"Perfect," Beth agreed.

Riley pulled her laptop out of her tote bag and set it on the table. She opened it and they were both quiet for a few minutes as Riley checked email and was typing away on her keyboard. She paused for a moment and looked up with a smile. "The stroll starts next weekend, doesn't it?"

"Yes, it kicks off Friday night with a tree lighting downtown."

"And how many rooms do we have rented?"

"At the moment it's just Franny and Aidan and another couple that is checking out tomorrow. I have one more room booked for stroll weekend, but that leaves five available."

Riley bit her lower lip, thinking. Beth smiled as she watched her daughter trying to work out a solution to their lack of guests. After a long moment, she smiled and looked excited.

"I think I can get those rooms rented. Chatham's stroll isn't as well known as the Nantucket one. It also sells out and is more expensive to go there. I can get some blog posts up today and for the next few days and maybe we can offer some kind of special?"

"What did you have in mind? I've already dropped the rates as low as I can go," Beth said with concern.

Riley smiled big. "Yes, I've been thinking about that and I actually think we should raise the room rates in general, but especially for that weekend. If we position the inn as a bit more exclusive we can charge more and it could make it more in demand. We can price it a bit above the other inns in town, kind of reposition it. People often equate price with quality and in this case I think they are right."

"You do?" Beth wasn't sure about this idea at all. It worried her that if she raised prices, her bookings could decrease even further.

"Trust me, Mom. We can make some little tweaks that will add value. Now that I'm here, I can make the quiches from scratch, for instance, and the muffins, too. We could do a chocolate turndown service. That won't cost much, and people love it. All we have to do is leave a little chocolate for each person in the room."

"I like it when places leave chocolate," Beth agreed.

"And I thought for stroll weekend, we could experiment with having wine and cheese before the dinner hour in the living room or cookies and hot chocolate."

Beth liked that idea, too. "That could be interesting."

Riley's eyes lit up. "I love the concept. It will bring the guests together and everyone can enjoy the warmth of the fire and the beautiful tree all decorated for Christmas. By including these extras, we can bump our rates a bit. And after the holiday maybe we keep the wine and cheese going—depending on how people like it?"

"And then we could keep the rates up, too?" Beth asked.

Riley nodded. "Yes, exactly. I will post all over social media about the special stroll package. What do you think?"

"I think it's a great idea. I hope others do, too."

Riley grinned. "I think they will."

CHAPTER FOUR

"Promise me you'll stay in Chatham through the holidays."
Ella's eyes had been insistent. It was difficult for Franny
to refuse her sister anything, but especially when she was lit-
erally on her deathbed. Ella was seventy-eight, five years older
than Franny. Ella had lived in Chatham all her life. She'd lost
her husband, Victor, the year before, and in the past year, she
seemed to be fading. She had been battling skin cancer, which
had somehow spread from her nose to her neck, and she didn't
want to go through the traditional treatments of chemo and
radiation.

She'd called Franny when the hospice nurse said she only
had a week left. Franny had visited more often this past year,
staying for a week or two each time, and they spoke on the
phone every day, even if just for a few minutes. Franny knew
the end was coming but it was still so hard. She wasn't ready
to lose her sister. But she knew Ella was ready to go and to
be with her beloved Victor. They'd been married for over
fifty years. Franny hated the thought of staying in Ella's house
without Ella there. She nodded, though, and agreed, since it
was important to her sister. "Of course. I can do that."

"I don't think you should stay here, though," Ella said
softly.

That surprised Franny. She smiled and gave her sister's hand a gentle squeeze. "Where do you suggest I stay, then?"

"Well, of course you could stay here, but I don't think I could do it. I'd be too sad. And I don't want you to be sad, Franny. I've had a truly wonderful life, the very best. I want you to feel nothing but happiness when you think of me. I would stay at that bed-and-breakfast on Main Street—the Chatham Coastal Inn. The owner is a lovely woman. You'll like it there." She had sighed and closed her eyes for a moment. It was the most she'd said at once in a very long time and it had clearly taken a lot of energy that she didn't have.

Franny nodded. "I'll find it. But you're not going anywhere just yet. I'll see you in the morning."

Ella opened her eyes and Franny saw a twinkle of good humor there. "Maybe you will, maybe you won't. Good night, Franny. Love you." Her eyes drifted shut again and Franny stood. The hospice nurse entered the room and waited for Franny to leave so she could check on her sister.

"'Night, Ella. Love you, too," Franny said softly.

The hospice nurse let her know in the morning that Ella had passed peacefully in her sleep. It was a shock at first because Franny thought she would have at least a few more days with her sister, but she realized that Ella was ready to go. And she'd made it easy for Franny. Ella had already paid for her funeral and picked everything out, right down to the music she wanted—her instructions were for only happy music, nothing gloomy or sad. She really wanted people to celebrate her life.

And so they did. Ella had thought of everything and left a detailed list for Franny of who should be notified—she still had quite a few friends in town. Franny wrote an obituary and oversaw everything, from the wake to the funeral and the gathering after. The past few days had been a blur. Franny had taken her sister's suggestion and checked into the Chatham Coastal Inn.

Beth, the owner, was a lovely woman, as her sister had said. Franny felt her frustration as she'd hobbled over to the front desk on her crutches. Beth's daughter was helping, though she seemed to have her hands full with the two little girls that raced through the living room laughing.

Franny had settled into her room, which was on the second floor. It was very comfortable with a queen-size bed covered in a puffy cream-colored comforter with cranberry and navy accent pillows. There was a little nook to the side of the room that had a small table facing a bay window that looked out over the ocean and the busy street below. There was a plush armchair and ottoman that faced a wall-mounted television. And there was also a small refrigerator, microwave, and coffee maker. She could manage here quite nicely.

After a lobster roll for lunch at the Chatham Squire restaurant, Franny walked down Main Street until she reached the law office for her sister's attorney. They had an appointment to go over Ella's will and her estate paperwork. Franny wasn't looking forward to the meeting but knew as Ella's only remaining relative that it was a necessary step.

The law office was just past the bookshop that Franny had discovered on an earlier trip to visit her sister. Both she and her sister loved to read and Franny had spent a solid hour in the shop browsing the shelves and taking note of the staff recommendations. She'd picked up a few books and when she finished one, passed it along to her sister. Though that was on earlier visits, since more recently Ella didn't have the energy to read. Franny made a mental note to stop in the store after her meeting. If she was going to stay in town through the holidays, she would need a few more books.

She reached the law office and stepped inside. A young

woman at the front reception desk looked up and smiled when she saw Franny.

"Hello there. How can I help you?"

"I have a meeting with Jessica."

"Of course. Please have a seat and I'll let her know that you're here." She stood and walked out of the room as Franny settled into a leather chair and picked up a magazine from a side table. *Chatham Living by the Sea* was a thick magazine and Franny was impressed. It was full of gorgeous photography—beautiful homes and landscapes and articles that looked interesting. She loved looking at the pictures of home interiors. It had always fascinated her to see how people decorated their homes and gave her ideas she wanted to try. Maybe she would pick up a copy for herself at the bookshop. She was admiring a stunning all-white kitchen when the receptionist walked back into the room.

"Jess will be right out," she said as the phone rang and she reached for it.

A moment later, Jessica walked over. Franny had already met her at the wake and then again at the funeral. She was a stylish woman in her mid-fifties.

"Hi, Franny. It's nice to see you again. Let's go chat."

Franny stood and followed Jessica into her office and sat in the leather armchair in front of Jessica's desk. Once they were both seated, Jessica pulled a stack of papers out of a folder.

"Now, I am aware that as your sister's executor you already have a copy of her will and know that she left everything to you and a small amount to her favorite charity, the local animal shelter."

Franny nodded. She hadn't wanted to go over the will earlier but her sister had insisted. So they'd discussed it once. The only remaining relative was Franny. There was the Chatham house and a healthy bank account. Franny sighed. She didn't need her sister's money. She was fortunate that she was comfortable financially. She'd been a widow for almost ten years now and still oversaw the family business. After a year had passed she would consider selling her sister's house or possibly hold on to it and visit in the summers. She didn't have the energy to touch anything there just yet.

"Yes, Ella went over her wishes with me a year or so ago. I don't imagine anything has changed since then?"

Jessica smiled. "Well, the will itself is pretty much the same. But your sister left some letters for you, with instructions that you are to open them in order, one a week."

"What are they?" Franny couldn't imagine. Her sister hadn't mentioned anything about the letters.

"They are all sealed, so I haven't read them, but she told me that each one has some memories and something she'd like you to do. She said it's very important that you open them in order and that you don't skip ahead." She handed the stack of four letters to Franny. Franny looked at the creamy envelopes, the thick and heavy paper with her sister's delicate handwriting. She wondered what Ella had been thinking. It wasn't like her to be so mysterious. Franny was curious to open the first letter—to open all of them. But she would do as her sister requested and space them out. And she'd wait until she got back to the inn and could read the first letter in private. It would be like hearing her sister speak again and Franny wondered what she had to say that was so important.

"Thank you." She tucked the letters into her oversized purse. Jessica had a stack of paperwork for her to sign. It didn't take long, and twenty minutes later, she was done and Jessica walked her to the door.

"Don't hesitate to call if you have questions about anything." Her eyes were as warm as her smile and Franny appreciated it.

"Thank you, dear." Franny headed out and took her time strolling back to the inn. It was a warm day for the first week of December and there were quite a lot of people out and about. She popped into the bookshop and bought a copy of the *Chatham Living* magazine to read that evening. When she walked back into the inn, both Beth and her daughter Riley were sitting at the front desk. Beth had her leg up on a chair and was sipping a mug of tea while Riley typed on a computer. They both looked up when Franny stepped inside.

"Did you have a nice lunch?" Beth asked.

"I did. Can't go wrong with the lobster roll at the Squire."

Riley and Beth nodded in agreement.

She told them about her visit to the attorney's office. "All the paperwork is done now. But my sister wrote me a series of letters, four total, and I'm to open one a week." She smiled. "I haven't the foggiest idea what she was up to, but I am looking forward to reading that first letter. I'm going to head upstairs and make myself a cup of cinnamon tea and see what she has to say."

Riley looked intrigued. "How fun! I hope the letters are good news or that they bring you comfort. Please keep us posted."

"Yes, please do. You've made us curious now, too," Beth added.

Franny laughed. "I will."

She made her way to her room, heated up some water for tea, and once that was done, she settled in her comfy chair and opened the first letter.

> *My dearest Franny,*
> *If you're reading this, I've recently passed. Please try not to be too sad. Know that I am with Victor and Henry now and we all are with you, always. I got the*

idea to write these letters when Dr. Davis gave me the news that the cancer had spread and that I likely only had a few months. When that time drew near, I sat down and started writing.

There are things that I want to show you over the next few weeks. I want to share my Chatham with you, to show it to you through my eyes and to leave you with something really special. I can't share what that is just yet but when you get to the last letter, I think you will appreciate that I've kept the best for last.

So, the first thing I want you to do is one day this week, get yourself a hot cup of coffee to go and drive to the Chatham Light. Sit there and look out over the ocean, sipping your coffee, gazing at the beautiful lighthouse and remember when we were young and used to walk to the lighthouse, sit on the wooden bench, and dream of our futures. You still have many years ahead of you, Franny. Dream big and enjoy what life gives you.

Love,
Ella

Franny's eyes welled up and a single fat tear slid down her nose and landed in her lap. She laughed. "I'll do that, Ella. I'll go right now." It was still early afternoon and the sun was shining. Although plenty cold outside, it would be the warmest time of day to head to the beach.

CHAPTER FIVE

Franny headed downstairs and both Beth and Riley looked at her curiously. She'd only been upstairs for a few minutes. She walked over to them and sat for a quick moment.

"It seems like each week my sister will want me to visit some of our favorite places, to remind me why she loved it here so much—and why I used to, too. We both grew up here. I moved away to Albany, New York, when I married, and Ella stayed. My husband and I visited for at least a week or two most summers and often saw Ella and her husband on the holidays."

"Do you think she's hoping you'll move back to Chatham?" Beth asked.

"Possibly." The thought had definitely occurred to Franny. "I know she was hoping I might move here when my Tim passed. But we had an established business in Albany and I took over running it."

"Are you still involved in the business?" Riley sounded surprised.

Franny nodded. "I'm not as hands on as I once was. I've turned most of the responsibilities over to several managers who do a wonderful job. I pop in the office one day a week now and keep abreast of everything by email and Zoom. So,

I probably could move here at this point, if I wanted to. I'm not sure that I do, now that Ella is gone. I still have plenty of friends in Albany."

"Maybe you'll just want to come for longer stretches, like a month or two in the summer?" Beth suggested.

Franny smiled. "That is what I will most likely do. I'm not in any hurry to sell my sister's house and thought in a year or so, maybe I will feel more comfortable about staying there."

"Do you want a paper cup to take a coffee with you?" Riley asked.

"Oh, that would be lovely. Thank you." Franny had assumed she'd have to stop by a coffee shop.

Riley hopped up and returned a few minutes later with a big paper cup full of black coffee, the way Franny liked it. Franny said her goodbyes and headed out. She'd been using Ella's car since she'd arrived. It was a late-model navy-blue Mercedes sedan. And it felt bittersweet to drive it, as she thought of Ella every time she looked at it. Ella had always loved that car. Franny had to admit it was fun to drive. She'd always had more practical cars herself, Hondas or Nissans. She'd once thought luxury cars were a silly indulgence, but she understood now. It rode beautifully and the leather seats were so soft. Franny drove slowly down Main Street and headed toward the lighthouse.

A few minutes later, she reached it, and pulled into a parking spot. Even this time of year on a chilly December day, there was someone else there, too. A man sat in his car, sipping his coffee and reading the paper. Franny had brought her copy of *Chatham Living* magazine along. She'd read about half of it so far. But first she wanted to just sit and take in the view.

The lighthouse stood tall as it looked out over the water. The sun was shining brightly and it really was a beautiful day—chilly, but clear. Franny knew the history of the lighthouse—she and Ella had long been fascinated by it and looked it up one day. She knew that it had been there since 1808 and there had originally been two lighthouses, located east of this one. She also knew that it was now run by the Coast Guard and was one of the few remaining lighthouses in the country that was operated twenty-four hours a day.

Originally the lighthouses were set back two hundred feet from the bluff, but the seas shifted and erosion in the 1870s was so bad that they lost thirty feet of bluff each year. By 1877 there was only fifty feet of bluff left between the lighthouses and the ocean, and the decision was made to build two new ones farther back, at the current location. In 1923, the lighthouses were separated and one moved farther down the Cape to Nauset. Technology had changed so they could now tell the lights apart by the interval of the light's rotation.

She and Ella had ridden their bikes here so many times as children. They'd put coins in the public telescope, which gave an incredible view of the harbor, and they'd sit and dream about their futures. Ella had always wanted to be a journalist and she'd done it for a time, working at the *Cape Cod Times* as a junior reporter before she had their one child, Henry. He was born with cystic fibrosis and though he managed as best he could, attending college and working in finance, he still passed in his early thirties. Victor had encouraged Ella to go back to work then. Not because they needed the money, but because Ella needed something to focus on. She'd taken a part-time job at the local weekly paper, the *Cape Cod Chronicle,* and had loved it, working there until she was nearly seventy.

Franny thought back to her own dreams. She'd wanted to be a lawyer back then, but after falling in love with Tim, she'd settled for working in a law firm as a secretary and then a paralegal. She'd enjoyed the work and the hours. When she left the office at five, she knew that many of the junior attorneys would be there for the better part of the evening. Tim had encouraged her to go to law school if that was where her passion lay. But her interests had changed and she preferred the balance of work during the day and spending time with her husband in the evening.

They'd never had children and it had always been just the two of them. Franny loved to cook and though they both had enjoyed going out to dinner, her favorite memories were of the quiet evenings they spent together at home, talking about their day and enjoying a cocktail. Tim had been a businessman and built a small shop into a big department store and then multiple stores. Franny had never worked in the business until the year before Tim passed. She'd learned the ropes then, at his insistence. He'd always believed in her and wanted the business to continue, in her hands, when he passed.

And she found it all so interesting. There was a learning curve, of course, but Tim had hired good people who were patient with her, and over the many years of discussions over dinner, she had a good understanding of the business. One of the first things she did, after Tim passed, was to add an online store. Tim had resisted doing it, but Franny knew it was where the future was headed. They didn't put the entire store online, but they put the things that were unique to them—the custom clothing that could only be found at their stores.

Franny sipped her coffee and gazed out at the water, at the few boats in the distance, fishing boats probably this time of year. Fishing was year-round in Chatham. But everyone else pulled their boats out of the water for the winter and stored them safely indoors or trailered in their yard.

Franny loved Chatham, but she'd separated herself from it since she married. For Ella there was no other place on earth that she wanted to live. Occasionally over the years, she'd suggested that Franny move home, but the timing had never been right. And now that she was in a position where she could consider it, Ella was gone. Franny sighed. There was a sense of peace here, she'd always felt it; from the minute she crossed the Cape Cod Canal there was a feeling of coming home, and of a weight lifted.

She could definitely spend most of the summer here. Possibly as soon as next summer, which was only six months away. She'd have to see how she felt then, and if she could stay in Ella's house without Ella there. Ella had a lovely home. It wasn't large, but it was on the ocean, farther down Shore Road. When Victor bought the property, they'd just married and were living in his parents' home in a cottage on the grounds.

The house on the property had been tiny and falling down, an old shack. The land was worth far more than the house. Tim had removed it and built a new one and it was Ella's dream house, with big windows, three bedrooms, and a screened-in porch where they ate their dinner most nights.

Franny's coffee grew cold as she sat there remembering and forgetting to drink it. Finally, after about an hour, she decided to move on and head home. Ella would be pleased as Franny's trip down memory lane had accomplished what Ella had intended. Franny was more open to moving home to Chatham—at least for the summer. She was even more curious about the rest of the letters now.

CHAPTER SIX

Riley and her mother set out for the Christmas tree lot at a quarter to four. Riley didn't think it would take them long to pick out a tree. And she wanted to make sure it wasn't too much for her mother. But she was getting around a little better now on her crutches.

The lot was less than five minutes away and there wasn't much traffic this time of year in Chatham. It was Saturday, though, so the lot was busy. Several other families were roaming the aisles to pick out the perfect tree.

"Did you have any particular kind in mind?" Riley asked as they looked around at the selection.

"Just something pretty and a little taller than we normally would get for the house. The ceiling is almost twelve feet in the living room at the inn."

Riley had forgotten that they'd probably want a tree at home, too. "I wonder if Aidan has room in his truck for two trees?"

"He definitely does."

Riley turned and laughed. Both Aidan and Luke had walked up behind them.

"Can I help pick out the tree?" Luke asked.

"Of course you can. We need a nice big one," her mother said.

They set off to the back row where the taller trees stood. There was a good selection and Riley thought any one of them would be fine. She looked at Luke, who was going from tree to tree and examining them closely.

"What do you think, Luke?" she asked.

"I think this one," he said decisively. It was the tallest, thickest one.

"Looks good to me. What do you think, Mom?"

Her mother's eyes twinkled as she appeared to consider the question carefully. "I think it will do just fine. It's a magnificent tree. Well done, Luke!"

He helped them pick out a smaller tree for her mother's house as well, and Aidan secured them both in the back of his truck. They dropped off her mother's tree first. While Aidan and Luke brought the tree inside, Riley went into the attic and found the tree stand and bag of ornaments. Aidan helped her to secure the tree in the stand and then they set off for the inn.

Once the big tree was in its stand in the corner of the living room, Riley opened the boxes of ornaments and silvery garlands. Her mother rested with her leg up, while Riley, Aidan, and Luke hung the ornaments and arranged the garland on the branches. Franny came downstairs when they were halfway done and Riley invited her to join them. She turned the television on and put it on the Pandora station and selected Christmas music.

It was fun and festive listening to the familiar carols as they decorated the tree. Luke and Franny seemed to be enjoying themselves immensely. Riley noticed that Aidan was quieter and she wondered what was going through his mind. He looked somber but smiled cheerfully when she caught his eye and she wasn't sure if she'd imagined it. Her mother looked relaxed but had a similar pensive look as she watched them. As if her thoughts were a million miles away.

Riley had noticed her mother's mood shift this time of year before. She'd asked her once or twice over the years if something was bothering her and her mother had always smiled cheerfully, just like Aidan was doing, and said everything was perfectly fine, that she was just tired or thinking of her to-do list for the next day. She wouldn't blame her mother for feeling a little down this year, though. It had to be annoying to be slowed down by a broken leg.

Once all the ornaments were on, Aidan helped her string the lights from the top of the tree. He got out the dreaded ladder that her mother had fallen off of and carefully climbed to the top. He placed their golden star on the tip-top then swirled the lights around the tree. Riley connected another string for the bottom half and when they gave the word, Luke plugged the lights in and they all stood back and admired the tree with its twinkling white lights and glittering ornaments. It was beautiful.

"Who's ready for some hot chocolate?" Riley asked.

"I am!" Luke said.

"I can't say no to hot chocolate," Franny said. She was smiling and seemed happier and lighter today, for the first time since her sister passed. Riley was glad to see it.

Aidan, meanwhile, was still staring silently at the tree. "Aidan, do you want hot chocolate?" Riley asked.

"Sure, why not." He turned her way and smiled and Riley felt a warm glow. Aidan's smile had always had that effect on her, but it was unexpected and unnerved her a bit.

"Mom, I know you're having some," she said quickly.

Her mother laughed. "Of course."

Riley set off to the kitchen and quickly made up five mugs of cocoa topped with mini-marshmallows. Aidan helped her to carry them out to the living room.

As they sipped their hot chocolate, the stately grandfather

clock in the hallway chimed that it was six o'clock. The time had gone by quickly.

Riley's mother looked around the room gratefully. "I really do appreciate all of your help. If you don't have dinner plans, I'd love to have you all join me. I took out a big container of frozen meatballs and sauce this morning that Riley and I were planning to heat up for supper. There's more than enough for all of us. If you don't mind spaghetti and meatballs, that is—nothing too fancy."

"I love spaghetti and meatballs! Can we go, Dad?" Luke asked excitedly.

"Sure. If you're certain it's no trouble?" Aidan said.

"None at all. Riley and I would be eating meatballs all week otherwise." She looked at Franny, who hadn't said anything yet. "Franny, please say you'll join us. We'd love to have you."

"Thank you, dear. I do enjoy a good meatball. What can I bring?"

"Not a thing. Our house is about a half mile down the road. Why don't you all plan on six thirty? That will give us time to get home and get some pasta cooking."

They all agreed to meet in a half hour and Riley and her mother headed home to get ready.

As soon as they got home, Riley put a pot of water on the stove to heat up for the spaghetti and poured the containers of meatballs and sauce into another pot to warm up. She set out a loaf of bread and butter and set the dining room table. Once the water reached a boil, she added a big pinch of salt and the spaghetti. Ten minutes later the pasta was ready and she drained it and put it back in the pot to keep warm.

Meanwhile, her mother insisted on helping and managed to

open a bottle of red wine and got some wineglasses out of the cupboard. She poured two glasses and handed one to Riley.

"It worked out well, today, I think," her mother said as she lifted her glass.

The wine was a Cabernet, Daou, which was one of Riley's favorites. Riley took a quick sip. "It did. We got the tree in and decorated in no time with everyone helping."

"Luke was cute. Maybe after dinner, he might want to help us get ours all decorated, too. It's a smaller tree and should go even quicker," her mother suggested.

Riley loved the idea. "Franny seemed to enjoy it, too. I'm glad she's coming."

They both turned at the sound of a knock at the door. Riley opened it and saw Aidan, Luke, and Franny standing there. Franny handed her a bottle of wine. "The boys were kind enough to offer me a ride. I picked this up earlier and thought the two of you might enjoy it."

Riley took the bottle and saw that it was a very good Cabernet. "You didn't have to do that. But thank you."

Luke handed her a white paper bag with a heavy box inside. "We brought chocolate. It's from the candy place down the street. Dad and I stopped there on our way home from Hyannis."

Aidan grinned. "We stocked up. Luke and I like our chocolate. I thought it might be good for dessert."

"Thank you, both. I'm sure it will be. Come on in, everything is ready."

They followed her inside and Riley set the wine and chocolate on the counter. "We just opened a bottle of wine, would you both like some?" she offered. "And Luke, we have milk or orange juice or water."

Luke wanted milk and Franny and Aidan both said yes to

wine. Riley poured for all of them and then made plates of spaghetti and meatballs for everyone and brought them to the table. Her mother had found the cheese shaker and set that on the table as well.

"There's plenty more, so feel free to help yourself to seconds," her mother said.

They chatted easily over dinner and everyone agreed that Riley's mother's meatballs were fantastic. They sat around the table for well over an hour, eating and enjoying the wine. Riley opened the bottle that Franny had brought and they all enjoyed a second glass. The first wine was good, but this one was bigger and richer. And after Riley cleared the plates and set out the chocolate, they agreed that it went really well with that, too.

There was an assortment of chocolates, a few pieces of milk chocolate, but most of it was squares of dark chocolate, which Riley preferred, and some pieces had almonds. It was smooth and creamy and made right in the shop. Riley loved going into the Chatham Candy Manor—the minute you stepped inside, the sweet smell of sugar and chocolate wafted over you.

"How was your trip to the lighthouse?" Riley asked Franny.

Franny explained to Aidan and Luke about her sister's letters first and then answered the question. "It was lovely. My sister, Ella, and I used to spend a lot of time there when we were children. I looked out over Chatham Harbor as I sipped my coffee and watched the fishing boats in the distance and I remembered our happy times together and the dreams we had. As I'm sure my sister intended, it reminded me of what a special place Chatham is." She looked at Luke. "Did you know that there used to be two lighthouses there?"

He looked skeptical. "There were?"

"There were." She briefly explained about the history of the lighthouse and that one of them was moved to Nauset.

"We should take a drive over there soon, buddy. It's been a long time and they have those cool telescopes you can look through," Aidan said.

"They do? When can we go?"

Aidan laughed. "Maybe tomorrow. Is that soon enough?"

"Okay."

"Looks like tomorrow will be another clear day, it'll be good for watching the harbor. Maybe you'll see a seal. They like to sun on the rocks," Franny said.

"Do you want to come with us, Riley?" Luke surprised her by asking.

"Oh, I'd love to, but we have company tomorrow. My sister and her family are coming for Sunday dinner."

Her mother looked thoughtful. "They're not coming until early afternoon," she said. "If Aidan and Luke are going to the lighthouse before that, you could join them."

"We could go anytime, maybe after breakfast, say ten or so?" Aidan said.

"Sure, that could work. Unless my mother needs me?" Riley glanced at her mother, who shook her head.

"Go and have fun. I will be fine by myself for a while."

And so it was decided. Riley thought it sounded fun and she hadn't really talked to Aidan in years. It would be interesting to catch up with him more. She noticed that Luke was beginning to look bored and was fidgeting in his seat. She glanced her mother's way and she seemed to be noticing it, too.

"Luke, do you have any energy left to decorate another tree?" her mother asked.

That got his attention fast. "Yes, the one we got today? Where is it?"

"That's the one. It's in the living room and the bag of decorations is right next to it."

They all headed into the living room with their wine and while her mother relaxed in her chair and watched, the rest of them worked together to decorate the tree. It didn't take long at all and a half hour later, it looked just as beautiful as the one in the inn.

"Well, we should probably get going," Aidan said as Luke yawned for a second time. Everyone was feeling full and tired. They said their goodbyes and Riley walked them all to the door.

"This was a lovely night. Thank you both," Franny said.

"It was fun, thank you," Aidan agreed.

"It was our pleasure," Riley said. "Thanks so much for helping us with the trees. We really appreciate it."

She watched them go and closed the door feeling suddenly exhausted and ready for bed herself. It had been a fun time and she was glad to see her mother enjoying herself and forgetting about her leg for a while.

CHAPTER SEVEN

Riley helped her mother with breakfast the next morning at the inn and Aidan and Luke didn't come down until almost nine thirty. They both made big bowls of Raisin Bran cereal and joined Riley and her mother at their table. Riley was sipping her second cup of coffee and her mother was stirring milk into her tea.

"We both slept in today," Aidan said as they sat down.

"That was so fun decorating the trees," Luke said. "The one here is the biggest tree I've ever seen." He sounded so impressed that Riley and her mother both laughed.

"When Riley was little, she and her sister used to crawl behind the Christmas tree and stay there for hours. There's even more room behind this one," her mother said.

"We used to love it there," Riley confirmed. "It was like our secret Christmas hideaway. I used to go by myself sometimes and read a book and look up at the lights now and then. It's a magical place." Riley hadn't thought of it in years, but she and Amy had both loved to snuggle up behind the tree.

Luke looked excited by the idea of it. "Dad, can I go behind the tree? That sounds awesome."

"Sure, buddy. Not now, though. We're heading out to the lighthouse as soon as we finish breakfast."

When they finished eating, Riley cleared the dishes and put them in the dishwasher. Her mother winced a little when she stood to head into the reception area.

"Mom, are you okay? I don't have to go, I can stay and man the front desk."

Her mother shook her head. "It's nothing. I just get stiff when I get up after sitting for too long. It's all part of the healing process. I'll just bring my tea to the front desk, prop my leg up, and read my book. It is never busy on a Sunday. I'll be fine."

"Okay, I'm sure we won't be gone long."

"Take your time. I'll see you when I see you."

Riley brought her mother's tea to the front desk and waited until she was settled and comfortable before they left for the lighthouse.

Aidan drove and they all hopped into the front seat of his truck. Luke sat in the middle. A few minutes later they pulled up to the lighthouse and park. Luke ran to the pay telescopes and Aidan and Riley both laughed at his enthusiasm.

"I often wish I had half his energy," Aidan admitted.

When they reached the telescopes, Aidan put some coins into both of them. He let Luke use one and he and Riley took turns with the other. There was a gorgeous view of the harbor without the telescopes, but with them, everything seemed so much closer and clearer.

"Luke, there are two seals sunning themselves. Do you see them?" Riley said.

"Seals? Where?"

"On the rocks. You have to look closely as they blend in."

"I see them! That is so cool."

After they'd had their fill of looking through the telescopes, they decided to walk down to the beach. Even though it was a cold December day, there were quite a few other people out walking on the beach and several dogs, too.

"Dad, how fast do you think I can go to the end of the beach and back?" Luke asked.

Aidan laughed. "I don't know but I bet you're pretty fast. I can time you if you want."

Luke's eyes lit up. "Yeah, time me. Okay, see ya!" He bolted off, running as fast as he could.

"I see what you mean about his energy." Riley smiled as they watched Luke racing along the water's edge, where the sand was flat but not too wet. "How is he doing since your wife passed?"

Aidan sighed. "Honestly, he seems to be handling it better than I have. It's been a struggle for me and it seems to hit me harder this time of year. We lost her in early December, three years ago, so as you can imagine, that first Christmas was brutal for both of us. Luke still misses her, like I do, but he seems to be doing well. He's a kid and Christmas just makes him happy. I have to keep reminding myself of that."

Riley felt for him. "My parents got divorced just before Christmas. It was years ago, and my mother has never said anything, but I think the holidays are hard for her still, at times. She never lets it show, though, when she's around us."

Aidan nodded. "I try to keep that in mind and force myself to be full of Christmas cheer for Luke's sake. I don't always manage it, but I do try."

"He seems like a happy, well-adjusted kid. I think you're doing a great job," Riley said.

Aidan looked her way, appreciation in his eyes. "Thank you. I'm sure your mom is happy to have you here this year. Though it stinks that you lost your job. How is the job market for what you do? I don't think I actually know what you do?"

Riley laughed. "I was a senior content manager for a marketing agency. I wrote mostly, blog articles, white papers, website copy. It was a fun job." She explained how her team was affected by the company's decision to use AI instead.

Aidan frowned. "That's rough. I'm sorry. But they're the exception, I would imagine? Most companies aren't using AI that extensively yet?"

"I don't think so. There should still be plenty of jobs, but things are changing and I am considering moving into a job that uses other skills as well as writing. That might be safer long-term."

"Will you wait until after the holidays to start looking? I don't imagine there's much hiring going on right now?"

"It definitely slows, but I am going to update my resume today and start applying for some jobs online. I got my last job in December and I think there's actually less competition then as most people wait until after the New Year to even apply. And my old manager told me they were under the gun to fill the job in December or they would lose the headcount totally."

Aidan shook his head. "That seems crazy, but typical corporate behavior."

Riley laughed. "So true. I don't expect that much will happen this month but at least I'll feel like I'm doing something. There usually are a lot more jobs that open up after the New Year."

"And you're just looking in New York City?" Aidan asked.

Riley nodded. "Yes. That's where home is for me."

They were both quiet for a few minutes as they walked. Until Aidan spoke again.

"And you love it there? You always wanted to live in Manhattan. I'm sure you have a boyfriend?" He asked casually, but his eyes were distant and Riley felt a flash of sadness that took her back to high school when they'd had a similar conversation. She'd tried to explain how she needed to spread her wings and move off the Cape. She'd always dreamed of living in a big city. And New York City was the biggest on the East Coast. Yet, it was just a day trip away from the Cape, six hours or so, depending on what traffic was like.

"Yes, I have a boyfriend. Jack and I have been dating for a few years. He's an attorney at a big law firm and works long hours, so I don't get to see him as often as I'd like, but we make it work."

"I've heard that people on the partner track work a lot of overtime. Is it as bad as they say?"

Riley laughed. "It's worse. Jack actually keeps an air mattress in his office and has used it many times when he needs to pull an all-nighter for a big case. He often has to cancel plans last minute because of work. It's frustrating, but I'm used to it now."

Aidan frowned but didn't say anything. Riley realized it probably didn't sound so great.

"It won't be forever, just a few more years until he makes partner. And then probably a few more years after that. But it will slow down, eventually."

"Even if I didn't have Luke, I don't think I could work those kinds of hours. That's pretty intense. I work hard and go in early, but I like my nights and weekends off."

"I do, too," Riley said. "I couldn't do it either."

Luke came racing toward them, sending a spray of sand behind him as he ran. He stopped short in front of Aidan and was out of breath. "How'd I do? I think that was my fastest ever."

Aidan's face fell. "Shoot, I'm sorry, buddy. I forgot to check the time when you took off. It was super fast, though. I'm sure it was your best ever."

Luke grinned. He didn't seem to care that Aidan forgot to time him. He was just basking in the compliment of having his best time ever. Riley realized she'd probably distracted Aidan from checking the time. But it didn't seem to matter. The two of them were very cute and had a tight bond. It didn't surprise her that Aidan was a good father. He'd always been caring and thoughtful.

"Are you about ready to head back? I think you have a book report due tomorrow and you still need to finish the book?" Aidan asked.

"I do. Maybe I can read the book behind the tree? Like Riley used to do?" Luke suggested.

"That's fine by me if it helps you finish the book," Aidan said.

"It will. I know it will." Luke ran ahead of them to the truck and when they caught up to him, they headed back to the inn.

Her mother was reading a book at the front desk and looked up when she saw them. She smiled at Luke. "How did you like the telescopes? Did you see anything interesting?"

"We saw seals! It was so cool."

They said their goodbyes and Riley's mother left a note at the front desk with her cell number in case a guest needed to reach her or in the unlikely event that someone walked in looking for information. Riley knew that rarely happened, but once in a while it did, and then people would just call the number and her mother would help them.

As they walked to the car, Riley's thoughts turned to Aidan and Luke. It had been so nice to spend time with both of them. It was like the years fell away with Aidan and they chatted as easily as ever. She was reminded why they'd always gotten along so well. Aside from being as attractive as ever in a boy-next-door kind of way, she also realized they shared a similar outlook on many things, especially having a work-life balance.

She sighed. It was too bad that things hadn't worked out with them. But now she had Jack. Besides, even if she were single, the main obstacle between them was still there—Aidan's life was here in Chatham and Riley's was in Manhattan.

CHAPTER EIGHT

Riley dropped her mother off at home and then set out to the grocery store with a shopping list her mother had written up. She quickly made her way through the store buying everything needed for the inn for the week: various fresh fruits, breads, cereals, frozen quiche, and muffins. She wanted to experiment with baking some fresh quiche and muffins, but her mother wanted these as backups. Riley couldn't blame her as her baking skills were a little rusty.

She grabbed the biggest chicken she could find and the makings for mashed potatoes and stuffing, and a can of cranberry sauce and a jar of gravy. Her mother had suggested a simple roast chicken for Sunday dinner and Riley looked forward to how it would make the house smell.

When she got home, her mother was sitting at the kitchen table peeling potatoes. Riley put everything away and got started on the chicken as it would need to roast for an hour and a half or so. She knew her mother's recipe by heart as it was one she'd made often over the years. She stuffed half a lemon in the chicken cavity along with sprigs of rosemary and thyme, and drizzled olive oil on the outside and a sprinkling of salt and pepper, then popped it in the oven.

When the chicken was almost ready, she made the stuffing from a box, adding plenty of butter, and put the slightly cooled cooked potatoes through a potato ricer so they would be nice and fluffy. She folded in plenty of melted butter and milk and turned the heat on under the pot to keep the potatoes warm.

At one o'clock sharp the front door opened and her four-year-old nieces, Bethany and Emily, rushed in and threw their arms around her. Riley bent down and hugged them both. Her sister, Amy, and her husband, Rob, were right behind them. The girls looked adorable in matching pink dresses. Amy looked nice, too, in a pretty, multicolored, but mostly pink Lilly Pulitzer sweater over skinny jeans. The bright colors stood out against her sleek blond chin-length bob. Amy always looked impeccable. No matter how hard she tried, Riley never managed to achieve the same effortless level of elegance. She glanced down at her own top, an oatmeal-colored all-cotton fisherman-knit sweater. It was one of her favorites, and she paired it with dark jeans and dark brown leather boots. She spotted a sprig of rosemary stuck to her sweater—and quickly brushed it away as Amy pulled her in for a hello hug.

Rob was next and Riley smiled as he hugged her, too. Rob had been part of the family since high school when he and Amy started dating. They were just always together and even though Riley had wondered more than once over the years if Amy had missed out by not dating anyone else, she couldn't deny that the two of them were perfect together. Rob was easygoing, likable, and handsome, too. He was of average height and build, with dark brown hair and eyes, and a friendly smile. Amy helped Riley in the kitchen while her mother visited with Rob and the girls.

"I'm so glad you all were able to come over today. I feel like I haven't had a chance to catch up with you since I got here," Riley said.

Amy laughed. "You haven't! But I get it. When I was helping Mom at the inn I didn't have a spare moment. So, I'm grateful you're here. How is it going so far?"

"It's nice to be home. She is getting around a little better on her crutches, but it's still too much for her to manage without help. It's been fun actually."

Amy smiled. "You always did like working with people. You were so much better at restaurant work than I was."

Riley laughed. That was an understatement. Amy had lasted all of two months one summer as a waitress. She'd hated it and wasn't very good at it. She left for a job as a bank teller and was much happier working with numbers and counting money. Riley had loved waitressing and had spent each summer working at various restaurants on the Cape. She didn't always love it when customers were difficult, but the majority of the time they were nice and tipped well.

"Well, if I don't find a new content job, I can always go back to waitressing," Riley said. She was joking, but it was nice to have that skill to fall back on, as a good server could always find work.

"You'll find something. You're good at what you do. Don't panic if you don't land something before the holidays. I'm sure you will after the New Year," Amy said.

"I hope so."

Riley took the chicken out of the oven and let it rest for a few minutes while she heated up the gravy and stirred the mashed potatoes while Amy checked the stuffing. When everything was ready they brought the food to the dining room table and everyone helped themselves. Amy made plates for the girls, and then for herself.

While they ate, Rob told them funny stories about his week. He worked as an ER doctor at the Cape Cod Hospital. It was a stressful job but he managed to find humor in it and some of the situations really were comical. Like the father who brought his ten-year-old son in because he was worried that he wasn't tall enough—as if that was an emergency!

"How are bookings going? Is it picking up at all with the stroll weekend coming up?" Amy asked their mother over coffee and dessert.

"We still have rooms available but Riley's already updated the website and our social media pages and a new booking came in this morning while she was at the grocery store."

Riley didn't know that. "That's great news, Mom!"

"I forgot to tell you earlier. It is good news. I'm sure it will pick up this week, too. We were sold out last year for Christmas Stroll. I think we will be this year, too."

"We're doing something different starting stroll weekend, too," Riley said. She told her sister about the chocolate turndown service and the wine and cheese happy hour on the weekend. Amy looked intrigued.

"If you don't think that is going to take too much time, I actually think it's a really good idea. It will give the inn more of a special, high-end feel," Amy said.

Riley was glad that her sister liked the idea. "I don't think it will take too long. I can make the rounds right before five and put chocolate on their pillows."

"I stayed at a hotel once that did that and it was such a treat," Riley's mother said. "I love the idea. But if it turns into too much work, Riley, please let me know."

Riley nodded. "I will. I think it will be fine, though."

"I like the happy hour idea," Rob said. "How will you do it? Will you limit guests to one glass?"

Riley and her mother looked at each other. They hadn't discussed the specifics to that level yet and it was a good question.

"I'm honestly not sure," she admitted.

"I've been thinking about it some, and I think we should

limit the time. Do it from five to six and offer everyone a glass, but I'm fine with a little more, topping off their glasses a bit, possibly. We will play it by ear.

"We'll have cheese and crackers, and maybe bread and salami or something. We can vary that. And we can use small glasses—that will give the illusion of having more."

"That's a good idea, honey. Otherwise we risk overpouring so the glasses don't look empty."

Riley laughed. "Definitely. Imagine if we used your giant wineglasses, we'd all be drinking bowls of wine." Her mother had some gorgeous red wineglasses that were only meant to be filled maybe a quarter of the way—if they filled them to the top it would be almost half a bottle of wine.

"Maybe we can take a ride to the Dollar Tree tomorrow to pick up some wineglasses. I noticed the last time I was there that they had some smaller ones," her mother suggested.

"How's Jack?" Amy asked.

"He's good. Busy as ever. You know how it is," Riley said. Amy had once worked in a very corporate environment, with high stress and constant deadlines. Soon after graduating, she'd lived in Boston with friends for a year before she and Rob got engaged and moved in together. They'd stayed in the Boston area for five more years before Amy got pregnant with the girls and Rob accepted the position with the Cape Cod Hospital.

Amy looked thoughtful. "He must take breaks on the weekend, though, even when it's busy? Why don't you see if he can come for a visit this weekend? It would be fun to meet him finally and Christmas Stroll is a great weekend to come."

"Oh, that is a great idea. Riley, please ask him. We'd all like to meet him. It has been almost two years now," her mother reminded her.

Riley nodded. "That's a great idea. I'll definitely ask him.

He does work weekends sometimes, so he might not be able to make it."

Her mother smiled. "He should be able to slow down a little this time of year, I would think?"

Riley smiled at the thought. She doubted that the holidays even registered with Jack. He was so focused, all of the time. But he did say he'd make the trip to meet her family at some point, so this weekend might be a good time.

Later that evening, after Amy, Rob, and the kids went home and her mother was settled in the living room watching a movie on Netflix, Riley called Jack. He picked up on the first ring.

"Hey! How's everything on the Cape?" They'd talked twice, briefly, since Riley had arrived. Jack wasn't much for chatting on the phone but he'd called to say hello and she'd checked in as well, but never knew if she was interrupting. But she figured a Sunday night was a good time to catch him.

"Good. Mom's getting around a little easier and Amy and her family were here today for Sunday dinner. They asked about you."

"Oh, that's nice. Please tell them I said hello."

"I will. But we were thinking, maybe you can tell them in person. This coming weekend is a big deal in Chatham. It's the Christmas Stroll weekend, lots of Christmas activities downtown. Is there any chance you could visit? You could fly into Hyannis and I could pick you up. It's a quick flight," she added.

Jack was quiet for a long moment and Riley was sure he was going to say no, that he was too busy. But he surprised her. "I guess I could do that. We're winding up this case, which gives me a little bit of a break, and I've been pulling so many late nights that I could leave early on Friday and catch a flight that afternoon. Would that work?"

Riley was shocked into silence for a moment. "Yes! That would be great. There's a tree lighting ceremony downtown at six or six thirty. If you get in that afternoon, we should be able to make that and my whole family will be there."

"Perfect, I'll catch a flight that will get me in around four, then."

They chatted a bit more and Riley was still smiling when she ended the call. Jack was finally coming to Chatham. She was sure that her family would love him.

CHAPTER NINE

Dear Franny,

In my second letter, I would like to request that you participate in this year's Chatham Christmas Stroll, beginning with the tree lighting. Do you remember how much fun we used to have going together when we were younger? It's such a magical event filled with Christmas spirit and I want for you to experience that again. Victor and I made sure to go every year. Sometimes it was just the two of us, but often we went with friends and then had people over for supper or went out as a group. It's a time to come together with friends and family and experience the joy of the season.

Lots of love,
Ella

Franny folded the letter and slid it back into its envelope. She hadn't been to the Christmas Stroll in so many years. This was an easy enough request. She was happy to go and soak up a bit of holiday cheer. She finished dressing and headed downstairs for breakfast. It was Monday morning and Beth and Riley were sitting at their usual table eating breakfast.

Franny loaded up her plate, poured herself a cup of coffee, and joined them.

Once she was settled, Beth asked, "Have you opened this week's letter yet?"

Franny took a sip of her coffee before answering. She noticed that Beth had her laptop beside her and was finishing a bagel, while Riley was still working on a bowl of cereal. Franny had helped herself to a slice of ham-and-cheese quiche and a few pieces of cantaloupe.

"I did, just before I came down for breakfast." She smiled. "This week's instructions are to go to the Christmas Stroll activities this weekend, starting with the tree lighting ceremony on Friday."

"Well, that's fun. We're all going to the tree lighting. You're welcome to join us," Beth said.

"We're starting something new this weekend, with a chocolate turndown service and wine weekends, where we have a wine and cheese hour in the living room from five to six," Riley told her.

"We'll walk over to the tree lighting after that. I think it's at six thirty," Beth said.

"Oh, that all sounds lovely. I'd be happy to join you. Thank you," Franny said.

"What do you have planned for your week?" Riley asked.

Franny took a bite of quiche before answering. "Relaxing. I have no plans other than to explore Main Street and maybe go on some morning beach walks and to catch up on my reading. I haven't taken this much time off in a very long time." Franny knew she needed the break, too. Even though she wasn't in the office daily anymore, she still was on top of everything by email and Zoom meetings when necessary. She'd talked to her managers and they'd supported her taking the time for herself through the holidays.

"We can manage, Franny. Enjoy your time in Chatham," they'd assured her. And so she'd stopped obsessively checking email and daily sales numbers. She had good people in charge of the department stores and it was time she trusted them to do what she knew they were capable of. From what she could see, they managed just fine without her there, which was a relief and a blessing. Since meeting with her sister's attorney and deciding to stay in Chatham through the New Year, she'd been sleeping better. She felt more relaxed and at peace.

She still had daily moments of intense sadness as she remembered her sister, but that was easing, too, and settling into something more peaceful. She knew it was her sister's time to go and that she hadn't been sad about it, so Franny tried to shake those feelings when they crept over her. She instead focused on remembering her sister as the happy, carefree person that she was and Franny knew in her heart that Ella was happy now with her beloved Victor.

"I think I'll get my morning walk in when I leave here and stop in the bookshop on the way back. I'm ready for something new to read."

"What do you like to read?" Riley asked her.

Franny laughed. "Everything. It just depends on my mood. I love a good family-focused story but then I usually switch to something more suspenseful. I've been reading a lot of psychological thrillers lately."

Beth looked intrigued. "You don't find those too scary?"

Franny shook her head. "No. I don't read the violent gory ones, just the domestic suspense, where it's all about the unexpected twists. I like a good memoir, too, or biographical novel. I just read one that was based on the life of Estée Lauder that was fascinating. What do the two of you enjoy reading?"

"I read a mix, like you, but my favorite are romantic comedies," Riley said. "I recently read *The Undomestic Goddess* by

Sophie Kinsella and laughed so much that Lily stared at me. I'm working my way through her other books now."

"I am reading the newest Lisa Jewell," Beth said. "I loved her women's fiction books years ago and now am addicted to her suspense ones."

Franny nodded. "She's one of my favorites, along with Lisa Gardner and Freida McFadden."

Beth smiled. "I think we have similar taste. I've left some of my favorite books in the living room for guests to borrow and there are few books from all of those authors. You're welcome to take a look and borrow any you haven't read already."

"Thank you. I will look there before I head to the book-shop so I don't buy any you already have. I'll still pick up a few, though." She grinned. "There's no such thing as too many books."

When she finished breakfast, Franny said goodbye and headed into the living room. There was a nice assortment of books on the shelves, but Franny had read most of them. There were a few that looked intriguing. She took two of them up to her room before heading out on her walk.

It was an absolutely gorgeous day. Cold but clear and sunny. Franny had added a thick knit cashmere hat and gloves before heading outside and was glad for their warmth as she walked. Main Street was quiet as it was still early, and most of the shops didn't open for another half hour or so. So, she walked to the end of Main Street and then turned around and made her way back. By the time she reached the bookshop, it was open and she stepped inside.

Sun streamed through the big bay windows that faced Main Street, filling the shop with light. A little electric stove sat in the corner, glowing merrily and throwing a bit of heat, too. Franny stood nearby for a moment, enjoying the warmth after walking in the cold. She always felt a sense of excitement when she entered a bookshop, as she awaited the discovery of the perfect story that would transport her into another world. She gazed around the shop, at the front tables piled with new releases, and the carefully curated shelves with the many notecards with staff notes about books they especially loved.

Franny always felt drawn to the front tables where the newest books were displayed. She recognized many of the author names, as most were popular bestsellers. But sometimes there were interesting debut books there, too. She picked up a few with covers that caught her eye, then read the inside flap to learn more about the story and then if it sounded good, she would flip to the opening page. And that's where she often held her breath in anticipation—would this be a book she would instantly fall in love with?

Franny could usually tell just by reading the first few paragraphs—sometimes just the first sentence or two—if she was going to like a book. It was hard to explain but it was just a feeling she got from the way the author put their words together—sometimes their voice spoke to her or reassured her that she was in capable hands and that she needed to go on this particular story's journey.

When it was an author Franny already knew she loved, she just glanced at the blurb and that was enough. She found two of those books, and added a new author, and decided she was good for a few days. And then she'd want to return and go through the same process again. As she was about to head to the register, a young woman walked over to her and smiled.

"Good morning. Are you finding everything you were looking for?" The woman wore a name tag that said Sara and Franny recognized her from the last time she was in.

"Yes, thank you. Actually, you recommended a book the

last time I was in here. I think it was by your sister, Hannah. It was wonderful."

Sara's smile widened. "Oh, I'm so glad! I'm biased, of course, because she is my sister, but I really love her books, too. She has a new one coming out tomorrow, actually. It's a Christmas release and it's set here in Chatham." Hannah's last book had been set in New York City, so Franny thought that was interesting.

"I'll have to come back next week for that one. I love a good Christmas story." Franny would be sure to leave that one in the library when she finished as she thought Riley might like Hannah's writing style. Her other book had been a romantic comedy.

"She's actually going to be doing a signing here on Saturday," Sara said. "Hannah lives in Chatham now."

"Oh, well, then I will make a point of stopping by." Franny had a feeling that her sister would have approved and perhaps she was even meant to read Hannah's Christmas book. She smiled at the thought. She was getting caught up in the magical spirit of the holidays. She'd always loved this time of year.

Sara rang her books up, ran Franny's credit card, then handed her a pretty paper bag with her books and a complimentary bookmark. Franny had removed her gloves to handle the books and put them back on as she braced to step outside into the cold.

It wasn't as bad as she'd feared as the wind had died down and the sun was shining even more brightly. If one didn't know better, and was just looking out the window, it would almost look like a summer day. Except that snow was in the forecast, and as Franny began walking back to the inn, a few snowflakes appeared and whirled and danced around her on their way to the ground. It was just a light flurry, fun to watch, and as soon as the flakes hit the ground they quickly disappeared.

Out of the corner of her eye, Franny did a double take when she saw a familiar figure on the other side of the street. She caught a quick glimpse of his face and it stopped her short, like she'd seen a ghost. She hadn't seen Joe in decades. This man's hair was silver but in the split second she'd seen his face, he looked the same. She watched him for a moment as the snow intensified but he didn't turn around again, so she couldn't make sure it was him. Her phone rang, pulling her attention away. She fished it out of her purse and saw that it was an unfamiliar number and her phone identified it as a telemarketer. She didn't need to answer that. She dropped it back into her purse and glanced back across the street, but the man was gone.

She thought her mind must have been playing tricks on her. Or the man had just been a look-alike. Joe, her high school sweetheart, couldn't possibly be in Chatham. Last she'd heard, he'd moved to the West Coast with his family and he had no other family left in Chatham. Franny hadn't thought of him in years. She wished him well, wherever he was.

She had nothing but fond memories of Joe. They'd dated in high school and he'd been her first love, but his family moved when Joe was a junior in high school. They'd both promised to keep in touch. There had been a few letters at first, but those had faded away. Joe's last letter had come at the end of senior year and simply said that he was going to college in California. She had committed to going to Wellesley College, just outside of Boston. She missed Joe, but she also accepted that their lives were going in different directions and they were too far apart. And then in college, senior year, she met her husband and they fell in love. Franny had no regrets.

The snow blinded her for moment, clinging to her glasses and making it hard to see. She decided to step into the nearest shop for a break. In front of her was a cute wine and cheese shop that she'd been meaning to visit. She stepped inside and holiday bells hanging on the door jingled cheerfully as she walked in.

The shop was small but well stocked with a wide variety of wines in box shelves along all the walls. In the center of the shop was a refrigerated oval with an extensive assortment of cheeses, many that Franny had never seen or heard of before. A friendly woman who looked to be in her mid-thirties smiled when she saw Franny and welcomed her to the shop.

"Are you looking for anything in particular? I was about to slice up some samples of the Humboldt Fog aged goat cheese if you'd like to try it?"

Franny nodded and took her glasses off for a moment, to shake off the melting snowflakes. "I'd been meaning to stop in here. I'd love to try a taste. I haven't had that one before."

The woman unwrapped a small round cheese and sliced into it. She put a small wedge of the cheese onto a cracker and handed it to Franny. "This is one of my favorites. It reminds me of a mix between goat and brie cheese. My name is Anna. Let me know if you'd like to try anything else."

Franny glanced at the cheese and agreed that the textures seemed to resemble both. It had layers of firmer white goat cheese, and a surrounding layer of softer, almost runny cheese, and a black line in the middle, which almost gave it the look of cake layers.

"That black is ash and it's edible," Hayley explained.

Franny took a bite and experienced a rush of flavors and textures, a tangy hint of goat cheese and the smooth richness of brie. It was delicious.

"I'll take one of those, and a box of the crackers, too, please."

"Of course." Hayley paused then asked, "Have you tried Saint-André? It's a very buttery, sleek triple cream. It goes really well with those crackers, too."

Franny agreed to try the Saint-André, too, and loved it. "I'll take one of those and also that wedge of Manchego." Manchego was one of her favorite cheeses. It was a little softer than a Parmesan but had a similar nutty flavor and was delicious on its own with a glass of red wine.

"Perfect. And did you need any wine to go with your cheese?" Hayley asked.

Franny smiled. "What would you suggest?"

"Daou Cabernet is nice and reasonably priced. If you want to go to higher level, you might like their sister wine, Duckhorn Cabernet. Or a nice Pinot Noir like Belle Glos. Or if you want an absolute steal of a wine, we just got a bunch of Cocobon in—it's a red blend of Merlot, Zinfandel, and Petit Syrah. It's only seven ninety-nine and I swear it tastes like a thirty-dollar bottle."

Franny was intrigued. "I love discovering a good cheap wine. I'll take a bottle of that and one of the Daou, too, please."

Hayley rang everything up and by the time Franny stepped outside with her bag of wines and cheeses, the flurries had stopped and the sun was shining again. She set off to walk the short distance to the inn and looked forward to making herself a cup of hot tea and settling in with one of her new books and maybe a little cheese and crackers for lunch.

CHAPTER TEN

After Franny left and there were no other guests expected for breakfast, Beth refilled her coffee cup and opened her laptop to check email and any bookings that had come in the night before. Riley quickly put everything away in the kitchen and then poured herself a fresh cup of coffee, sat at the table with Beth, and opened her own laptop.

There were more emails than usual to go through, which was encouraging. Beth replied to several questions about the inn and weather this time of year in Chatham. Then she clicked over to the reservation software to see if there were any new bookings. She'd been about to take a sip of coffee, but put her cup down instead when she saw the booking activity.

"Riley, we're full now, and have a few new bookings for the following week as well. I'm not sure what you did, but it worked, and fast, too."

"Really? That's awesome." Riley looked happy to hear it. "It was the content marketing mostly, I think. I put up a few blog posts focusing on Christmas Stroll and all the fun activities here over that weekend. And I found some old pictures from past strolls. There were some good ones with lots of snow and holiday festivity. I also ran a small Facebook ad, using your email list and making a look-alike audience and ad so Facebook would remind anyone that has stayed here before as well as similar profiles—people that might be open to a Christmas weekend."

Beth laughed. "That sounds complicated, but I really appreciate it, honey. If this is what you can do, I'm sure you will get snapped up fast."

"Thanks. Let's hope so. I saw a few positions online last night that looked interesting and sent some resumes in. We'll see if I get any bites."

"Now that we are fully booked, maybe I should call someone to come take a look at those two rooms that need repairs. Jess gave me the name of someone a while back when I mentioned it to the girls. Her boyfriend, Ryan, knows a guy that does carpentry jobs of all sizes. I think I have his number here somewhere." Beth opened her purse and fished around in it until she found the scrap of paper she'd stuffed into a side pocket.

"Definitely call him. If he's able to fix the rooms before the weekend, you can rent those rooms out, too," Riley said.

"Oh, I doubt he will be available that soon. I'll call him, though."

Beth punched the numbers into her cell phone and after two rings a deep voice answered, "Andrews Construction."

"Hello, I was referred to Sean Andrews, if he's available?"

"You've got him. How can I help you?" His tone was friendly and businesslike.

Beth explained that Jess had referred him and that she needed some minor repair work done to two rooms.

"How soon are you looking to have this done?" he asked.

"The sooner the better."

"I could come out this afternoon and take a look if you like. See what you need and give you an idea of how long it will take. You're in luck—I just had a project pushed out so I am available this week."

"Great!" They settled on two o'clock that afternoon and Beth filled Riley in when she ended the call.

"If it just takes a few days, you might be able to sell those rooms, too!" Riley seemed excited about the idea and Beth was, too. If she was able to rent out two additional rooms for the weekend, that would come close to covering the cost of the repairs, she imagined.

Sean arrived at a few minutes before two, which both Beth and Riley thought was a good first impression. Many of the locals that worked in various areas of construction on the Cape had a relaxed approach to work—missing a day or showing up late wasn't a big deal.

Riley let him in and brought him into the living room where Beth sat on a chair with her crutches by her side.

"I'm sorry that I didn't get the door myself. This is my daughter, Riley. She's in town for the holidays and is helping me out a bit since I broke my leg."

Sean gazed at the cast on her leg. "I fell off a ladder," she explained. "Not my finest moment. I should have been more careful."

Sean looked sympathetic. "It happens more often than you'd think. Ladders can be dangerous. Hopefully you'll heal up quickly."

"Yes. Hopefully. The two rooms are on the ground level, so I can show you." Beth got to her feet and settled onto the crutches. She led Sean to the two rooms that were on the side of the inn. She explained about the repair work needed as they walked. "We had a bad storm a few months ago, and water got through the flashing and I think some of the hardwood in the floors might need to be replaced. It got waterlogged and swollen and now it's discolored, too."

"I remember that storm. It was a doozy. Kept us busy for a

while." Sean smiled as Beth opened the door to the first room and he stepped inside. She pointed out the areas of concern. He looked in both rooms and then wanted to go outside to check the flashing where they suspected the water came in.

"Mom, he's kind of hot. I didn't notice a ring. Do you know anything about his situation?" Riley asked. Beth glanced to the door, where Sean stood just outside. "The door is shut, he can't hear us." Riley sounded amused.

Her daughter was right. Beth had noticed right away that Sean had an attractive ruggedness to him. He was almost a foot taller than Beth, who was barely five foot three. His skin was tanned from working outside and she'd noticed the laugh lines around his mouth and eyes and they looked good on him. His hair was dark brown and his eyes were lighter, hazel maybe. She'd noticed his eyes right away as they took in the surroundings. He was lean and muscular. His work clearly kept him in good shape. She hadn't noticed the lack of a wedding ring. Beth almost never noticed that, though. Especially as she wasn't looking. At one point she was, years ago, for about a year. She did all the things, including online dating and set-ups from friends. And she'd had a few dates. But there were no real sparks and it just seemed like so much effort that she took a break from it. It was easier to just worry about it later. But months turned into years more quickly than she'd ever anticipated and now she was in her mid-fifties and still alone.

She had good friends and went out often with them, but they were all coupled up now. Her one remaining single friend had met someone on Instagram of all places. He was a podcaster that she admired and she slid into his DMs, as they put it—not intending for anything romantic, just to tell him how much she enjoyed his show. But after a few back-and-forth exchanges, the podcaster asked her on a date and a month later, she moved to Key West to live with him. Now a few months later, they were engaged. It seemed like a whirlwind to Beth, but she'd never seen Rachel so happy.

Beth had actually considered trying online dating again, and then the next day she fell off the ladder. So once again, she took that as a sign that it wasn't her time yet. She wasn't sure if it ever would be. And she hadn't cared much until recently. Suddenly she was noticing how coupled up everyone was and how alone she was. It would be nice to have someone to do things with: dinner, watch TV, stroll along Main Street, or relax at the beach.

"Okay, so you definitely have an issue with your flashing." Sean had returned, and his voice snapped Beth back to attention. She turned to face him. "It needs to be replaced and part of the drywall where the water came in should be replaced, too. But the good news is you don't need to replace the hardwood. It's just a little swollen and that will continue to dry out as long as it doesn't get wet again."

Beth nodded. It was all Greek to her, but she trusted Sean as he came so highly recommended. He quoted her a price that was reasonable and even a little lower than she'd expected. "I can start first thing tomorrow, if that works for you. If you want to think about it or get a few other quotes, though, that's fine, too."

Beth didn't hesitate. "No, that sounds good. Let's do it. If you could start tomorrow, how long do you think it would take to finish?" It sounded like a lot of work to her, so she doubted it would be ready in time to rent out the rooms. But maybe for the following week.

"It won't take me long. Maybe by end of day Wednesday. Thursday at the latest. The material you have here is common. I have some on hand and if I need more I can get it without waiting. Same with the flashing materials. Fortunately your walls are painted white so that's an easy match once we're done."

"Mom, that means you can rent two additional rooms for this weekend. That's huge!" Riley sounded as excited as Beth felt.

"That is great news. I didn't really think it was possible."

Sean grinned. "I'm pretty certain I'll be done by end of day Wednesday."

They agreed that Sean would start first thing the next day.

"We put breakfast out for guests at eight, feel free to join us if you like," Riley invited him.

"Yes, please do. There's always plenty," Beth said.

He nodded. "Maybe I'll take you up on that. At least for a hot coffee anyway. I'll see you both tomorrow."

They walked him out and Beth was in a great mood. "If we can really rent out those two rooms so quickly, that would be wonderful."

"I was thinking the same thing. I'll make a new blog post saying that we're almost sold out but that two newly renovated rooms will be ready. I'll make them sound extra special."

"Perfect. Thanks, honey."

Beth breathed a sigh of relief. She'd been concerned that the inn had been so slow, and she'd also worried about spending money she didn't have on repairs. When she'd fallen off the ladder, it had really scared her. Fortunately it had just slowed her down, but the timing couldn't have been worse. But now, thanks to Riley's help and after meeting with Sean, she was feeling much more optimistic about everything.

CHAPTER ELEVEN

Sean arrived at ten minutes past eight the next morning. He'd told Riley's mother that he usually began work around eight thirty but that he'd stop by a little earlier for coffee first. Franny was the only other guest in the dining room. Aidan and Luke had breakfast in their room during the week as Luke had to be at school by eight and Aidan headed into his office after that.

Franny was eating light, just some buttered toast and sliced melon. Riley was about to slice into the quiche for herself and her mother. She'd tried her hand at making the spinach, onion, red pepper, and goat cheese quiche the night before, following her mother's recipe carefully. She hoped that it tasted as good as it looked. She handed one of the plates to her mother and set her own down on the table.

"Sean, help yourself to whatever you'd like. Riley made that quiche. I'm sure it's delicious," her mother said.

Riley laughed. "It's her recipe so it should be."

Sean raised his eyebrows as he reached for a coffee cup. "I was just going to have coffee, but a homemade quiche is tempting. I might have to try a slice."

Franny agreed. "That does sound good. Please cut me a small slice if you don't mind."

Sean cut two pieces, one generously sized for himself and a smaller one for Franny. He brought them both to the table, along with his coffee, and settled in.

Franny took the first bite and announced that it was delicious. "Well done, Riley."

"Thank you." She took a bite and happily agreed. The flavors reminded her a bit of spanakopita, with the red pepper adding a bit of sweetness.

"Do you have any kids?" Riley asked Sean. She figured it was a roundabout way to see if he was single. She was curious as he seemed about her mother's age, so his children, if he had them, would probably be close to Riley's and Amy's ages.

He nodded. "Two girls. Anna is twenty-eight and Becky is thirty-one. They both live in the Boston area near my ex-wife."

So, he was divorced. He might have a girlfriend, though. If not, Riley couldn't help but wonder if he might be a good potential date for her mother. Her mother was so cute and nice. Both Riley and Amy wanted her to meet someone, but she never wanted to discuss it when they brought it up. Riley supposed she didn't blame her. When she was ready, she would do it, or not. And maybe she wasn't Sean's type. But she could tell her mother was at least a little bit interested. Riley had noticed that her mother was wearing her favorite sweater and she'd taken a little more time with her hair. Maybe it was just lip moisturizer, but it looked like she had a little color on her lips, too.

"That's nice that they are nearby," her mother said. "Do they come to the Cape often?"

"Not a lot. They usually get down a few times over the summer and I see them on Thanksgiving or Christmas, depending on the year. They have their own lives. Both have serious boyfriends." Sean polished off his last bite of quiche and finished his coffee, then stood. "Well, I should get started. Thanks for breakfast."

"Let us know if you need anything. Just call my cell if we aren't here. We usually head to my home after breakfast is done. But I'm right down the road, so we can be back quickly if you need us," her mother said.

"Will do. I think I have everything I need. But I will holler if I have any questions." He smiled and his whole face lit up. Riley noticed her mother's eyes widen at the sight of that smile. "Enjoy the rest of your day, ladies."

Riley dropped her mother at home after breakfast and grabbed her laptop and walked up Main Street. She planned to get a caramel macchiato at the coffee shop next to the bookstore and to spend some time online focusing on her job search. She'd read that not all jobs were posted and if she did a little research on LinkedIn she could reach out to newly hired marketing directors that might need to hire staff. She knew that often happened when new leadership arrived.

She had a stop to make first. She needed to stock up on chocolates for the turndown service that weekend. Her mother had given her the inn's credit card to buy an assortment. They figured two nice pieces of chocolate per person would be ideal.

Riley stepped into the store and inhaled the sweet scent of rich chocolate. She wasn't hungry in the slightest but it made her want something sweet. She picked out a bunch of chocolates, both dark and milk, some truffles and raspberry filled. No nuts, though. Too many people had allergies so they decided it was best to avoid them. Riley had no issues with nuts, and splurged on a dark chocolate pecan turtle for herself, to enjoy with her coffee.

She brought her bag of chocolates with her to the coffee shop and the manager, Caitlin, recognized her as she'd stopped in several times since she'd been back in town.

"Hi, Riley. Your usual—caramel macchiato with almond milk, extra foam?" Caitlin asked.

Riley nodded. "Yes, please." The coffee shop was warm and cozy and decorated for the holidays with a big Christmas tree in the corner and stockings with all the employees' names pinned to the wall behind the register. There were twinkling candle lights in the windows and the overall feeling was festive and welcoming. Most of the tables were taken with people enjoying coffee and muffins or bagels but Riley found one in the back corner that was free and set her laptop on it, while she waited for her coffee. It didn't take long and a few minutes later, she was sipping her sweet foamy drink and surfing the internet.

She checked the job listings first and there were a few new ones that looked interesting. She hadn't heard back yet from any of the jobs she'd applied for but she knew things moved slowly this time of year. She spent an hour or so on LinkedIn and did find a few newly hired marketing directors at interesting tech companies. She went ahead and sent them a note and attached her resume, asking them to keep her in mind as they considered growing their teams.

She grew tired of that, and switched over to Facebook to see what her friends were up to. To her surprise, she saw that Jack had posted a picture of himself out with some work colleagues. They were at a bar around the corner from his office. It was a fun place and she'd gone there a few times with Jack when they'd first started dating.

They rarely went to places like that now, though. Usually it was out to dinner, which was fine with her, or takeout and an early night at home, as he was often too tired to stay out late. She was glad to see he was getting out more while she was gone. He'd been so heads-down focused on work lately.

She noticed there were lots of comments on his post, other

coworkers chiming in on what a fun night it had been. She guessed it had been the night they'd finished the big case they'd been working on for so long. She glanced at the comments and was about to scroll down to the next post when one comment caught her eye. It was from a very pretty young woman, Brittany. Riley wasn't the jealous type but she picked up a flirtatious tone. *It was so great hanging out with you. We need to do this more often!*

But then she told herself she was being silly and it was likely nothing of any significance, just normal coworker banter. She scrolled down and looked at pictures from other friends, nights out, pictures of food at restaurants, new outfits, all the things one posted on Facebook. She liked her neighbor Phoebe's picture of her new cat. She and Phoebe were about the same age and had bonded over the misery of schlepping to the basement to do laundry. Both of them dreamed of having an apartment with a washer and dryer in the unit. But that was so rare and Manhattan apartments were ridiculously expensive to begin with. That was the one thing Riley didn't love about living in the city.

She did love her apartment, though. It was small, but it was cute and had high ceilings, which gave the illusion of more space. If she and Jack eventually married, they could pool their resources and get a bigger, better apartment. But that felt like it was far off. Neither one of them had mentioned marriage. Riley knew it wasn't on Jack's radar until he was closer to making partner. So realistically at least another year or two before they had the discussion, she imagined. Which was fine with her. She'd never been one of those girls that obsessed about getting married. And truthfully, sometimes she wondered if Jack was the one. She loved spending time with him. They had a good time and they shared a lot of the same values, and he was handsome.

But she hadn't missed him that much since she'd been in Chatham, and part of her wondered if that was normal. Maybe she should miss him more? Or maybe she was just being practical. She knew this was just a temporary visit and Jack was so busy these days that she didn't see him much anyway. And she'd be seeing him this weekend. She was looking forward to showing him around Chatham and experiencing the magical Christmas festivities with him. She was also eager to introduce him to her family and curious to hear what their impressions of him were. It was really an ideal time for him to visit.

CHAPTER TWELVE

"Is that a new sweater?" Beth turned at the sound of her daughter's voice. Riley had just walked into the kitchen and was still in her pajamas. It was early. Beth woke early most days and today she'd felt up to experimenting and was trying a new breakfast casserole recipe. She was comfortable enough on her crutches now that she could maneuver around the kitchen and get everything she needed onto the counter. She'd just poured the mixture into a buttered glass casserole dish and was about to slide it into the oven.

"Sort of. I bought it a year ago and found it hanging in my closet with the tags still attached. I just stumbled across it this morning and decided to wear it." It was a gorgeous cashmere sweater, a little dressier than Beth usually wore, which is why it was still hanging in her closet. But it was a bright, cheery red and it matched her festive mood. And when she tried it on, she remembered why she'd fallen in love with it—the color and the cut were very flattering.

"Cool. It's a pretty color. What are you making?"

"A sausage and cheese strata. It has eggs and buttery brioche bread. I found a loaf in the freezer yesterday and thawed it out. Bread freezes beautifully and I thought it might be fun to try this recipe."

"It sounds delicious. Not exactly low-cal," Riley said.

Beth laughed. "Not at all. But that's part of the fun of going on vacation and staying in a bed-and-breakfast—indulging a bit."

"True. Plus, there's always fruit and cereal if people want healthier options."

Riley headed off to shower and change and by the time she returned to the kitchen Beth was just taking the strata out of the oven. It was golden brown and bubbling a bit. She set it on the counter to cool and fifteen minutes later, she and Riley were headed out the door. Beth had covered the casserole with foil to keep it warm and Riley carried it carefully as they walked to the car.

While Riley went to the kitchen to start getting breakfast out, Beth went to check on the progress of the two rooms Sean was working on. She was pleasantly surprised to see that it looked like most of the carpentry work was completed and now he just had to finish up and then paint. She breathed a sigh of relief. It would definitely be done on time. Which was a good thing, because while the strata baked, Beth had checked her email and overnight both rooms had been booked. The inn was now completely full for the Christmas Stroll weekend.

By eight, everything was set up in the dining room and both Beth and Riley helped themselves to the sausage strata. It smelled amazing and tasted even better. Beth looked up each time they heard footsteps. They hadn't discussed it, but she was hopeful that Sean would come early again and join them for a few minutes, at least for coffee. She'd made the strata with him in mind.

Franny was the first one down. She was an early riser, too. She excitedly helped herself to some of the strata and a few pieces of melon and coffee.

"This looks wonderful. I've always loved a good strata. I used to make it on Christmas Day." She grinned as she speared a cube of melon. "The fruit cancels out the calories, right?"

Riley and Beth looked at their own plates and laughed, as they'd thought the same. "It's like getting a popcorn with extra butter and a Diet Coke," Riley agreed.

A few minutes later another older couple, Rita and Tom Smith, joined them. They were from Connecticut, a suburb near New York City, and they were in town for an early Christmas visit with their daughter and her family. They loaded up their plates with strata and joined them.

"My daughter invited us to stay with her, but they don't really have the room. She offered to clear out their office so we can use the pull-out sofa there, but if I know Abbie, she has stuff piled on that sofa and it would be a project to clear it out. This way, we have a nice quiet room and they're just a few miles away. It works out better for everyone."

"She has two children now, a year apart," Tom added.

"How old are they?" Beth asked.

"One and three. So she really has her hands full. We'll head over there from here. I told Abbie we'd watch the kids all day to give her a break. She booked a hair appointment and a pedicure in Hyannis."

"I bet she appreciates that," Beth said.

"She does. She deserves it," Rita added as she cut into her strata and took a bite. "Oh my goodness, this is so good. I'm going to need the recipe, if you don't mind sharing?"

Beth smiled. "Of course. I'll email it to you."

At that moment, she heard heavier footsteps as Sean walked in. He waved hello and went to pour himself a coffee.

"Please help yourself to the strata. It's a new recipe and I'd love your opinion," Beth said.

Sean grinned. "Happy to help." He filled his plate with a big slab, skipped the fruit, and joined them at the table, sitting next to Franny.

Beth introduced him to everyone. "Sean is helping us with some repair work." She glanced his way. "It looks like you got most of it done yesterday, other than the painting?"

He nodded. "I have a few more touch-ups, but after that it's just painting that wall so it all blends in. I should be done by midday."

"Really? That's great news!" Riley said.

Sean ate quickly, drained his cup of coffee, and stood. "Thanks for breakfast. Whatever that was, it was delicious. I'm going to get started. I'll give you a call when I finish up."

"Thank you." Beth watched him go, noticing how his red plaid work shirt contrasted with his dark hair, and how his well-worn jeans emphasized his lean physique. She brought her attention back to her breakfast and saw Riley watching her with an amused smile. Beth ignored it and asked Franny what she had planned for the day.

"I'm going to get my morning walk in, and around eleven I'm heading to the library for a local author event about a non-fiction book on the history of the lobster. There may be a recipe or two as well."

Beth smiled. "That sounds fun."

Once everyone finished breakfast and went on their way, Beth helped Riley to clean up. She didn't trust herself to carry dishes and maneuver the crutches, but she was able to stay by the sink and rinse everything off as Riley brought it to her, and load it all into the dishwasher.

"Are you ready to go?" Riley asked when everything was finished.

Beth shook her head. "I think I'm going to stay here. Sean

will likely finish around lunchtime and it seems silly to go home and then have to come back so soon. I have my laptop and can keep myself busy until then."

Riley smiled and Beth knew her daughter was aware of her attraction to Sean. The new sweater was a dead giveaway. It was also the second day in a row she'd taken the time to blow her hair dry so it looked smoother and had more style. Normally she let it air dry and then pulled it into a messy knot.

"Okay. I told Amy I'd swing by for coffee this morning, so I'm going to head there now."

"Tell her I said hi, honey. I'll call you when everything is done."

CHAPTER THIRTEEN

The first thing Riley noticed when she stepped into Amy's house was the quiet. Her sister lived in a classic Cape Cod–style home, with gray weathered shingles and white shutters and flower boxes by the windows. It was a modest-sized house with three bedrooms and two and a half bathrooms. The girls shared a bedroom now but Amy had said in another year or two they might consider moving to a slightly larger house so each girl could have their own bedroom and they'd have a guest room, too.

Riley followed Amy into the kitchen, which was immaculate. Amy's house was always spotless and Riley didn't know how she managed it with two small children. She didn't have any help either. Unlike Riley, who tended toward clutter and put off cleaning as long as she could, Amy found it relaxing and claimed that she actually enjoyed it.

"Is this when you do most of your housework—when the girls are in pre-K?" Riley asked as she settled onto one of the chairs surrounding the kitchen's center island. She'd always admired the island—it was topped with a sleek quartz that looked just like marble, but didn't stain the way marble did. Amy slid a mug of hot coffee her way, fresh from the Keurig machine. She made herself one as Riley took her first sip, then joined her.

"I get everything done now in the mornings after I drop the girls off. Any shopping I need to do. That was always a challenge. Other than grocery shopping, I did most of it online. It's not easy bundling up two toddlers and navigating a store with them." Amy laughed. "I don't miss that at all."

"Do you think you'll go back to work once the girls are in school full-time?" Riley asked. She knew the kids kept her sister busy, but Riley couldn't imagine not working at all.

"Maybe. I'm not sure. If I did, I'd still need daycare for after school. At least until they're old enough to be here by themselves and I'm not sure how I feel about that. They'll have after-school activities they will need rides to and I like being here for them when they get home."

Riley nodded. "You don't miss it, though? Being in an office and having a career?"

"Not as much as I thought I would. I'm lucky that we're in a position where we can afford to have me home. And when we did the math, with the cost of daycare for two kids, well, there wasn't much left over after that. It made more sense for us for me to be here."

"You enjoy it, too," Riley said. Her sister seemed happy and content.

"I really do. But I know it's not for everyone. My friend Jamie doesn't understand it at all. She couldn't wait for her maternity leave to be over so she could get back into her office. She loves her work and being around adults. But she has a great arrangement, an in-home daycare right up the road from where she lives."

"And it's probably better for her kids than if she were to stay home and be miserable," Riley said.

"Exactly. I have thought that maybe at some point I might find something part-time, mother's hours or maybe even something I could do from home." She smiled. "I have no idea what that could be, but something could turn up."

"Speaking of jobs. I've been sending out tons of resumes, and I have a phone interview lined up for Friday. If it goes well, they said the next step is a video interview and then a final in-person," Riley said.

"Oh, that's great news! I wasn't sure if you'd even get any interviews this time of year."

"I wasn't either. Although I did land my last job in December, so I knew it was possible."

"Maybe it's actually a good time to look. I bet most people assume nothing happens and put their searches on hold. What kind of company is this one for?"

"It's a tech company—an Internet of Things software company. I need to research it more tonight to get a better understanding of what they do. But it has to do with artificial intelligence and devices talking to each other."

"You mean like our thermostat that we can change from an app on our phone?" Amy asked.

Riley nodded. "Yes, something like that."

"That's a little ironic—you lost your job because of AI and now you're interviewing with a company that has an AI product."

Riley laughed. "I know. It's just a first interview though, so it will be good practice for me, even if it goes nowhere."

"Well, good luck. That would be a nice Christmas gift if you lock up a new job before the New Year."

"It would be. I have enough in savings to carry me through the winter if need be, but I'd rather get back to work and get settled somewhere sooner rather than later."

The conversation shifted to Jack's visit that weekend.

"I'm so glad we'll finally get to meet him. I was starting to wonder if maybe things weren't that serious between you. You haven't mentioned him much since you've been back," Amy said.

"I've just been busy helping Mom." Riley knew it was true, though. She hadn't talked about Jack much other than to let them know he'd agreed to visit, finally. "Things are fine with me and Jack. I don't get to see him as much as I'd like. His schedule is intense. Lots of late nights and sometimes weekends, too."

Amy made a face. "That sounds awful. For both of you. I don't think I'd like that—dating someone who is so unavailable."

"It's not so bad, really." Riley had grown so used to it that she hadn't given it much thought. "I'm usually exhausted at the end of the day and Lily is easy company," she said.

Amy looked at her and raised an eyebrow. "You're thirty, not fifty."

Riley laughed. "It will be nice to have him here this weekend. It's a great time to show him Chatham and have him meet everyone."

"He'll think you grew up in a Hallmark Christmas movie when you show him Main Street," Amy said.

"It is so pretty here this time of year," Riley agreed. "I'm glad he'll be here in time for the tree lighting. You guys should come by the inn at five for our new wine and cheese happy hour. Friday is the first day for it. We can walk over to the tree lighting after. And I'll make sure to have hot chocolate for the girls while we have our wine. We have another child there, too. Aidan's boy, Luke."

Amy looked intrigued at the mention of Aidan. "I almost forgot that he was staying at the inn through the holidays. How is he? Have you had a chance to chat with him at all?"

"A little bit. It's a hard time of year for both of them. His wife has only been gone for a few years. Three, I think. He seems a little down, to be honest, but he tries to hide it, for Luke's sake. I guess she died a few weeks before Christmas."

"Oh, I didn't realize that. I remember how hard it was for Mom when her divorce was finalized right before Christmas. It took her a long time to get over that. I think the holidays still make her a little sad, though she tries not to show it, too."

Riley nodded. "I know. I used to hear it in her voice when we'd chat on the phone. She seems happier this year, though. Especially now that those two rooms are repaired and rented for the weekend."

"Oh, that's great news! I think she likes having you around, too. You're good company for her, especially at this time of year," Amy added.

"It's good for me, too. Otherwise, I'd be alone and depressed in my apartment all day. Keeping busy and being around Mom and everyone at the inn has been fun. And seeing you and the kids, too, of course." Riley was close to her sister and they talked often on the phone, but it was so much nicer to visit in person.

"What else do you have planned today?" Riley asked.

Amy glanced at the clock. "I have just about enough time to run to the post office and do some grocery shopping before it's time to pick up the girls. What about you?"

"I thought I might head over to the coffee shop and jump online for a while before I have to head back to the inn. Mom is there, waiting for Sean to finish up. We'll probably grab lunch at home after that."

They chatted a few minutes longer, then Riley stood to leave and Amy walked her to the door. "We'll plan to meet you at the inn. Wine and cheese sounds great to me," Amy said.

Beth was sitting in the dining room, sipping a cup of cinnamon tea and engrossed in the latest Lisa Jewell novel, when she heard the now-familiar footsteps approach. It was a few minutes past noon when Sean walked into the room and announced that the project was done.

"It's all set, if you want to come and take a look?"

Beth grabbed her crutches and pulled herself up. She followed him to the two rooms where Sean pointed out the repairs he'd made. He showed her the flashing outside and in the rooms everything looked brand-new, as if nothing had been touched. The walls were painted with two fresh coats of white.

"Those will dry today and by tomorrow you'll be good to go," he assured her.

"Thank you so much. Both rooms are rented as of Friday so that's just perfect." Beth was impressed and grateful that he'd gotten the work done so quickly.

"I'll write you out a check," she said as they walked back to the dining room. She fished the inn's checkbook out of her purse and wrote Sean a check, confirming that the amount he'd quoted earlier was the right amount. It didn't seem like enough to her.

"That's it. I'm heading off to another job this afternoon. So this worked out great for me, too."

Beth handed him the check. She held his gaze for a moment and was so tempted to invite him to join them on Friday for wine and cheese, but she chickened out. She also didn't want the questions it would surely invite from the girls as to why he was there. But she felt so drawn to him. She still didn't even know if he was available or even remotely interested in her.

"Are you going to the tree lighting on Friday?" she asked casually.

He nodded. "I might check it out. Depends on what time this job finishes up on Friday. Though I think I should be done by then."

Beth smiled nervously, feeling suddenly flustered and not quite herself. "Great. Maybe we'll see you there, then."

He grinned, and the laugh lines danced across his face. She tried not to stare but it was hard to look away. She knew he had to go, though. She stood to walk him out. "Thanks again, for fitting us in so quickly."

"It was good timing," he said. "I'll see you later."

Beth watched as Sean walked out the door and smiled to herself as she texted Riley to let her know she was ready for a ride home. She hadn't been so flustered by a man in forever. She'd actually wondered if she was even capable of feeling that way again. It was good to know that she was. Even if it never went anywhere with Sean, it was still a good sign to her that she was ready to think about dating again.

CHAPTER FOURTEEN

Riley was glad that Jack texted her that he was taking an earlier flight. It would get him into Hyannis at three thirty, which was perfect timing to get home to Chatham, settle in, and then head to the inn, where Riley was going to do the first chocolate turndown service and then the wine and cheese happy hour at five.

She didn't hit any traffic on the way to Hyannis even though it was a Friday. This time of year, the Cape was so much quieter. It was nothing like the summer when the population doubled and traffic could be annoying at times. Still, it was never as bad as in Manhattan. But that was why Riley didn't bother with having a car in the city. It was too expensive and it was often faster to walk.

She parked and made her way into the small airport. She was glad that the weather was good. It was a clear day, cold but sunny and there was a possibility of flurries later, which would add to the festivities downtown. She knew Jack had grown up in Chicago, so he was used to city life. He'd never been to Cape Cod. She guessed it would seem very small-town to him. But she hoped he would like it and also like her family. She couldn't imagine anyone not liking her mother and sister. She was very curious to see what they would think about Jack. He was definitely different from other boyfriends she'd had in the past. He was more career focused and driven, really a workaholic.

Riley admired his work ethic, but wished at times that he would relax a little and have a bit more balance to his life. Jack was such a creature of habit. They typically went out once during the week and once or twice on the weekend. Usually it was Saturday night as by the time Friday rolled around, Jack was exhausted and wasn't up for much beyond crashing on the sofa with takeout and going to bed early. Once in a while, he invited her to join him on a quiet Friday night, but usually he preferred to decompress alone and she knew that he often brought work home with him and kept going so that he wouldn't have to work over the weekend.

She spotted him as he came off the small plane and grabbed his overnight bag off the trolley as he walked toward her. He looked good. He always did. Jack had a clean-cut preppy look about him and was wearing tan pants and a pink button-down shirt with a navy cashmere sweater over it. His hair was shining from the gel he'd used to slick it back and it looked like he'd had it cut this week. It was a little shorter than usual. He smiled when he spotted her and pulled her in for a hug and kiss when he reached her.

"How was your flight?" she asked him.

"Fine, fast. Not bad at all, really." He looked around him, at the traffic going by on route 28 and the familiar fast-food restaurants in the distance. "So this is Cape Cod? I thought it would look a little different."

Riley grinned. "Wait till you get to Chatham. This area is like the city of the Cape. It's not all like this. You'll see." They walked to her car and Jack threw his bag in the back seat and climbed into the passenger side. Riley pulled out of the airport and onto route 28 and headed toward Chatham. Jack told her all about his week as she drove. He was just starting a new case and it was interesting. His focus was on corporate litigation and he couldn't share client specifics, but he told her enough that she could understand what he was working on.

She took him along the back roads into Chatham so that they drove along the shore, past the Chatham Bars Inn and the lighthouse, and he was impressed by both. And by the huge mansions along the water.

"Is your mother's place on the water?" he asked.

Riley smiled. "No. These homes are worth millions. Ours is much smaller but it's not far from the beach. And it's right on Main Street, so it's an easy walk to downtown."

A few minutes later, she turned onto Main Street, came around a corner, and pulled into her mother's driveway. Jack grabbed his bag and they headed inside to meet her mother.

She was waiting for them in the living room and got to her feet when they walked into the room. Riley introduced Jack and he reached out his hand and flashed his most charming smile. "It's a pleasure to meet you, Mrs. Sanders. Riley mentions you often."

"It's lovely to meet you, too, Jack. Thank you for making the trip to see us. Would you like a coffee or tea?"

"I can get it, Mom, sit down and relax," Riley said.

Her mother laughed. "Very well. I'll take a green tea, with a bit of honey."

"I wouldn't mind a coffee," Jack said.

"Have a seat. I'll be right back." Riley headed to the kitchen while Jack settled on the sofa near her mother. She made her mother's tea first to let it steep while she made coffees for her and Jack. A few minutes later, she returned with the tea and coffees and sat next to Jack on the sofa.

"Your mother was just telling me about the repairs at the inn. And that you helped her get the rooms rented out quickly," Jack said.

Riley nodded. "It worked out well. There were a lot of people searching online for the Chatham Christmas Stroll and they found the blog posts I put up."

"It won't be long before you land a new job." Jack sounded sure of it.

"Hope so. I had a phone interview this afternoon, just before I left to get you at the airport," Riley said.

"How did it go?" Jack asked.

"I think it went okay. It's hard to tell sometimes. They said they will let me know about next steps."

"You might want to check the job listings on my company's site. I heard they might need someone with your background. I don't know much more than that, but the details should be up on the site. It might be fun to work at the same company," he said.

"Thanks, I will look later." A thought occurred to her. "Are you sure your company doesn't have rules about employees dating each other?"

"Hmm. Not that I am aware of. Seems like that is how a lot of people at my company meet their partners. We spend so much time there."

Riley laughed. "That is an understatement."

Jack laughed, too. "Since we're already dating, I don't think it will be an issue as we'll be up-front about it," he added.

"Do you like what you do, Jack? Riley says you often work long hours," her mother asked.

He nodded. "Fortunately, I do. And I know the hours are working toward making partner. So, hopefully it will be worth it."

When they finished their coffees, Riley showed Jack where they were sleeping upstairs and he brought his bag up to the room.

When they came downstairs it was time to head to the inn.

Riley drove them over and showed Jack around, giving him the tour of the downstairs, including the two rooms that had been repaired, as the guests hadn't checked in yet for either. They'd let her mother know they'd be there shortly before five. They were beautiful rooms. All of the rooms at the inn were very cozy and elegantly decorated with seascape watercolor paintings and thick white comforters and pretty accent pillows in shades of blue and green. A small table made of polished dark pine was by a window, and matching chairs with seafoam-green cushions sat on either side.

"Doesn't look like either room had work done," Jack said.

"I know. Sean, the carpenter my mother found, did a great job," Riley agreed. They made their way back to the kitchen and Riley opened the drawer where she'd stashed the chocolates. She counted out nineteen boxes. She'd had the candy shop put two chocolates in each box, and every room, except for Franny's, had two people staying in it.

At a quarter to five, Riley planned to start the turndown service with the two rooms that had been repaired, since they were vacant. By the time she got upstairs to the other rooms, the guests would likely have headed to the living room for wine and cheese.

"If you want to join my mother in the living room, I'm going to go do the turndown service quickly and then I'll join you," Riley said.

Jack raised his eyebrows. "You're going to do it? Doesn't your mother have people for that?" His tone was dismissive as if the work was beneath her.

"She has help, but Ethel finished up hours ago. This won't take me long. I'm just fluffing pillows and dropping off candy." Riley smiled. "I'll be along shortly. You can pour me a glass of red wine if you like."

"All right. See you in a bit, then." Jack made his way into

the living room where her mother was getting ready for the wine and cheese service. Riley put the little chocolate boxes in a bag and set off to start the turndown service. It didn't take long. She went into each room and folded the comforter back, fluffed the pillows, and placed a box of chocolate in the middle of the main pillows.

After she finished the two unoccupied rooms, she went to the two other downstairs rooms, knocking first to make sure she didn't interrupt anything, before using the master key to let herself in. She worked quickly and a few minutes later, headed upstairs. Half of the rooms were empty but a few were occupied. Franny happily let her in and watched as she turned the bedspread down and laid the box of chocolate on her pillow. Franny's eyes lit up. "I may need to open that box now to see what's inside."

Riley laughed. "It's chocolate. Truffles today."

Franny opened her box and nodded approvingly at the selection of one milk chocolate and one raspberry dark chocolate truffle. "This is a lovely treat. Thank you, dear."

"You're very welcome. Will we see you in a few minutes for wine and cheese?"

"I'll be there. I'm looking forward to it."

Aidan and Luke's room was next, and they were both there, as well. Aidan invited her in, looking amused. "Is this the chocolate service you mentioned?"

She nodded. "Unless you don't want it?" she teased.

"We want it! Don't we, Dad?" Luke said.

Aidan laughed. "I guess we do."

It took Riley just a few minutes to turn down the comforter, fluff the pillows, and set the two boxes of chocolate down. Luke immediately ran to one of them and grabbed it. "Can I open it now?" he asked.

"You can open it, but wait until later to eat it," Aidan said.

Luke opened the box eagerly then looked up. "What about if I just have one now and save the other for later?" He tried to negotiate.

Aidan nodded. "Sure, that's fine. Maybe I'll do the same." He picked up his box and opened it. Riley was happy to see that so far the chocolate turndown service seemed to be a hit.

"Will I see you both downstairs in a few minutes? Luke, there will be hot chocolate and cheese and crackers."

"Can I have hot chocolate?" Luke asked.

Aidan smiled. "Absolutely. And I am just about ready for wine."

Riley glanced at a clock on the wall and saw that it was a few minute past five. "You guys should head down. I just have a few more rooms to do and I'll be right behind you."

They headed downstairs as Riley left for the next room. Five minutes later, she was done and made her way to the living room. Her mother was at the front desk, welcoming the two new arrivals and giving them the keys to their rooms.

"Once you're settled in, please join us for wine and cheese hour in the living room," she told them.

When Riley reached Jack, he was chatting with Franny. He handed her the wine she'd requested earlier. It was a red blend that Riley had picked up at Trader Joe's in Hyannis on her way to the airport. It was inexpensive but also smooth and delicious. She took a small sip and glanced around the room. Everyone had a glass of wine in hand, or in Luke's case, a mug of hot chocolate. When she glanced their way, she caught Aidan's eye and she waved him over and introduced him and Luke to Jack. She did not mention that she and Aidan had dated many years ago, just that they went to high school together.

"Have you two been dating long?" Aidan asked after Jack stepped away to get more cheese.

"Almost two years." Riley knew that sounded like a long time.

"So you guys are pretty serious, then?" Aidan asked.

Riley nodded. They were exclusive, but it didn't feel overly serious, because she didn't usually see Jack more than once or twice a week. And they'd both been fine with that. But Riley was starting to wonder if she might want more. Especially now that she wasn't working and had more time to think about where things stood with their relationship.

Jack returned with a plate of cheese and crackers and Riley helped herself to a slice of cheddar on a cracker. A moment later, her sister and Rob and the girls walked in. Riley went to say hello and introduced them to Jack. Riley and Amy left him chatting with Rob while they went to the kitchen with the girls to make their hot chocolate with mini-marshmallows.

"He's cute," Amy said. "Was that tall guy by the cheese and crackers Aidan? I noticed a young boy standing by him."

"Yes. I'm sure he'll remember you. I'm surprised you haven't run into him over the years. Chatham is a small town."

Amy laughed. "Just wait until you have kids one day. I don't go anywhere. And we didn't move back here until shortly before then."

"Okay, you have a point. And he has Luke, too, so he's probably not out and about either."

"Everything changes when you have kids. Once in a blue moon Rob and I get a sitter and go out, but that's only been in the past year or so. It was just too hard to pull it off before then. We were both so busy and exhausted that the last thing we felt like doing was getting dressed up and going out to dinner."

"Well, you should take advantage of my being here for the next few weeks. I'm happy to watch the girls anytime so you two can have a date night."

Amy looked intrigued by the offer. "I just might take you up on that. The girls would love it and it would be fun for us."

"Just let me know. I'm wide open after this weekend."

Aidan walked over and introduced himself to Amy. "It's been a long time, but I thought I recognized you. Riley told me you're back in Chatham now, too, and have twins."

"It's great to see you, Aidan. Riley told me you were here and you have a child, too, a nine-year-old boy?"

"Yes, Luke."

Riley left the two of them to chat and went to walk around the room, topping off people's wineglasses and encouraging them to help themselves to more cheese and crackers.

When she reached Franny, she held out her glass and offered her thanks. "This is just lovely, Riley. I told your mother as well. It's so nice to see everyone this way and the room looks so festive."

Riley had to agree. They'd added electric candle lights in all the windows and she'd run a string of mini-lights across the fireplace mantel. The tree glowed merrily in the corner and soft Christmas carols played in the background.

"It is nice. I'm glad you're enjoying it. You're coming with us to the tree lighting?"

Franny nodded. "I wouldn't miss it."

"Good. We're heading out shortly." Riley finished her walk around the room. She brought the now-empty bottle to the kitchen. The wine and cheese had been a big hit. A few minutes before six, Riley brought the cheese tray into the kitchen. It was mostly empty at this point. She dumped the remaining few crackers and pieces of cheese in the trash and rinsed the platter with soap and hot water.

She walked back into the living room and addressed the group. "Thanks so much for coming to our first wine and cheese hour. It's six now, so some of us are going to walk down-town to the tree lighting. All are welcome to join us."

People began leaving and either headed up to their rooms or out the door. Riley quickly cleared the empty glasses and brought them into the kitchen and gave them a quick rinse.

When she returned to the living room, everyone looked ready to go. They put on their coats, hats, and mittens and headed out the door. Riley glanced at her mother, who was settling herself onto her crutches.

"Mom, are you sure you can manage? I could probably drive you closer."

But her mother shook her head. "I'm fine. It's not far and I'll just go slow."

Everyone headed out and slowly made their way down Main Street. There were so many people walking in the same direction that they had to go slowly. So, her mother managed to keep up just fine.

Riley noticed that many of the shops were now decorated for Christmas with lights in the windows and it looked so pretty as they walked along. When they reached the tree, there was a big crowd gathered. Carolers sang "Jingle Bells" and then it was time to turn the lights on. The crowd cheered when the tree lights were plugged in and the huge tree lit up. It was a magical sight and Riley felt a rush of joy as she saw the looks of wonder on the girls' faces and on Luke's as they stared at the tree.

They strolled along a bit after that. All the shops were open and some were handing out mulled warm cider. They stopped at the coffee shop, which had stayed open later than usual. Caitlin was outside and was dressed like an elf, all in red, and was holding a silver tray of iced gingerbread cookies shaped like Christmas stockings. She offered a free cookie to everyone that came by. The girls and Luke were first in line to get one.

"Riley, what do you think? Can I tempt you with gingerbread?" Caitlin asked with a grin.

"Of course. Thank you." She reached for a cookie and grabbed one for Jack, too, and handed it to him.

"So, what do you think of Chatham and my family, so far?" she asked.

"Very nice, all of it. Your mom is a sweetheart." He grinned as he took in the crowded Main Street and twinkling lights everywhere. "This is like a Hallmark Christmas movie."

CHAPTER FIFTEEN

Beth was having a wonderful evening so far. The wine and cheese hour had been a success and she always loved spending time with her girls and her grandchildren. The twins were at a fun age and they looked adorable in their matching red velvet dresses with their black tights and boots. They wore black wool peacoats and had red hats and mittens.

Beth looked around, but didn't see Sean anywhere yet. It was crowded, though, and it wasn't like they had any definite plans to meet up. Still, she'd hoped that she would run into him. But once the tree was lit and the crowds dispersed to stroll along and visit the shops, there was still no sign of Sean. She was disappointed but put it out of her mind and focused on having fun with her family. She was glad that she was able to move about more easily now on the crutches, too.

They stopped into the candy store, which was giving out samples of fudge. It was really good and Beth bought some to nibble on later. She offered to get some for the girls but Amy shook her head. "I think they've had enough sugar with the hot chocolate. I want them to eat dinner when we get home."

"Are you sure you don't want to come out to dinner with us?" Riley asked Amy.

"No, I think it's best if we get the girls home. It's so busy tonight, we'll never get seated if all of us go."

Beth knew she was right. She was happy that they'd been able to join them for the tree lighting.

"Don't forget, you're coming to our house for Sunday dinner this week," Amy reminded her.

Beth smiled. "I'm looking forward to it. Let me know what I can bring."

"Maybe something for dessert?" Amy suggested.

"We can make chocolate-chip cookies or brownies," Riley said.

"Either sounds good to me," Amy replied.

When they exited the candy store, Beth felt her stomach do a flip when she spotted Sean, walking with an older woman. They were heading her way and he smiled when he saw her.

"I thought I'd missed you," he said when they reached her. "Beth, this is my mother, Angela."

"It's so nice to meet you," Angela said. She was soft-spoken with sharp eyes that swept over the group and took it all in. Beth introduced her to everyone. She noticed that Angela was about the same age as Franny, and Angela had known Franny's sister. The two of them were chatting away like they'd know each other for ages. A few minutes later, Amy said she and Rob were going to take off.

"I think Luke and I are going to head home as well. It was great to meet you all," Aidan said.

That left Riley, Jack, Franny, Sean, and Angela. "We were thinking of grabbing a bite to eat. Would you like to join us?" Beth asked.

Sean hesitated and seemed unsure, but Angela answered without hesitation. "We'd love to. I'm starving actually. Where are we going?"

The Chatham Squire was across the street, so they decided

to try that first. There were six of them, so they had to put their name in. "I don't think it will be too long," the hostess said. "We have a larger party that is on dessert now."

They made their way toward the back of the bar so they would be out of the way.

"What would everyone like? This round is on me," Sean said.

"Oh, you don't have to do that," Beth protested.

But Angela laughed. "Yes, he does, actually. I'll have a Chardonnay."

They all told Sean what they wanted and he went to the bar and placed their order. Jack helped him to deliver the drinks and they'd only had them for a few minutes when the hostess came and found them to let them know their table was ready.

She led them to a big round table in a corner. Franny and Angela sat next to each other. Sean sat next to his mother on Beth's right, with Riley to her left. She noticed with amusement that Franny and Angela were deep in conversation.

"From what I can gather, they know some of the same people, or used to. My mother is about Franny's age, I think, and they went to high school together," Sean said.

"Ah. It really is a small world," Beth replied.

Their server told them about the specials, which were grilled swordfish or a New York strip steak with two sautéed shrimp. Beth and Riley both went with lobster rolls. Franny got the fish and chips, Angela went with a scallop roll, Sean got a burger, and Jack ordered a fried fisherman's platter.

"Riley says the seafood in Chatham is great, so I figured this way I can try it all," he said.

"Do you like seafood?" Beth asked Sean.

He laughed. "You'd think I would, growing up here, but I can't stand any of it. I'm a meat and potatoes kind of guy. That strip steak sounded good, but I was in the mood for a burger."

"How did your other project go?" Beth asked him.

"Good. It was a quick and easy one. I just needed to install some crown moldings in a few rooms. A friend recently bought a house and wanted to make a few updates."

"I love crown moldings."

"Yeah, it turned out nice. Really dresses up a room," Sean agreed.

"Is this normally a slow time of year for you?" Beth wondered.

He nodded. "It is. Spring, summer, even fall is very busy, and a lot of my work is outside. Then it slows way down in the winter months. Which is fine by me. I usually enjoy the quiet and take a little time off. Sometimes I go south for a few weeks."

"He visits me," Angela said. "I have a condo in Naples, Florida, and usually head down after the holidays in January and stay through April. By then, I'm ready to come back to the Cape."

The way his mother spoke, it didn't sound like Sean had a girlfriend as she made it seem like Sean visited alone. She wondered how long he'd been divorced. But she didn't want to ask in front of everyone. That seemed too nosy and too personal. So, instead, she asked how he knew Ryan, Jess's boyfriend.

"Ryan and I go way back. We grew up on the same street. I've met Jess a few times. She said the two of you are good friends?"

Beth nodded. "We are. We lost touch for years when she moved to Charleston after graduating college and getting married. But we reconnected again when she got divorced and moved home."

They continued chatting and she learned that he was a few years ahead of her in school, which is why she hadn't known him growing up. Their food arrived soon after and they all dug in. Beth laughed at the expression on Jack's face when they set the fisherman's platter in front of him. It was a huge tower of fried seafood, clams, shrimp, scallops, and fish, topped with fried onion rings and fries on the side.

Jack loved it. They all did. Beth wasn't sure yet what she thought of Jack. He seemed nice enough, but there was something there she couldn't put her finger on. She wasn't sure he was quite right for Riley. Though she couldn't say why not. Maybe she just didn't know him well enough yet to judge. They hadn't had a chance to talk much since he'd arrived. Hopefully she'd get a chance to dig a little deeper over the weekend. As long as he made Riley happy, that was the main thing.

"Do you have a busy week next week?" Beth asked Sean.

"I do. I'm normally pretty fully booked, this past week was unusual with the cancellation. That doesn't happen often."

She smiled. "Well, it worked out very well for me. I'm so grateful you could fit us in."

"I'm glad you could get those two rooms rented. Weekends like this don't come along often in the winter," Sean said.

"You're so right about that. It has been slow. Riley has been a godsend. She did something with online marketing that really helped to get the word out. I'm lucky to have her around for the next few weeks."

Riley overheard and smiled her way. "It's fun for me, too. It's nice seeing how the marketing can directly affect a small business. I don't usually see that part."

"What kind of a company do you work for?" Sean asked.

"I worked for a marketing agency, so we had lots of clients. We did the marketing, but never directly saw the results. They just laid off my whole team, so I'm job searching at the moment."

Sean looked sympathetic. "I'm sorry to hear that. I hope you find something good soon."

"Thanks. I had a phone interview earlier and I just got

an email before we left that they want to do a video call next week. So, that's a start, at least."

"Oh, that's great news, honey." Beth was happy for her. She knew how stressful it was to be out of a job and looking for a new one. Riley didn't seem too worried about it yet, which was a good thing. Beth was sure she'd find something pretty quickly.

"I don't think Riley will have any trouble finding something new." Jack echoed her thoughts and Beth liked that he sounded so confident. "I told her we have an opening at my company she should apply for, too. It just opened up."

"I'll definitely check that out," Riley said.

Beth couldn't help wondering if that was a good idea. She thought it might be too close for comfort to be working at the same company as someone Riley was dating. But maybe it would be fine. She knew Jack worked for a very successful law firm. No doubt the benefits there were good. Beth also wondered if Riley's career growth might be limited at a law firm. But Riley was smart to look into it and explore as many options as possible.

When they finished, Jack packed up his leftovers. He'd barely eaten half of his meal, which was huge.

"It was very good. Riley was right about the seafood here," he said.

When the server brought their bill, Jack took it and handed her his credit card before any of them had a chance to even reach for their wallets. Sean frowned and Beth could tell he wasn't comfortable with it.

"Can we split it at least?" He handed Jack his credit card but Jack waved it away.

"I've got it. Least I can do, since Beth has welcomed me into her home for the weekend," he said.

"All right. Thank you, then," Sean said.

They all chimed in, thanking him, and Jack smiled and looked pleased. When the server handed him back his credit card, Beth noticed that it was a Black Mastercard, one of the special invite-only cards. Beth appreciated the gesture, it was very nice of him. And she knew he could easily afford it. Riley had told her once what Jack's salary was and it was a huge amount, even for New York City where everything was so expensive. Being a corporate litigation attorney at a top law firm in the city paid very well indeed. And Riley had said that when Jack made partner, his salary would go way up and he would share in firm profits each year, which would be a significant amount. If things progressed with Riley, they would be just fine financially. Beth still wasn't sure about him, though.

When they stepped outside, it had started to snow while they were eating and the ground was covered in a fine dusting of snow. Sean looked concerned when he saw it.

"Will you be able to manage okay with your crutches?"

Beth tested the ground and it didn't seem slippery yet. "As long as I go slowly, I should be fine. We're parked at the inn so it's just a short walk."

"We parked down that way, too, a little beyond the inn."

They set off walking in pairs along the sidewalk. Riley and Jack took the lead, followed by Angela and Franny, who were laughing and chatting up a storm. Beth went slowly and it really wasn't too bad. Though it wouldn't be much longer before it would be slippery. The snow was coming down more heavily now, in big, fat flakes. She loved to see it and it added to the magic and festivity of the evening. Now that she'd had a chance to chat with Sean, she liked him even more, and she wasn't sure but she thought she possibly sensed a spark of interest from him, as well.

They chatted easily as they walked, and the time went by almost too quickly for Beth. In less than ten minutes they reached the inn. Angela and Franny were still chatting away and Riley and Jack were already at Riley's car. Sean stopped for a moment, to say good night.

"Thanks for inviting us to join you. That was a fun time. And my mother enjoyed it." He grinned. "It looks like she and Franny are best friends."

"I'm glad to see it," Beth said. "Franny could use a friend here. She's going to be in Chatham through the holidays."

"What would you say about having dinner again soon—but just the two of us?" Sean asked.

Beth smiled and felt a rush of happiness. "I'd really like that."

"Great, I'll give you a call in a few days and we'll make a plan."

Beth said goodbye to Angela and carefully made her way to Riley's car and climbed in the back seat with her crutches. She felt very full and content—and excited about what was to come. It had been a magical evening, more than she'd expected.

CHAPTER SIXTEEN

Riley was floating on a happy cloud of Christmas spirit. The evening had been so fun and she was glad that Jack got to meet her family and experience the Chatham Christmas Stroll. He seemed to enjoy himself—especially that fisherman's platter. They put it in the refrigerator when they got home and she said it would heat up easily in the oven for lunch the next day.

They collapsed on the living room sofa and Riley clicked on the television while they waited for her mother to join them. Riley had been happy to see that Sean seemed to be as interested as her mother was. It was the first time in years that she'd seen her mother excited about dating someone. It was about time as far as Riley was concerned. And Sean seemed like a nice guy, down to earth. He'd brought his mother to the Christmas Stroll, after all. That was a sign that he was a decent guy.

She flipped through the channels to find something they'd both enjoy. Jack didn't seem to be paying attention, though. He was on his phone, furiously texting someone. She shot him a look, wondering what was so important. He paused texting for a moment to explain.

"It's Brittany, from work. She gave me the heads-up that we have a problem with our big case that we thought was all set.

A new issue has come up that needs to be addressed. She's still in the office, working on it."

Riley glanced at the time. It was almost ten. "She's seriously in the office at ten on a Friday night?"

Jack shrugged as if it was no big deal. "They got the call just before five and two of them have stayed late trying to resolve it. But it's bigger than they realized. She's heading home shortly and just wanted to give me the details."

"Is there anything you can do about it from here?" Riley wondered.

"I can try. I have my laptop with me."

Of course he did. Riley could see that he was anxious to dig into it and see if he could get the work done.

"You could do it in the morning. We don't have to be anywhere," she said.

Jack glanced down at his phone, which had dinged again with a new message. "I could. But they're heading back into the office tomorrow morning, too, and I'd like to see if I can help before that."

"You want to work on it now?" Riley wasn't surprised. This was who Jack was. Work was always his top priority.

"Yeah. You don't mind, do you? I can go in the kitchen so I won't bother you or your mother."

"Sure, do what you need to do." Riley's tone was flat. She wasn't mad but she was disappointed.

Jack ran upstairs, got his laptop, and disappeared into the kitchen. Riley turned her attention to the TV and landed on the Hallmark Channel where a new Christmas movie was about to start. Her mother had gone to change into her sweats and looked around when she walked into the room.

"Where's Jack?" she asked.

Riley glanced toward the kitchen. "Work emergency. Fortunately he brought his laptop with him."

Her mother glanced at the time and said nothing.

Riley sighed. "I know. Two people from his work are still in the office, so he felt bad and wanted to help, if he could."

"Well, he's certainly committed," her mother said. She leaned her crutches against her chair and settled into it, pulling her favorite fleece over her lap. Lily took that as an invitation and jumped into it. Her mother laughed and petted her while Lily purred loudly before flopping down and snuggling into the fleece.

"So, that was a fun night," Riley said. "Do you think you'll see Sean again?"

Her mother smiled. "He suggested dinner sometime next week. Just the two of us."

"Oh, that's wonderful! He really seems like a nice guy."

"I think so. We'll see how it goes." Her mother seemed excited but also cautiously optimistic, which Riley thought was probably a good thing. Her mother still needed to learn more about Sean and getting to know him slowly seemed smart. It was hard to judge when you first met someone what they were really like. Riley had been crazy about Jack at first, as he could be very charming and they'd had some romantic dinners at impressive restaurants in the city. He had been lots of fun and though she knew he was a successful attorney, she'd had no idea then how much of a workaholic he was. Or how driven. It was something she admired about him but lately it was also becoming something of a concern.

Riley went up to bed an hour later and Jack was still working away in the kitchen. She tossed and turned for a while and finally fell asleep. She never heard him come up to bed. When she woke around seven to get ready to serve breakfast, Jack was fast asleep. He didn't stir as she moved around the room. After she showered and changed, he was still dead to the world. She left him a note to help himself to coffee and whatever he wanted to eat in the kitchen and said they'd be back around ten thirty or so.

Breakfast was busy at the inn, but it was quiet for the first hour as everyone seemed to be sleeping in. Except Franny. She joined them a little after eight and had a bowl of oatmeal and blueberries with her coffee. Riley had made an artichoke and spinach quiche, but both she and her mother ate lightly, just having fruit and toast. Franny was excited about her new friend and let them know that she and Angela had plans to meet up soon.

"She invited me to attend her book club next Wednesday night. Isn't that nice? We both love books and I'd mentioned that I was missing my club from home. Hers is down a few people so she said they'd be happy to have me. Even if it's just a temporary thing. And it turns out the book they are discussing is one I already read recently."

"That sounds fun," Riley said. "Do you have dinner or is it just a discussion?"

"It's drinks and dinner. Sort of a potluck. The host makes the main meal and everyone else brings an appetizer or salad or dessert. I told her I'll bring a cheese and cracker selection. I love that wine and cheese shop on Main Street. They have some unusual cheeses."

"I love that shop, too," Beth agreed. "The young woman that works there has recommended some wines that I've liked quite a bit. They're reasonably priced, too. And the owner is super nice, as well. This is his passion. He opened the shop recently after retiring."

"Oh, how fun, to do something like that. I'll have to make a point to stop in again and let him know how much I love his shop," Franny said.

Riley's mother and Franny chatted about their favorite wines and cheeses while Riley sipped her coffee and wondered how the rest of her weekend with Jack was going to go. She didn't have a good feeling about it after his late night working. She had been looking forward to relaxing with him the rest of the weekend. She'd thought they might head out somewhere tonight for a romantic dinner, maybe at the Impudent Oyster, one of the best restaurants in the area. And she was looking forward to him joining them for Sunday dinner at Amy's house. She thought it would be a good chance for Amy and Rob to get to know him better. They hadn't had a chance to really talk to him much last night.

"What do you have planned for Jack for the rest of the weekend?" Franny asked. Riley smiled. It was almost as if Franny had read her mind.

"I was thinking maybe dinner at the Impudent Oyster if we can get in. If not, we'll find somewhere else."

"Oh, that will be lovely." Franny took a sip of coffee then changed the subject. "Did you hear they're talking about a big storm now either late tonight or early tomorrow? Does the inn have a generator by any chance in case we lose power?"

Riley and her mother looked at each other. "I hadn't heard that," Riley said.

Her mother frowned. "I haven't checked the news today. I saw something earlier in the week about a possible storm, but it didn't seem like a big deal then. We do have a generator, thankfully. I have one at my house, too. We've lost power a few too many times because of the winds in storms and I hate that. And with the inn, I didn't want guests to be without it either. Takes the fun out of a vacation."

"I remember when you got the generator for the house

first. It seemed like a big expense, but it really has been worth it," Riley agreed.

"It's not supposed to start until late tonight at the earliest, so you should still be able to have your romantic date night," Franny said.

Riley laughed. "I hope so."

CHAPTER SEVENTEEN

But after breakfast was over and they headed home, Riley found Jack back in the kitchen on his laptop. He looked frazzled as he ran a hand through his hair, which was tousled and going in every different direction. He hadn't showered yet or eaten anything, but he did have a half-empty coffee cup by his side. He looked up when he heard them walk in.

"Did you sleep all right?" Riley's mother asked. "There are bagels or I could make you some eggs if you're hungry," she offered.

"I was just thinking about toasting up a bagel, actually."

"I'll do it for you." Riley sliced a bagel and put it in the toaster. When it was done, she put it on a plate and handed it to him, along with a tub of cream cheese.

"Thanks." He spread a thick layer of cheese on the bagel, while Riley made another cup of coffee for herself. Her mother excused herself to head upstairs and do some laundry. Riley settled at the kitchen table with her coffee and watched Jack for a moment as he absentmindedly ate his bagel and stared at the laptop screen.

"Are you making any headway?" she asked.

He nodded. "Yes. Getting there. There's still a lot more to do, though."

"You won't have to work all day, will you? I thought we could drive around and I could show you more of Chatham and maybe tonight we could have a nice dinner at one of my favorite restaurants."

Jack turned and looked at her—frustration and exhaustion written clearly across his face. "Riley, have you seen the weather reports? We're getting a huge storm, either late tonight or tomorrow morning. If it's really bad I might not be able to get out of here on time. I hate to cut this short, but given the storm and what's going on with work, I think maybe I should head back this afternoon. I can't risk getting stuck here and I really should work on this tomorrow to get ahead of it for Monday. You understand, don't you?"

Riley sighed. She did understand. If the storm was really bad, flights would be delayed or even outright canceled. And she could tell Jack's attention was elsewhere. As usual.

"I can drive you to Hyannis after lunch. You might as well eat your leftovers before you go," she said.

Jack grinned. "You really are the best. I hate to go, but I don't think we really have a choice on this."

There was always a choice, but Riley knew what was most important to Jack, and it was becoming clear that it wasn't her.

Riley drove Jack to the airport after lunch and he was able to get on a three o'clock flight back to New York. He knew she was disappointed and pulled her in for a hug when he got out of the car.

"I'm so sorry about this, Riley. I really did want to stay the whole weekend. But it looks like Mother Nature had a different idea about that." His eyes twinkled and he searched hers, hoping for her to smile in return. But she couldn't manage it. There was nothing funny about the situation to her. She was disappointed that Jack didn't want to take his chances and spend time with her and her family. So what if there was a storm and maybe he'd have to miss a day of work? But she knew that was impossible for him to even consider. Work always came first. Always.

"Have a safe flight back, Jack. And good luck with your case."

He kissed her goodbye and she kissed him back. But there was no joy in it for her. She watched him walk into the airport with his carry-on bag and then she drove away. She felt restless and irritated and decided to stop at Trader Joe's, which was right near the airport. They could use more cheese for upcoming wine and cheese hours and roaming the aisles at Trader Joe's always cheered her up. She was a little bit hungry, too, which was always a dangerous thing in a grocery store. She stocked up on a bunch of different cheeses, including her favorite cheddar that had a hint of a Parmesan taste to it. And she found a new one, a cheese spread that used the same cheese.

She bought more of the wine that had been a hit with everyone and she found a few new ones to try as well. She grabbed some grapes and a few boxes of crackers and then checked out.

She noticed as she drove back to Chatham that the wind had picked up and the sky was dark. They were definitely in for a storm at some point. Maybe Jack had made the right decision—the responsible decision, to head home early. As much as she hated to admit it. Though it could still turn out to be nothing. One never really knew.

Riley dropped everything off at the inn before heading home. She walked through the living room on her way out the door and stopped short at the sight of two small feet in dark green socks sticking out from under the tree. She walked closer to get a better look, and then smiled. It was Luke, snuggled in the corner behind the tree. He was lying on his back, reading a book.

"Hey, Luke, how do you like it back there?" she asked.

"Is that Riley?"

"It is. I just stopped by for a minute. We'll be back soon, though."

"It's so awesome back here. My dad said it was okay if I read here for a while."

"It's totally okay. I used to love it back there." Riley remembered the many happy hours she and Amy spent behind the Christmas tree over the years. And she'd done what Luke was doing right now so many times when she'd been by herself. She could stay back there for hours with a good book. "What are you reading? Anything good?"

"*Diary of a Wimpy Kid*. I'm on book three."

Riley smiled at the excitement in his voice. "I've heard of that one, and you're already on book three. It must be pretty good."

"It's awesome!"

Riley laughed. "Well, I'll let you get back to your reading. We'll see you in an hour or so for hot chocolate."

"Cool. See ya later, Riley."

CHAPTER EIGHTEEN

Riley headed home and found her mother folding laundry. They both looked toward the window as the wind howled and the panes shook a little.

"Jack got off okay? No delays?" her mother asked.

"He got out fine. If this keeps up, though, they will probably cancel flights, I imagine," she said.

"Seems like he did the right thing going home early. I'm sorry, honey. I know you're disappointed. At least we got to meet him."

"You did. What did you think of him?" Riley asked.

Her mother was quiet for a moment before speaking. "He's clearly very driven and successful and smart. And he has good taste in girlfriends." She smiled. "I do wish we'd had more time to get to know him better. Hopefully he'll come back again to see us."

"Hopefully." Riley wasn't going to hold her breath that it would happen anytime soon. Jack was just too busy, and going into winter now, the weather was going to continue to be unpredictable. "On a different note, I spotted Luke reading behind the Christmas tree when I left. It was cute. Reminded me of when Amy and I used to do that."

Her mother smiled at the memory, too. "I'm glad he feels

comfortable enough at the inn to do that. I know he misses having his own tree this year."

A short while later, they headed back to the inn. Riley cut the cheeses and set up the platter with grapes and crackers and several of the cut cheeses, while her mother opened the wine bottles they planned to serve. Riley brought everything into the living room. Then she left her mother to oversee it while Riley made the rounds to drop off the chocolates and turn down the bedcovers in each room.

When she reached Aidan and Luke's room, there was no answer, so she guessed they'd already headed to the living room. A few of the guests had asked that she just leave the chocolates outside the door, so she was able to finish up even faster. She headed back to the living room and saw that almost everyone was there already, including Aidan and Luke.

She felt a wave of sadness that Jack wasn't with them. That they weren't heading out to dinner after the wine and cheese hour. He was probably back at his apartment by now. She imagined he was probably working a little or just relaxing at home. Or maybe he was out with friends. It didn't matter much to her either way at this point. She sighed and took a sip of the Cabernet her mother had handed her.

"Are you okay, honey? You looked a million miles away," her mother said softly.

Riley smiled. "I'm fine, thanks. This wine is really good. Which one is it?"

"I think this one is the Josh. It's a nice easy-drinking Cab. And it's inexpensive, too."

"I like it." Riley turned at the sound of Aidan's voice. He'd walked up beside her. Luke was beside him, holding his mug of hot chocolate with both hands.

"Hey, Aidan," Riley greeted him as the lights flickered for a moment. She could hear the wind howling even more loudly outside.

"Guess we're in for a good storm." He reached for a slice of cheddar and cracker and popped it in his mouth. "Where's Jack?"

"He headed home this afternoon instead of tomorrow, to beat the storm. Just in case it turns into a big one." The lights flickered again and Luke looked excited.

"Do you think the lights will go out all the way?" Luke asked.

"They might," Riley said. "But we have a generator, so if they do, our power should kick right back on."

Luke looked disappointed, but Aidan didn't. "I didn't realize that. Good to know."

Riley glanced around the room. Just about all of the guests were in the living room now and all seemed to be enjoying the wine and cheese hour. Her mother was making the rounds and talking with everyone, and was managing just fine with her crutches. Riley knew she enjoyed chatting with everyone and overall was so much happier since she'd opened the inn. It was the perfect career for her.

Riley wondered where she would end up and hoped her next company would be a place she could stay longer and grow with the company. She had the video interview coming up on Tuesday, but so far, there had been no other bites on her resume. Jack had sent her the link to the opening at his firm and she'd been on the fence about even applying, but until she landed something, she realized she should keep an open mind and apply for just about everything.

"Dad says if there's enough snow that we can make a snowman tomorrow. But I have to get your permission first. So, can we?" Luke asked.

Riley laughed. "I'm sure my mother would be very excited if you built a snowman for us."

"Maybe you can help!" Luke suggested.

"Maybe. It depends what time. We might be going to my sister's for lunch tomorrow. But I'll be free for a little while after ten, when breakfast service ends," she said.

"Let's wait and see how it looks tomorrow, buddy," Aidan said.

Luke wandered away to get more cheese and crackers and Aidan immediately apologized. "I'm so sorry. I don't want you to feel like you have to do that with us."

But Riley didn't mind. It was nice to feel wanted. "I don't mind. I've always liked building snowmen. It's been a while since I've done that."

He laughed. "Probably not too many opportunities in the city, I imagine."

"Nope. Not on my street," she agreed.

"I am sorry your dinner plans got canceled tonight. Luke and I were thinking of getting a few pizzas. If you're interested in sharing, there will be plenty. Your mother is welcome, too, of course." He looked so kind and friendly and she thought it was nice of him to invite them.

"That sounds pretty good, actually. We could go to my mother's house where we won't be interrupted by people coming and going."

"If she doesn't mind, that sounds great. And we'll drive over. Normally I'd say a half mile is an easy walk, but it might get messy out there."

"I don't think she'll mind at all, but I will go check to make sure." Riley went off to find her mother and ran the pizza idea by her.

"Well, that's certainly fine for me. I hadn't given supper much thought and I don't really feel like cooking."

"I don't either," Riley agreed. "I'll tell him it's a go, then."

On her way back to find Aidan, Riley ran into Franny, who was in search of more cheese and crackers.

"All your cheeses are good, but this one that tastes a bit like Parmesan and cheddar together is my favorite. I don't think I'm going to need any supper," she said.

"That one is my favorite, too," Riley said.

"A few more and I'll be ready to head upstairs and hunker down for the evening. I started a new book this morning, a suspense novel, and I'm eager to get back to it."

"It's definitely a good night to stay in," Riley agreed. "I'll see you at breakfast tomorrow, Franny."

At six, Riley put the cheese and crackers and wine away and said good night to everyone. Aidan asked what kind of pizza she and her mother liked and then called the order in. "I'm having it delivered here and then we'll just bring it right over," he said. "I'm guessing we'll be by in a little over a half hour."

He was close. About forty-five minutes later, Aidan knocked on the door carrying three big pizzas. Luke was right behind him. And the snow had started. It was coming down lightly but the winds were strong and it would no doubt intensify as the night went on. They stepped inside and handed the pizzas to Riley, who set them on the kitchen table and went looking for some paper plates and napkins.

There was one plain cheese pizza, one pepperoni, and one with sausage, mushrooms, peppers, and onions. They all looked and smelled delicious. Once Aidan and Luke took off their coats and shoes, they joined Riley and her mother in the kitchen and everyone helped themselves. Aidan and Luke both had Cokes and Riley and her mother had water. They took everything into the living room. Aidan and Luke sat on the big comfy sofa, while Riley took the love seat, and her mother sat in her usual chair.

"We could watch a Christmas movie," her mother suggested. "Have you seen *Christmas with the Kranks*? That's one of my favorites. It's very funny."

"Luke hasn't seen that one. I agree, it is funny. I'd love to watch it," Aidan said.

Her mother turned the movie on and they started watching while they ate. Riley noticed how good Aidan was with Luke, encouraging him to eat a second slice. He also offered to get more for them. Her mother passed. She was content with the two slices she'd taken. Riley, however, opted for a third and decided to try one of the sausage slices.

She had only seen the movie once and it was years ago. She'd forgotten how funny it was. They all laughed throughout the whole movie. By the time it ended, Luke was almost asleep.

"I should probably get this guy home to bed," Aidan said. He sounded as though he would have liked to stay longer. And Riley would have liked it, too. Aidan was easy company and it was fun sharing pizza and watching a Christmas movie with him and his son. She tried to imagine doing the same with Jack someday, but the image that came to mind was Riley and their child on the sofa watching the movie together while Jack was in the other room on his computer. She told herself she was just feeling bitter because he'd gone home early. But it didn't look that bad out. Maybe it was just a little snow and a lot of wind.

"Good night, Aidan, and Luke," her mother said. "Thank you both for the pizza. Please take the leftovers home with you. Riley and I don't need all this pizza."

"Are you sure?" Aidan said.

Riley laughed. "Definitely. Please take it. And thank you. It was delicious." She combined the leftover pizza into one box and handed it to him. "See you at breakfast, maybe, tomorrow."

Aidan smiled. "We will definitely see you then."

She watched them step outside. It was very cold and the snow was falling steadily now. "Drive carefully and watch your step. It might be slippery."

"Will do. Good night, Riley."

Riley waited until they were in their car and backing out of the driveway before she closed the door. It wasn't the night she'd hoped for, but it had still been fun and the company had been good. Before she drifted off to sleep, her thoughts lingered on her cozy evening with Aidan and Luke and for a moment she felt guilty that she was thinking about Aidan instead of Jack. But just for a second or two before she fell fast asleep.

CHAPTER NINETEEN

Riley woke to clear skies. It had stopped snowing sometime overnight, but there was at least a foot of snow on the ground. The plows had come by, but her mother's car was surrounded by snow and needed to be shoveled out. While her mother was still sleeping, Riley bundled up in her warmest jacket, gloves, and hat and grabbed a shovel from the basement.

It took her almost an hour to fully dig the car out and clean all the snow and ice off the car windows. By the time she finished, she was ready for coffee and a hot shower. When Riley came back downstairs, fully dressed with her hair blown dry, her mother was sitting in the kitchen, also showered and changed and stirring sugar into her coffee.

"Thank you for shoveling, honey. There must be close to a foot out there," her mother said.

"More than that in spots," Riley agreed. The wind had caused the snow to drift and in some places it was almost two feet high and in others just a few inches. It was good to remove the snow early as she had done, before it had time to harden and became icy and heavy. "You might want to stay home this morning, Mom. It's pretty icy out there. I can manage on my own."

"We can throw some salt down to help with that. And I'll

be careful. I want to get over to the inn and see how badly they are snowed in. I have rubber tips, too, so I should be fine," her mother insisted.

Riley didn't like it, but agreed. "Okay, we'll just go super slow then."

They left earlier than usual to allow for extra time getting there and navigating the snow. Riley grabbed the scrambled egg dish her mother had made while Riley was in the shower. It was a quick veggie, cheese, and egg scramble and even had some hash brown potatoes mixed in. It was one of Riley's favorite breakfast dishes that her mother made and her stomach rumbled at the scent of it as she carried it to the car.

It didn't take long to get to the inn as it was only a half mile down the road and there were few other people out driving. Riley was relieved to see that the inn's driveway had been plowed and the company her mother hired had also shoveled the walkway to the front door. Riley pulled up as close as she could to the walkway.

"Let me get out first," Riley said. "I'll be right behind you in case you slip."

She left the egg dish in the car so she would have both arms free to help her mother if needed. She would run back out to get the eggs once her mother was safely inside.

It was early still, just seven thirty, so they had plenty of time to get in and ready for breakfast service. Her mother went slowly and made it inside with no issues, much to Riley's relief. Riley ran back for the eggs and brought them right into the dining room and turned on the warmer.

They got everything else ready and brought it into the dining room, before fixing themselves plates of eggs. Her mother had made a huge amount and they knew that less than half of the guests would want the hot dish. Many people just had coffee or something light for breakfast. Riley always woke up starving. Plus she'd worked up an appetite with all the shoveling. She made herself toast to go with the eggs and took a little side of cantaloupe as well. And more coffee.

The dining room was busy from eight when Franny came down. She was followed soon after by a steady stream of guests, all of whom were concerned about the storm, especially as most of them would be driving home that day. Riley's mother kept several shovels at the inn for times like this when guests would need to dig their cars out a bit. The plow service had cleared out the driveway and the small parking lot behind the inn, but each car still had a good amount of snow to shovel.

Around nine thirty, Aidan and Luke came down. Aidan ate quickly then went to shovel his car out so he'd be able to drive to work easily the next day. Luke stayed and had a second blueberry muffin and chatted with Franny and Riley and her mother. Franny had come down early, but she had no plans that day and she enjoyed chatting with everyone, too.

"I'm glad I don't have to worry about going anywhere anytime soon," she said. Aidan had asked which car was hers and when she said a light blue Camry, he said he'd clear around her car as well.

"Oh, you don't have to do that," she protested.

Aidan just smiled, though. "I'm going to be out there anyway. It's no trouble." He glanced at Luke and Riley. "I think the two of you said something last night about wanting to build a snowman? We can do that when I get back if you like?"

"Awesome! Riley, you're still going to help us, right?"

Riley smiled. "Of course. I even wore my special snow pants." She'd found them in her closet. They were many years old, but they still fit, though maybe not quite as loosely as they used to.

"That sounds fun," Franny said. "I will watch you from the window and cheer you on silently."

Riley's mother laughed. "I'll join you."

Aidan returned a half hour later and Luke ran to the door, ready to go outside, but Aidan stopped him. "Not so fast, buddy. Dad needs a cup of coffee to warm up first."

Riley jumped up and poured it for him. She knew he drank it black, like she did. She handed it to him and he smiled gratefully. "Thank you."

His eyebrows had snowflakes on them. It was flurrying a little and his nose was red from the cold. He sat with them for about ten minutes, until he felt thawed out and ready to head outside again. Riley pulled on her hat, mittens, and coat and they made their way to the front yard. There was plenty of snow there and they found a high drift and shaped it into the bottom half of the snowman. They all took turns scooping up snow and adding it until they had a good-sized ball for the midsection. The last step was the head and Luke scooped up a big mound of snow that Riley helped him to shape into a ball and then Aidan carefully placed it on top.

"We need to make his eyes, nose, and mouth," Luke said.

Riley thought for a minute. There was too much snow on the ground to use small stones, as they were buried. "I'll be right back." She went to the door and asked her mother to get a few things for her and a moment later, she walked back holding a pair of sunglasses, a carrot, and an old pipe that someone had left at the inn.

Aidan laughed. "We're going for a cool smoker dude. Not sure what kind of message that sends."

Riley laughed, too. "We had to work with what we had." She placed the sunglasses on the snowman and Luke loved it.

"He looks wicked cool with those dark glasses."

Aidan put the carrot into position and handed the pipe to Luke. "Your turn."

Luke carefully slid the pipe into the snowman, just below the carrot, and they all stood back to admire their work.

"I think that looks pretty good," Riley started to say but the words were cut off by a snowball that smacked her on the top of her arm. She didn't see who threw it, but Aidan was frowning and Luke was giggling, so it was pretty obvious.

"Luke, you shouldn't have done that," Aidan said. He tried to sound stern, but Riley could see a smile playing at the corners of his mouth.

But Riley had already scooped up a ball of snow and while Luke was looking at his dad, she caught Luke by surprise by tossing a snowball his way and hitting him on his side. He spun around with a big grin. "See, Dad, she doesn't mind. Riley is cool!"

Riley laughed. "I've always liked a good snowball fight." She scooped up another handful of snow, shaped it into a ball, and hurled it at Aidan. He ducked, but not in time. The snowball hit his elbow. They all tossed snowballs at each other for a few more minutes until Luke flopped on his back, signaling that he'd had enough.

"Are you making a snow angel?" Riley asked him.

He looked confused. "What is that?"

"I'll show you." She sat in the snow and lay back so that her legs were straight. She put her arms to her sides, then moved them up all the way until they met at the top of her head. She moved them back and forth a few times, then jumped up to see her handiwork. "See, looks just like an angel with its wings spread."

Aidan watched in amusement as Luke followed Riley's lead and then hopped up, all excited to see his snow angel.

"Dad, you do it, too," he demanded.

"I don't know if I still remember how to do that. It's been a long time," Aidan joked. But he got down in the snow and made a snow angel, too. The snow flurries stopped as they headed back inside.

"What are you up to for the rest of the day?" Riley asked once they were all out of their wet coats and shoes.

"We are taking it easy today. Luke has a book report he needs to work on and I have a book I just started last night that is pretty good. I think there's a football game at one that we'll probably watch, too. What about you?"

"We're still heading to my sister's house for Sunday dinner, I think, and then we'll hunker down at home after that."

"Who wants hot chocolate?" Riley's mother called from the kitchen.

"I do!" Luke said.

"I think I might have one, too," Riley said.

"Why not? Make it three." Aidan looked enthused about the idea as well. They went into the kitchen and then brought their mugs of hot chocolate into the living room and sat by the Christmas tree. It had been a fun morning and the hot chocolate warmed Riley up quickly as she sipped it and looked out the window. Everything was covered in white and it looked so pretty. She also noticed that it had started snowing again.

"We should probably head home soon," her mother said. "I'm not sure what this snow is going to do. We might want to postpone dinner with Amy if it keeps up."

Riley agreed. She was still worried about her mother slipping on her crutches. They said their goodbyes and on the way home, Amy called, also thinking it might be good to wait until next Sunday.

Once they were settled at home, Riley turned on the Weather Channel and she and her mother sat in the living room watching the coverage. The storm had intensified and was now expected to go on for the rest of the day and would bring five or six more inches. Which would mean more shoveling. But by then, hopefully, it would already be starting to melt. If it slowed by the afternoon, she would go back out there and try to get most of the shoveling done. She was very glad that they'd decided not to go to her sister's house. It was perfect weather to hunker down, drink cinnamon tea, and watch movies or read. Or both.

CHAPTER TWENTY

Riley's video interview went well on Tuesday afternoon. She was a little nervous at first because instead of being one person on the call, there were three. But they were all nice and the interviewer explained that the other two attending would be her coworkers on the marketing team. The company made an educational software product that helped elementary- and middle-school children improve their reading skills. Riley's job would be focusing on content marketing to reach parents—so writing for blogs and the website, and would include some ad copy duties as well.

It also sounded like there would be a good amount of growth and that these two coworkers would actually report to Riley. So, she understood why they were on the call and appreciated that the company had thought to include them. Many times that wasn't the case and a new manager would simply be announced—hired with no input from the people they would manage.

The interview lasted about an hour and when it finished, Riley was told that someone from HR would be in touch to see about scheduling a final round.

"We do have a few other people we are talking to, though,

so don't worry if you don't hear right away. We will probably schedule in-person interviews next week."

That would be the week before Christmas. Riley assured him that was fine. She knew things rarely moved quickly this time of year. She was encouraged that they told her she'd be going back for a final interview. She still hadn't had bites on anything else yet and she kept sending her resume out for any positions that looked at all interesting.

Jack called that night to say hello and he was in a great mood. It was a little past six, early for him to be home.

"Did you get everything straightened out for your big case?" she asked.

"We did, and we found a few things that will make our case even stronger, so it looks even better for us now. We have a meeting set with the other side on Thursday and hopefully this will never make it to trial. They should want to settle given how strong our case is now."

"That's great, Jack." Riley was happy for him.

"I've got some other good news for you, too. I spoke to Sharon in HR and told her you'd applied for the marketing job and she's moving your resume to the top of the pile. They always do when someone internally refers them. You should be hearing from her in the next day or two about a phone interview."

"Thank you." Riley still wasn't sure she wanted to work at a law firm, especially the same one that Jack worked at, but an interview was an interview and she was grateful for his help.

"Let me know how it goes. I'm sure you will ace it. Sharon says they are anxious to get this filled."

"Great, I will. Thanks again, Jack." They chatted a bit longer, and then he had another call beep in, someone from work, of course. Riley ended the call and pulled up the job listing again for another look. The job itself sounded fine and very similar to the one she'd just left. It was a content marketing role and would be focusing on writing case studies, blogs, newsletters, website copy, and annual reports.

She wondered why it was open. She'd forgotten to ask Jack. It was always good to know. The interviewer with the other company had said the position was open due to an internal promotion and the person in the role had moved into product marketing. That was appealing to Riley because it showed that there was lateral growth and the chance to move into other areas.

It would be fun to get back to the city for the interview. She could check on her apartment and see Jack. Maybe they'd have a nice dinner and catch up before she headed back to Chatham the next day. She'd leave Lily with her mother for the night. Both of them would like that. Her mother adored Lily and Riley had a feeling she might get a cat once they went back to New York permanently. Her mother had always had a cat, but her last one, Whiskers, had passed a few months ago. She'd had him for twenty-one years, and was crushed when he passed. She hadn't been ready for a new animal yet, but Riley thought she might be soon.

Almost as if she'd been summoned, Lily appeared by Riley's side and meowed loudly. It was her *I want a snack* meow, which Riley immediately rose to fulfill. They went downstairs where Riley kept Lily's bag of treats. She gave her a few and noticed her mother sitting at the kitchen table, holding her phone and smiling.

"How did your interview go, honey?" she asked.

"Pretty well, I think. They mentioned the next step, which would be a final, in-person interview next week."

"Oh, that's great news. Maybe you'll have something lined up before the end of the year. Wouldn't that be nice?"

Riley smiled. "It would be. So, what are you looking so happy about?"

"I just hung up from talking to Sean. He called to make plans to go to dinner Friday night." She looked excited, but a little nervous, too.

"Do you know where you're going?" Riley asked.

"I think Mahoney's in Orleans." Mahoney's was a great choice for a first date. Orleans was the next town over and Mahoney's served very good food in a relaxed, pub-like environment. Riley thought her mother would be more comfortable there than somewhere more formal.

"That's a perfect place. What will you wear?" Riley asked.

Her mother looked a bit panicked. "I have no idea. It's been so long, I might need a little help finding something in my closet."

"You have plenty of options. I'll help you find something. Let's go take a look."

They went upstairs and into her mother's room. Riley pulled several tops out of her closet as well as several sweaters from her chest of drawers. Her mother tried on several outfits, and they finally agreed that the deep blue cashmere sweater and a newish pair of dressy dark jeans would be perfect. It was casual but dressy at the same time. Riley hoped the date would go well. Her mother had been alone for too long—it was time for her to meet someone nice.

CHAPTER TWENTY-ONE

Franny added a cinnamon tea bag to her cup of hot water. Within a minute the sweet fragrant scent tickled her nose. She let it steep for a few minutes, then discarded the tea bag and took a small sip. She savored a cup most afternoons, as she sat in her comfy chair by her second-floor window and watched people walking and driving by below on Main Street.

This was actually her second cup of the day as she was killing time before she had to leave to go to Angela's house. She and Sean's mother had connected the night of the tree lighting and had been messaging ever since on Facebook. Angela had invited Franny to attend her monthly book club, which was meeting that night. She'd said they rotated houses depending on whose turn it was to host.

Franny was a little nervous as she didn't know any of the women, other than Angela, but she was also looking forward to it, especially as she'd already read the book. It was a twisty psychological thriller and the ending had taken Franny completely by surprise. She was eager to discuss it. Angela had said that she was making a chicken dish, and a few of the others were bringing sides or salad, so Franny said she'd bring an appetizer. She'd stopped by the wine and cheese shop earlier in the day and picked up an interesting assortment. A few that she'd already tried and liked, and she also grabbed a few boxes of crackers and a jar of fig jam.

Her stomach rumbled a bit as she thought about the cheese and jam. She'd eaten lightly that day at lunch, just a cup of soup from the coffee shop. She'd also treated herself to a pumpkin spice latte that Caitlin had suggested. It was made with a homemade syrup and had a thick dollop of whipped cream on top of the foam. It was heavenly. She'd lingered there for a bit, reading the new book she'd discovered at the shop next door. It was impossible for Franny to go into that bookshop and walk out empty-handed. She'd chosen two new books and spent most of the afternoon reading one of them.

They were meeting at six and by five thirty, it was dark outside and time to go. Franny didn't think it would take too long to get to Angela's house, but she wanted to take her time in case she got lost. She headed downstairs and climbed into her sister's old car. It was small but it had a lot of pep and was fun to drive. It was bittersweet driving the car now as she thought of her sister the instant she stepped into it. Franny smiled, though, as she knew her sister would approve of her stepping out of her comfort zone a little to go to the book club.

She put the address in the car's GPS and pulled onto Main Street. Angela lived near the Chatham Bars Inn on a side street just off Shore Drive. As Franny pulled into the driveway, she saw that the house was set on a hill and she imagined that during the day Angela had a lovely distant view of the ocean. There were already several cars there. Franny parked behind one of them and gathered her bag of cheese, crackers, and jam.

Angela opened the door a second after Franny knocked and looked delighted to see her. She pulled her in for a welcoming hug.

"I'm so glad you were able to join us."

Franny handed her the bag of food. "Do you have a plate I can use to set up the cheeses?"

"Sure, right this way." Franny followed Angela into the kitchen where there were three women standing around an island that had a platter of shrimp cocktail and another with some chips, salsa, and guacamole on it. Angela handed Franny a big wooden cheese tray and introduced her to everyone. Franny nodded and hoped she'd remember their names. Lynn, Barbie, and Jackie all looked to be about Franny's age. They were friendly and while Franny arranged her cheeses, she listened as they all chatted.

She learned that Lynn was newly widowed, Barbie was happily married, and Jackie had lost her husband around the same time that Franny did and she was happily single.

"Maybe someday I'll feel like dating, but honestly, I keep my eyes open and it's slim pickings around here," Jackie said.

Angela laughed. "You should join our ladies' golf league. There are always interesting men at the club. We usually stay for a bite to eat and a drink after we play. It's a fun time."

"I'll think about it," Jackie said.

"You don't have to be good," Angela added. "They'll give you a handicap first time you play." She glanced at Franny. "Do you golf?"

"I do. My husband loved it, so we used to play often, and I was on a league for a number of years. I haven't played in a few years, though. I've been thinking that I might want to give it a try again."

"Oh, you should! If you're ever here in the summer, we'll have to play," Angela said enthusiastically.

Franny finished arranging the cheese and crackers the way she wanted them and opened the jar of fig jam.

"What kind of cheeses are those?" Barbie asked.

"This funny-looking one with the charcoal stripe is

Humboldt Fog, an aged goat cheese. I tried it for the first time last week and really liked it. Manchego is a favorite, it's Spanish and reminds me of a softer Parmesan, and this one is Saint-André, a buttery triple cream. I thought it might go well with a little bit of jam." Franny made herself a cracker with some of the creamy cheese and a dab of the jam. She took a bite and sighed. "Oh, these work well together."

"Franny, what kind of wine would you like?" Angela asked. "We have Cabernet or Chardonnay open."

"Cabernet, I think." Franny liked red wine in the winter and it went well with the rich cheeses.

Angela handed her a glass of wine and went to welcome two more women that had arrived, Sheila and Erin. Sheila was a little older than the others and had known Franny's sister.

"I'm so sorry for your loss. I knew Ella from the garden club."

Franny smiled, thinking of Ella's flower garden that she'd always been so proud of.

"She always had such a green thumb. I wish I could say the same." Franny couldn't seem to keep anything alive, except for the cactus that Ella once gave her because she knew it was unkillable.

They all chatted and nibbled on appetizers until Angela said it was time to make plates and sit down to dinner. Everyone helped themselves to the lemony chicken piccata and the roasted potatoes and Brussels sprouts with bacon. Sheila had brought a loaf of sourdough bread from Pain D'Avignon, a local bakery that supplied many restaurants on and off the Cape.

Everything was delicious and they discussed the book as they ate. Most everyone had enjoyed it.

"I thought it was a fast read, hard to put down," Barbie said.

"I loved the twists and the one at the end totally shocked me," Erin said.

"I liked it, but I thought the final twist was a little far-fetched. It seemed to come out of nowhere," Jackie said.

"You know, I thought that at first," Lynn said. "But then I went back and reread it from the beginning and it was set up, she'd mentioned the connection with the sister early and I had just missed it."

Jackie furrowed her brow. "Really? I'll have to go back and look. If that's the case then never mind and color me impressed. She got me good."

"I really enjoyed it," Franny said. "I loved her sly sense of humor."

"I loved her voice, too," Angela agreed. "I've already one-clicked another book of hers."

Franny laughed. "I did, too. As soon as I finished I went looking for more."

A few of the others said they'd done the same thing. After they finished discussing the book, Angela asked for suggestions for next month and they decided on a historical saga, *The Lioness of Boston,* based on the life of Isabella Stewart Gardner.

"If you're still here, we'd love to have you join us again," Angela said.

"Thank you. I'm not sure I'll still be here, but that book does sound wonderful." Franny made a mental note to see if the bookshop on Main Street had it in stock.

When they finished eating, everyone helped to clear the table and then Angela set out a tray of fudgy brownies. Franny thought she was too full, but they looked so good that she nodded when Angela asked if she'd split one with her.

"Is Sean still dating Marcy?" Sheila asked.

Angela made a face. "No, he's not, thankfully. Did someone say otherwise?"

"I didn't think he was. But I was behind her in line at the coffee shop a few days ago and overheard her chatting with the woman with her. She'd asked how things were with Sean, like she thought they were still together."

"Really? That is odd. And what did Marcy say?"

"She just smiled and said Sean is great and she was going to be seeing him soon."

"Hmm. That's news to me." Angela didn't look happy to hear it.

"Who is Marcy?" Franny asked.

"She's a woman Sean dated for almost a year. I was never crazy about her. I told Sean she was looking to lock him down. He said he was up front with her that he wasn't looking to get serious with anyone. But she thought she could change his mind. As far as I know they've been broken up for a few months."

"Maybe she's hopeful that they will get back together?" Franny said.

"Possibly. I haven't talked to Sean in a few days. He seemed quite interested in Beth, from the inn. I thought I sensed some sparks there."

"I thought so, too," Franny said.

"I'm sure it's nothing to worry about," Sheila said. "It could be that I heard wrong."

"You probably heard right," Angela said. "It's almost the holidays; wouldn't surprise me if she reaches out looking to get back together."

"Do you think Sean will give it another chance?" Franny asked. She hoped not, for Beth's sake.

"I wouldn't think so. But you never know what people will do," Angela said.

CHAPTER TWENTY-TWO

Beth could hardly eat all day on Friday, she was so nervous about the date with Sean. She was looking forward to it, of course, but she worried that she was so out of practice that she might mess the whole thing up.

She admitted as much on the phone to Jess, who'd called to wish her luck.

"Don't be ridiculous," Jess assured her. "You're just nervous and it's normal. Sean is a great guy. He's one of Ryan's best friends and I've met him several times. I have to admit, I may have secretly hoped the two of you would hit it off when I recommended him for your repair job."

Beth smiled. She wasn't surprised by the admission. Jess had been overly enthusiastic when she'd suggested Beth call him for the repair work. She hadn't thought anything of it at the time, though.

"I'm sure it will be fine," she said.

Jess laughed. "Just relax and have fun. Think of it as being out to dinner with a new friend. Don't put so much pressure on yourself. If it works out, great. If not, then no big deal."

"You're right." Jess's advice calmed her somewhat.

"Call me tomorrow to let me know how it went," Jess said.

"I will." Beth ended the call and checked her appearance in

her bedroom mirror. She'd tried on a few other options, but came back to the blue sweater and jeans that she'd picked out earlier with Riley. She checked her makeup, adding a swipe of rosy pink lipstick and running a brush through her hair one last time.

Sean arrived right on time to get her, at six thirty. Riley was at the inn, handling the wine-and-cheese hour. Beth had offered to help as usual, but Riley didn't want her to feel rushed and they were only half full this weekend now that the stroll was over.

Sean knocked on the front door and when she opened it, he grinned. She saw the warmth in his eyes and relaxed a little.

"You look pretty," he said and something shifted inside her. It was a simple thing to say but it had a powerful effect on her. She hadn't felt appreciated like this in a very long time.

"Thank you. You're looking sharp yourself." Sean was also wearing jeans with a navy button-down cotton shirt that looked really good on him.

"I'll just grab my coat." Beth looked around and saw it hanging over a chair in the kitchen. She pulled it on, along with her hat and gloves and they headed out. They went in Sean's car, a big blue truck that he also used for work. The front area where they sat was clean, though, with comfortable leather seats. It didn't take long to get to the restaurant as there was no traffic in December on the Cape. They chatted easily as they drove. Sean told her about his work week and his latest project.

"It's a fun one—custom built-in bookcases for a home office and a desk."

"I didn't realize you did that kind of woodworking." Beth was impressed.

"It's a great time of year for this kind of project because I'm not as busy. I used a dark wood and just finished polishing it up today. It came out pretty sweet if I do say so myself." She could hear his enthusiasm and love for what he did.

"Did you take any pictures? I'd love to see it."

He laughed. "You might be sorry you asked. I took a ton of pictures. I'll show you over dinner."

They arrived at the restaurant a few minutes later. There was a wait for a table as the restaurant was busy, but there were two open seats at the bar.

"Do you want to have a drink first? We could eat there as well, unless you'd rather wait for a table?" Sean asked.

"The bar is fine." Depending on the restaurant, Beth was usually happy to eat at the bar and Mahoney's had a gorgeous one. It was long and made of polished hardwood. The bartender had been there for as long as she could remember. She didn't go to Mahoney's often but whenever she did it was almost always the same bartender. As soon as they sat down, he came over and gave them menus and took their drink orders.

"I'll have a glass of Cabernet," Beth said.

"Maybe we should get a bottle. I was thinking of having red wine, too." They decided to try a bottle of Readers, a Cabernet from Washington State. While the bartender opened their wine, he told them about the specials.

"We have a stuffed haddock with Newburg sauce and a veal chop." He poured a small amount in Sean's glass for him to taste.

Sean sipped and nodded. "That's fine. Thank you."

The bartender filled Beth's glass and then Sean's. "I'll give you some time to look at the menu."

Beth took a sip of her wine. It was smooth and delicious. She glanced around the room. The restaurant was very busy but she liked the overall feel of the place. It was welcoming and warm with soft lighting, dark wood, and leather seats. She turned her attention back to the menu. There were a lot of seafood dishes as well as chicken and steak. She was tempted by one of the specials, though.

"What do you think?" Sean asked her.

"Everything looks good, but I may go for that stuffed haddock. What about you?"

"That veal chop sounds pretty good, but I think I'll get the New York strip steak. Any interest in sharing an appetizer? The tuna nachos are always good and the calamari is excellent."

"I love fried calamari."

They put their orders in and while they waited for their food, Sean pulled out his phone and showed her the pictures of the office he'd just built. Beth was impressed. His work was beautiful. "I'd always want to work from home if I had that office," she said.

Sean laughed. "Thanks. I'm pretty happy with it and thankfully, my client is, too."

The bartender returned a few minutes later and set a plate of lightly fried calamari between them. It had a roasted garlic aioli for dipping. Beth dipped one of the rings into the sauce and took a bite. The calamari was cooked perfectly, nice and tender.

As they ate, they chatted easily about all kinds of things. Beth had worried that there might be some awkward silences but she was thrilled to discover that it was the opposite—they both found themselves rushing to talk and almost finished each other's sentences twice. Sean was fun to talk to and he made her laugh, especially when he talked about his mother.

"I love her dearly, but she is obsessed with my dating life and constantly tries to fix me up."

"Did you ever take her up on any of those offers?" Beth asked.

He grimaced. "Twice. Let's just say she'll never make a career out of being a matchmaker."

"I bet she says that the third time will be the charm?" Beth teased.

He laughed. "She does, actually."

"Did you tell her you were taking me out tonight?"

"No. The less she knows, the better. If she knew, she'd be grilling me for updates. She means well, but I'm too old for that."

They talked about their kids. He was close to his daughters even though he didn't see them as often as he would like.

"They're busy. I know at their age, I didn't get home much. I'll be seeing them soon, though."

"Will they come to Chatham or are you heading off-Cape?" Beth asked.

"My mother and I are heading up to my older daughter, Becky's house Christmas Eve. She will have a nice dinner that night, and then Christmas brunch the next day. I'll be back in Chatham by Christmas night. What about you?"

"Similar, but I don't have to go far. Everyone comes to my place Christmas Eve and Christmas Day we'll head to my daughter Amy's house. We'll have dinner there midday and then a light supper later at the inn. It's usually a relaxing day. I do most of my work the night before."

"Do you cook up a storm?" Sean asked.

Beth smiled. "We do a lot of appetizers, shrimp cocktail, cheese and crackers, stuffed mushrooms, and then we usually do a surf and turf, filets and lobster meat with butter."

"That sounds great. Ours is more casual. Neither of the girls is big on cooking, but they do a great job with takeout. There is an Italian place near them that makes up trays of pasta and antipasto."

"That sounds really good, too. Not cooking takes a lot of the stress away."

He nodded. "That's what they said. It's all good to me. I just show up and eat whatever they give me."

When their meals arrived, they were quiet for a minute as they took their first bites. Everything was delicious and they dove back into easy conversation for the rest of the meal and over dessert when they shared a crème brûlée.

The time flew by and Beth was having such a good time, better than she'd expected. They'd shared their relationship stories, too. Beth told Sean about her marriage ending years ago.

"It just didn't work out. We married young and it was the next step. We were in love at first, but over the years we grew apart. I've mostly focused on the girls since then. I've dated a little here and there but nothing serious."

"It's been similar for me. I married young—in my early twenties. We'd only been dating nine months. And it was fun, at first. We had kids right away, too, and I love them, but it changed things. As the girls got older we realized we just didn't have enough in common."

Sean took a bite of crème brûlée and then continued. "I was recently in a relationship that was heading toward being serious. Marcy and I dated for almost a year and she was ready to get engaged. She'd never been married. I wasn't there yet though, and I'd told her when we started dating that I didn't know if I'd ever want to get married again. She said she didn't care about that, but it turned out to be important to her. She gave me an ultimatum and I didn't want to be forced into something." He paused and took a sip of water. "I recognized that it wasn't fair to her if I wasn't there and didn't know if I ever would be. So we ended things. I thought it was amicable, but I'm not sure if she would agree."

"That's too bad." Beth smiled. "I'm honestly not sure I ever want to marry again. I did it once and I'm really fine on my own." Marriage was the last thing on her mind. She didn't want to get stuck in a bad marriage again. Best to avoid it completely.

Sean grinned. "I'm glad we're on the same page, then. I think it's different when you've been married before and you know what you don't want."

"Exactly," Beth agreed, as she scooped up another bite of the creamy dessert. She loved the crackle the layer of hardened sugar made as she dipped her spoon into it.

Sean grabbed the bill when it came and waved away Beth's offer to chip in.

"This is on me. It's my pleasure."

"Thank you."

It was almost ten by the time they arrived back at Beth's house. She thought about inviting him in, then decided against it as it was their first date. He walked her to her door, though, and she thanked him again.

"This was such a fun night. I really enjoyed it," she said.

Sean looked pleased to hear it. "Good. Maybe that means you'll want to do it again sometime?"

Beth laughed. "I'd love to."

He leaned in and Beth held her breath for a moment. He kissed her sweetly on the cheek. "I'll call you in a few days and we'll make a plan. Good night."

"Good night." Sean waited until she was inside and she watched out the window as he walked back to his truck and drove away. When she turned around, she saw Riley on the living room sofa, watching TV with Lily on her lap.

"I take it you had a good time? You look smitten," Riley said.

Beth made her way over to her favorite chair, set her

crutches down, and shrugged out of her coat. She collapsed into her chair and smiled. "It was a great night." She told Riley all about it and as she drifted off to sleep later that night the last thing she saw was Sean's smiling face. She couldn't wait to see him again.

CHAPTER TWENTY-THREE

The next morning over breakfast, Riley remembered something she'd forgotten to mention to her mother the night before. They were both more excited about her mother's date with Sean.

"So, I was chatting with Aidan and Luke during the wine and cheese hour and Luke asked if the big-screen TV in the living room worked. We decided it would be fun to watch Christmas movies there tonight." She glanced at Franny, who had just joined them. "And everyone staying at the inn of course would be welcome to join us. I thought I could make a big batch of hot buttered popcorn."

Her mother smiled. "That's a great idea, honey. And something fun to do."

"How did your book club go, Franny?" Riley had meant to ask earlier, but it had escaped her mind.

"It was a really nice time. Angela's friends are lovely. I was a little nervous at first as I didn't know them, but they were all very welcoming." She smiled. "They invited me to go again if I was going to still be here. But, of course I'll be home by then."

"Do you need to rush back? Maybe you would enjoy staying a bit longer?" Riley's mother asked.

But Franny shook her head. "I might never leave if I stay

longer. I should get back. I have a business and a home in Albany."

"Is everything going okay with your business while you're here?" Riley's mother asked.

Franny nodded. "It is. Very well actually. I'm lucky that I have good people working for me."

"Well, that's a relief. At least you don't have to worry about that."

"True," Franny agreed.

"What's it like where you live in Albany?" Riley asked. "Do you love it there?"

Franny looked thoughtful. "I did for a long time. It's a lovely area. But it's not the same with my husband gone. Some of my close friends have moved down south. There's still a few left, but I don't see them as often as I used to." She smiled. "They are trying to recruit me to move to Florida. I don't see that ever happening, but perhaps a vacation might be fun."

"That's a great idea," Riley agreed. She glanced out the window and saw a few flakes float by. Snow was in the forecast again but they weren't supposed to get more than a few inches. Still, it was cold and she shivered at the sight of it.

Her mother laughed. "Florida sounds pretty good to me right now. They say it's going to get into the teens tonight."

"It's nice and cozy in here. I love that electric stove you put in the old fireplace. It looks so real, and it throws a lot of heat," Riley said.

"Thanks, honey. I might push the thermostat up a little in here to make sure the lobby stays warm. Especially if we're going to be here later watching TV." Her mother hopped up and grabbed her crutches and made her way over to the thermostat.

A few minutes later, Aidan and Luke came into the dining room and filled their plates. When they sat at the table with them, Franny asked, "What do you two have planned for the day?"

"We're going to Edaville Railroad!" Luke said excitedly.

Aidan laughed. "That's not today, buddy. We're going tomorrow. I have to work for a little while today."

Luke looked disappointed. "That's right. I just got excited." He looked around the table. "Have any of you been to Edaville?"

They all nodded. "It's a magical place," Riley said. "I've been a few times. We used to love to go." It was a Christmas-themed amusement park, just off-Cape in Carver, with a railroad and lots of festive lights, rides for kids, and of course Santa was there.

"Do you often have to work on Saturdays?" Riley noticed that Aidan seemed a little stressed.

He shook his head. "Not usually. My client is under a deadline for a bank refinancing for his business and I told him I'd meet with him today to go over everything before his meeting on Monday." He ran a hand through his hair. "The girl I usually call to watch Luke sometimes, she was supposed to come by this afternoon, but she just texted me that she has the flu."

"You could leave him with us," Riley said. "I was planning to be here this afternoon anyway to make a quiche for tomorrow and to deliver the chocolates. Maybe Luke can help me?"

"I could deliver chocolates!" Luke seemed enthused by the idea of it.

Aidan looked unsure, though. "Are you sure? I don't want to put you out at all."

"It's nothing, really. Just text me ten minutes before you want to go and I'll head over then."

"If you really don't mind, that would be awesome. It won't be longer than an hour," Aidan said.

"It's all set then," Riley said.

CHAPTER TWENTY-FOUR

Aidan texted her at a quarter past three and Riley and her mother headed over to the inn. Luke was waiting for them in the lobby and ran over as soon as they walked in.

"Do we do the chocolates now?" he asked.

Riley laughed. "Not yet. We'll do that in a little while. Right now we need to make a quiche. Which means we have to make pie dough. And I thought it might be fun to make something sweet with the leftover dough. Do you like raspberry squares?"

Luke looked confused. "I don't know what that is."

Riley's mother smiled. "You are in for a treat."

Aidan came down a moment later, carrying his briefcase. He walked over to them. "Okay, I'm off. I'll see you in about an hour."

"Take your time," Riley said.

"Thank you. Luke, do whatever Riley and her mom tell you." Aidan playfully mussed Luke's hair.

Luke laughed and ran his hand over his hair to smooth it back into place. "Bye, Dad."

"Okay, who wants to learn how to make a quiche?" Riley led the way into the kitchen and Luke followed. Beth went into the tiny downstairs office to get her checkbook. She returned a moment later and sat down at the kitchen table with a stack of bills to mail out. Meanwhile, Riley got all the ingredients for the quiche and set about mixing up the pie crust. She showed Luke how to wash his hands thoroughly so he could touch the food and help. She handed him a rolling pin and demonstrated how to roll the ball of dough into a big circle of pie crust. Once he was done, she laid it in a quiche pan, lined it with aluminum foil, and then handed an open bag of beans to Luke.

"Want to pour these into the pie pan?"

He looked at her curiously before doing as asked.

"We're doing something called blind baking. We bake the crust a little so it won't be soggy when we add the filling. And the weight of the beans helps keep the crust in place." Riley popped it in the oven to bake.

Next, she mixed up the filling: the egg, milk, and heavy cream mixture that formed the base of the quiche. She let Luke crack the eggs after showing him how to do it so that he wouldn't get any shells in the bowl. She was impressed by how careful he was and that he managed to crack four eggs and only one small speck of shell got away from him. He looked disappointed but she assured him he'd done great.

"I almost always get a little shell in there. But it's easy enough to fish it right out." She flicked the annoying bit of shell away and gave him a big wooden spoon. "Okay, now mix that up good, while I get the rest of our ingredients."

Luke stirred energetically while Riley found the leftover cooked bacon from breakfast and the sliced onion and thawed chopped spinach.

"That looks perfect, Luke. Now we add our other ingredients."

She chopped the bacon into small bits and squeezed any remaining water out of the spinach before adding it into the egg mixture along with the onion and bacon. She then stirred in half a log of goat cheese.

"Okay, we have to wait for the pie crust to finish cooking and then cool a little. I thought we could make our raspberry squares now." Her pie crust recipe made two crusts but they only needed one for the quiche. She grabbed the other ball of dough and rolled it out into a square shape this time. Then she laid it across a buttered cookie sheet, sliced it in half, and got a jar of raspberry jam out of the refrigerator.

"I need your help spreading the jam. Do you think you can do that?" Riley asked.

Luke nodded and she handed him the open jar and fished around in the drawer for a knife.

"Okay, dip your knife in the jam and then spread it on the dough. Like this." Riley got some jam on the knife, then carefully spread it over the dough. She handed him the knife and he finished the rest of the jam layer. When he was done, she plopped the other square of dough on top of the jam and got two forks out.

"And now we poke the dough all over so it will cook perfectly." She showed Luke how to evenly poke holes across the top of the dough. Once he was done, it was time to take the pie crust out and slide the raspberry squares into the oven.

"While we let this pie crust cool a little, I think we should take a break. I could go for a hot chocolate, how about you?"

Luke nodded. "I love hot chocolate."

"Mom?" Riley asked.

He mother laughed. "As if you need to ask. Yes, please."

Riley quickly made three mugs of hot chocolate and added mini-marshmallows, then handed one to Luke and one to her mom. After about ten minutes, she had Luke pour the bowl of quiche mixture into the pie crust. Riley slid it into the oven and they joined her mother at the table to finish their drinks.

Riley's mom asked Luke about school and he told them all about it—the classes and teachers he liked and the ones he didn't—math and Mrs. Evans—because she always told him to stop talking.

"It's never my fault! If people talk to me I talk back," he explained.

Riley tried not to smile. Luke was chatty and had a lot of energy, and she remembered that Mrs. Evans was near retirement age and had always been one of the stricter teachers. Riley hadn't been overly fond of her either.

When they'd finished their hot chocolate, Riley checked on the raspberry squares and they needed a few more minutes. It was almost four thirty, so she decided to get the cheese and crackers ready to go. She pulled several cheeses out of the refrigerator and after taking the raspberry squares out and setting them on the counter to cool, she and Luke sliced the cheeses and she arranged them on a platter along with crackers and a small dish of Marcona almonds that were lightly oiled and salted.

When they finished with that, the front door opened and Aidan walked in. Luke glanced his way and waved. Aidan came into the kitchen and smiled appreciatively at Riley and her mother.

"Thanks for keeping an eye on him."

"No problem. We kept him busy," Riley said.

"Yeah? What did you guys do?" Aidan asked.

"I learned how to make egg pie! And raspberry squares." Aidan glanced at the pastry that was still too hot to eat. "Are they ready yet?"

"Not just yet. A few more minutes."

"We should probably get out of your hair. Do you want to head upstairs, Luke?"

Luke put his hands on his hips and looked determined. "Not yet. I want a raspberry square and I'm going to help deliver chocolates."

"I did say we were going to do that," Riley agreed. "I can send him up when we're done . . . or you can relax with my mom and have a raspberry square when we come back. It won't take us more than ten minutes or so."

Aidan smiled. "A raspberry square, huh? I guess I can't say no to that."

Riley opened a drawer and pulled out the bag of chocolates in their boxes. "Ready, Luke?"

He followed her to the rooms that were booked and they knocked before going in and fluffing the pillows, drawing back the comforter, and placing a box of chocolates on each pillow. Luke helped with the fluffing and placing the chocolates.

"This is so fun!"

Riley smiled as they raced to the next room and as predicted, ten minutes later they were done and headed back to the kitchen. Riley checked the quiche and it needed a little more time, but the raspberry squares were cool enough to eat. She cut out one for each of them and put them on small paper plates.

"I used to make these for the girls when they were little," her mother said.

"Every time we made pies, we made raspberry squares or turnovers, depending on how much extra dough we had," Riley said. "They weren't always pretty but they still tasted delicious."

"I've always liked a good raspberry square," Aidan said.

After they finished, the quiche was ready to come out, too, and Riley set it on the counter.

"Is that on the menu tomorrow morning?" Aidan asked hopefully.

Riley grinned. "It is. It's a new experiment. Goat cheese, onion, spinach, and bacon."

"Well, if it tastes anywhere near as good as it smells, it's a winner," Aidan said.

"I guess we'll find out tomorrow," Riley replied. It really did look and smell good.

"Okay, now we will get out of your way. At least for a few minutes," Aidan said.

It was a quarter to five, almost time for wine and cheese.

"Come on, buddy, say thanks to Riley and her mom for watching you."

"Thank you! It was fun."

"It was fun," Riley agreed.

"I really do appreciate it," Aidan said. "I'm going to drop my stuff off in the room and then we'll be back down a little after five."

CHAPTER TWENTY-FIVE

While Riley was rinsing the mugs and putting them into the dishwasher, her mother's phone rang. Riley noticed that her tone changed and a moment later she left the room, taking the stack of bills and her checkbook to her office. When she returned a few minutes later she had the same happy look on her face as when she'd come home from her date with Sean. Riley glanced her way, not wanting to be too nosy and ask who it was—especially if it wasn't Sean.

But her mother grinned and said, "That was Sean. We're going for dinner and a movie on Wednesday."

Riley was glad to hear it. And glad that Sean hadn't waited long to call. She'd noticed that her mother had glanced at the phone, anxiously checking the caller ID, every time it rang. "That's awesome, Mom."

At a few minutes before five, they brought the cheese and crackers into the big living room and set it on the table near the fake fireplace. Riley stood by it for a moment, letting the heat it generated warm her.

"Are you cold, honey? Should I turn the heat up a little more?"

"No, it's fine. It's plenty warm in here. I just love the feel of the heat." The temperature had dropped and it was in the mid-teens. Whenever Riley glanced out the window at the few scattered flakes that twirled in the light of the outside lamp she could almost feel the cold seep into her bones. She went back into the kitchen to grab the bottles of wine that she'd opened earlier. That would warm her up, too.

Riley poured a small glass of Grounded, an inexpensive Cabernet from Josh Phelps that Anna from the wine and cheese shop had recommended. Riley had tried it in the store and liked it, but now that she'd had it open for about an hour, it tasted even better, bigger and richer. She could almost detect the hints of cherry, cinnamon, and clove that the label promised.

"Oh, this wine is really good," her mother said as she reached for a slice of cheese.

"We'll have to add it to the list of ones to buy again," Riley said.

A moment later, Franny joined them and Riley poured her a glass of Cabernet as well.

"Thank you, dear. I have to say, I love these wine and cheese hours. I look forward to them all week," Franny said.

Riley's mother looked pleased to hear it. "Thank you. I think we may have to keep it going after the holidays as well. It has been very popular."

"It's a nice way to meet new people that might be passing through," Franny said. "Everyone has interesting stories. Like that young couple that was here last weekend. She'd never been to Cape Cod and her husband hadn't been in years. They were here to visit his parents."

"They hadn't seen them in years?" Riley asked.

Franny nodded. "They didn't go into why, just said that now that they were expecting, they wanted to try and mend fences. And it sounds like it worked. His parents were thrilled to hear that their first grandchild is on the way."

"That sounds like a happy ending," Riley's mother said.

"I think they only told me because they were both nervous. They were meeting his parents for dinner after the wine and cheese hour. She wasn't drinking, of course, but he welcomed a little liquid courage. It seemed to help for them to talk about it. I told them I was sure the dinner would be a success. And if it wasn't at least the food would be amazing . . . they were going to Cuvée at the Chatham Inn." Cuvée was one of the best restaurants in Chatham, and definitely the most expensive and high-end.

"Oh, I've never been there," Riley said.

"I haven't either," her mother admitted. "I have also heard it's very good. Don't they have those fancy tasting menus?"

Franny nodded. "I've been a few times over the years. Ella loved it there and we went a few years before she passed. They have a seven-course tasting menu with matching wines. It was all exquisite. Really a special occasion kind of place."

"That sounds heavenly," Riley said. "Maybe if I land a new job, we'll go to celebrate, Mom."

Her mother smiled. "*When* you land a new job, not *if.* I'm confident it won't take long."

Riley saw Aidan and Luke walk into the living room. Luke raced over and grabbed a slice of cheddar and a cracker.

"What should we get Luke to drink?" her mother asked. "We have some sparkling apple juice or we could do hot chocolate again?"

"Sparkling apple juice sounds good. One hot chocolate a day is enough, I think."

Riley went to the kitchen to get it for Luke and returned a moment later. She'd poured it into a champagne flute and Luke was impressed by the bubbles.

"This looks pretty cool." He took a tentative sip and nodded approvingly. "I like apple juice."

Their other guests arrived: the Pattersons, the Smiths,

and the Donovans. Riley enjoyed talking with all of them. As Franny had said, it was interesting to hear people's stories and what brought them to the Chatham Coastal Inn. The Pattersons and the Smiths were also visiting family, while the Donovans lived just outside of Boston and had only been married for a little over a year.

"We're actually celebrating our anniversary. We got married on the Cape last August and we just wanted to get away for the weekend. We've never been here this time of year," Bill Donovan said.

"We wondered if it might be too quiet and desolate. Our friends told us we were crazy to come this time of year. But we're actually loving it so far. It's so peaceful. No one ever mentions that," Adele Donovan said.

Riley smiled. "We love it here this time of year, too. It's a nice change from the summer crowds." And the rush of the city, too. Riley loved the energy of Manhattan, but she was enjoying the quieter pace of Chatham.

The hour flew by and by six everyone had left to head to dinner. Riley and her mother were planning to go home, heat up some leftover pasta, and then come back for movies at seven.

"Do the two of you have dinner plans?" Aidan asked.

Riley laughed. "We were just going to grab something at home."

"Well, I'd really like to treat you both to dinner. You saved me today and it's the least I can do. We were thinking of going to the Red Nun for burgers."

"Come with us!" Luke added.

Riley glanced at her mother, who smiled. "I love their burgers," she said.

And so it was decided.

Aidan drove and pulled the car up to the door so her

mother wouldn't have to walk far in the icy cold. Riley took her mother's crutches and helped her get into the front seat. She then climbed into the back and Aidan put the crutches in the way back of his SUV. It wasn't far to the Red Nun and while they were busy, they were seated immediately.

They all ordered burgers. Aidan also ordered a plate of nachos for them to share while they waited.

Everything was good, as usual. While they ate, Aidan asked about her job search.

"I have a final interview in the city this Thursday, and a first interview with Jack's company."

Aidan raised an eyebrow. "With your boyfriend's law firm?"

Riley nodded. "I'm not sold on it for a few reasons, but I figured I should at least talk to them. I'm not really in a position to be too picky. It's only the second company that has expressed any interest, so far."

Aidan picked up his cheeseburger and took a bite. He swallowed then said, "It's bound to pick up after the holidays. Working at your boyfriend's company might be a little too close for comfort. What if you hate it there?"

Riley had the same concerns. She nodded. "That has crossed my mind as well. But if it gets that far, I could just quit."

"That might be awkward for Jack?"

"It might be," she agreed. "But it's too soon to worry about that. I don't even know if I'll get past the first interview. And the other job sounds really good. I'm keeping my fingers crossed for that one."

Aidan smiled. "Well, I hope it works out for you, too."

After dinner, they made their way back to the inn. Franny joined them and they settled on the comfy sofa and chairs around the big-screen television. Everyone was too full for popcorn when they first started watching the classic Will Ferrell movie *Elf,* but halfway through when they took a short break, Riley went to the kitchen and returned a few minutes later with a giant bowl of old-fashioned popcorn that she'd cooked on the stovetop in olive oil. She'd drizzled melted butter all over it and a sprinkle of salt and brought paper plates with her. She wasn't sure if they'd still be too full, but the minute she put the bowl down, everyone reached for some popcorn.

It was almost nine when the movie ended. Luke was yawning by then, and Franny was, too. As they walked toward the stairs, Aidan thanked them again. Riley turned to Luke and smiled. "Have fun at Edaville Railroad tomorrow."

His eyes lit up. "Dad, can they come with us? That would be so fun."

Riley's mother glanced down at her crutches. "I think that might be pushing it for me."

"Me, too," Franny agreed. "I've been there many times. You'll have so much fun."

Luke stared at Riley, his eyes imploring her to go. He was impossible to say no to. And Riley hadn't been to Edaville since she was about his age. It sounded fun to her, and something to do on a quiet Sunday in December.

"Sure, I'd love to go with you guys."

Aidan looked surprised while Luke fist pumped the air. "Awesome."

Aidan smiled. "All right, this will be fun. We're planning on leaving around three, if that works for you?"

"I'll plan on it."

CHAPTER TWENTY-SIX

My dear Franny,

For my third request, I want you to go back to one of our favorite restaurants. Remember all those thick chocolate frappés and the platters of fried seafood and onion rings that we used to share? If I remember right that's where Joe took you on your first anniversary? I had many dates there, too. But my favorite times there were with you when we'd go after school or on a hot summer day. There's nothing like Kream 'N Kone in Albany, Franny. Before you head home, I just want to make sure you experience the delicious food and enjoy the memories.

Lots of love,
Ella

Over breakfast, Franny told Riley and Beth what was in her third letter.

"I just opened it this morning." She smiled. "My sister wants me to go to the original Kream 'N Kone in West Dennis. There's one in Chatham now, but it wasn't open when we were in high school. We used to love to make the drive there and sit on the deck that overlooked Swan River in warm weather."

"Kream 'N Kone has the best fried seafood around," Riley said.

"And the best coffee frappés," Beth added.

Franny nodded. "I was always partial to the chocolate ones."

"What do you think your sister's purpose is with these letters?" Riley asked.

Franny smiled. "I'm not entirely sure. Maybe just to remember and to appreciate the Cape and all the good times we had here."

"Well, that sounds like a lovely way to spend a Sunday afternoon," Beth said.

"Maybe not as exciting as Edaville Railroad, but it's more my speed," Franny said.

Riley grinned. "I really am looking forward to going. I remember how magical it seemed when I was there as a kid. It will be fun to experience that through Luke's eyes."

"Well, I am looking forward to a nice quiet afternoon," Beth said. "I have a new book that arrived yesterday. It looks like a fun romantic comedy and I plan to curl up with your Lily by my side."

Riley laughed. "She will love that. And I won't feel so badly for leaving her if she has you to give her attention."

Beth laughed, too. "She definitely doesn't lack for attention."

Aidan and Luke joined them soon after, and Aidan cut himself a big piece of the quiche that Riley had made with Luke. Luke had no interest in it and went for his usual bowl of Cheerios with a banana on the side. Luke was unusually chatty as he ate. He was very excited for the trip to Edaville.

"We saw on the news this morning that it might snow a little. That will be so awesome to ride the train in the snow. And Santa loves the snow."

"He does," Riley agreed.

"You're still sure you want to come?" Aidan asked with a wink. "It's not too late to back out. I wouldn't blame you."

Riley laughed. "I was telling my mother and Franny that I'm really looking forward to it."

He looked glad to hear it. A big smile spread across his face. "All right then. We'll see you back here at three."

"Have fun. Riley, be sure to take some pictures, so your mother and I can see how it's changed over the years. Maybe it's exactly the same," Franny said.

"I will, definitely," Riley assured her.

Later that afternoon, around one thirty, Franny set out for a late lunch at the Kream 'N Kone. She drove along route 28, the main road that ran most of the length of the Cape. She passed hotels, shops, and restaurants as she drove. There was snow in the forecast but not until later. Still, she could feel the dampness in the cold air and the sky was a deep gray. Snow was definitely on the way.

She passed by the Kream 'N Kone in Chatham, which had opened when she was in her early thirties. It was just as good but it didn't have the same feel and she knew it wouldn't invoke the same memories as the West Dennis location even though that building had a major fire in 2003 and had to be rebuilt up the road. It still brought back special memories And she knew that was more important to her sister than the food. Though the food was good too.

Even though it was December, there was still a small line at the counter when Franny walked in. She waited her turn, debated over what to get, and then placed the order she always seemed to place at the Kream 'N Kone—a scallop and clam plate and a chocolate frappé. It was a lot of food and she knew she wouldn't eat all of it, but she would give it a good try. She could never decide between scallops and clams, and at the Kream 'N Kone she could get both. When her name was called, she went back to the counter to pick up her order and brought her tray to a window that overlooked the Swan River.

The platter came with onion rings and French fries. Franny very rarely ate fried food, so when she did, she savored every bite. Kream 'N Kone had spoiled her for all other fried seafood and onion rings. The batter was so light and crispy and the onion rings were sliced thin and melted in her mouth. She took a sip of her frappe. It was thick and rich with chocolate ice cream and she was instantly transported back to high school.

She and Ella used to come here often. When they didn't have the fried seafood, they had burgers, but they always had chocolate frappés. They'd come with their girlfriends, too. It was part of their weekend nights out and lots of other students would be there, too. And that's where she first met Joe, standing in line to order a clam roll. It was a warm summer night and the line was long. He'd looked familiar to her and he recognized her, too.

"You're in my math class. Mrs. Hannigan."

Franny had instantly made a face at the mention of the teacher's name. And Joe had laughed. "She's not my favorite either."

They'd instantly bonded over their dislike of the cranky teacher. Franny had instantly been attracted to Joe's smile and warm brown eyes, his wavy dark hair, so dark it was almost black. Their orders were called at the same time and they realized they were sitting at adjoining tables. They'd managed to keep the conversation going over dinner while everyone talked around them. It was like they were the only ones there.

And before she and Ella left, Joe asked her to go to a dance with him.

And that was the beginning of their romance. Franny felt her eyes grow misty as she thought of him. On their one-year anniversary, he'd taken her back there for dinner. He was her first real love and she'd been devastated when he moved away soon after with his family. They'd both promised to stay in touch and they did for a while. But it was too much once they graduated and chose schools on the opposite ends of the country. Franny wondered if it might have been different if they'd had cell phones then or social media.

She dipped an onion ring into ketchup and popped it in her mouth. And she realized that everything really did happen for a reason. She wasn't meant to stay with Joe because soon after she started her junior year of college, she met Tim. And she knew right away that she was going to marry him. She smiled, remembering their third date. They'd gone for ice cream and he made a confession to her.

"I told my mother when I got home from our first date that I was going to marry you. She of course told me that was ridiculous and that I needed to get to know you better, to be sure." He pulled something out of his pocket and got down on one knee and opened his hand to show the small gray velvet box. Franny sucked in her breath.

Tim grinned. "So I waited until our third date. And I'm even more sure now. I love you, Franny. Is there a chance you love me, too? Will you marry me?"

And Franny hadn't hesitated. She knew, too. "Of course I will. I'd love to marry you, Tim. I love you, too!"

They'd gotten engaged and married the following year soon after graduation. And she'd had a long and very happy life with him. She'd truly been blessed to have found love twice. So, she didn't mind so much that she was alone now. She had her books and she kept busy. Life was pretty good.

She finished about half of her fried food and all of her frappé. She drove back to the inn feeling full, content, and nostalgic. It was bittersweet remembering Ella and all the good times she'd had with her sister. She missed Ella. She especially missed being able to pick up the phone and call her sister whenever she felt like it, which was several times a week, at least. They'd spoken often, even if it was just a few minutes, to catch up or share any funny or interesting things that had happened. It hit Franny when she least expected it, the wave of sadness that would wash over her. It didn't stay long, though, as Franny always reminded herself that Ella was in a better place now. She wasn't suffering and she was with Victor.

And Franny was enjoying her time at the inn. Her sister had been wise to ensure that she stayed around instead of going straight home to Albany. That would have been harder and she would have felt more alone. Here she was surrounded by friendly people who had quickly become friends and it helped. A lot.

A sense of peace came over her as she realized what her sister was trying to tell her. It was time for her to be in Chatham more. She didn't know if she would ever be ready to stay in her sister's house. She'd walked through it after the funeral and it just didn't feel right. It was her sister's home. Franny didn't think it could ever be hers. But, maybe she could buy a home of her own there. Just a small place. It didn't have to be as big as Ella's as it was just Franny. If she could find a small cottage with even a sliver of an ocean view she'd be happy with that. She could afford it. And eventually she would sell Ella's house, but not yet. Not for at least a year.

As she drove back to the inn, she grew more excited about

her decision. She would call a Realtor in the morning and start the search for her new cottage. She realized that in the past few weeks, she'd made new friends—everyone at the inn felt like family, and though Angela was a new friend, they'd connected immediately and she'd had such a good time at the book club. Many of those ladies also golfed, which was something Franny used to love. Perhaps she'd take it up again. It felt like this was where she needed to spend more time now.

CHAPTER TWENTY-SEVEN

The ride to Edaville Railroad in Carver took a little over an hour. Carver was near Plymouth, which was just over the Cape Cod Canal bridge. They sang along to Christmas carols as they drove and Aidan explained some of the history of Edaville Railroad to them.

"Did you know that the railroad started as a way for the owner to haul cranberries from the bogs he owned in the area?"

"No, I had no idea. I assumed it was always meant as an amusement park," Riley said.

"It kind of organically grew into that when people started wanting rides on the trains and it was popular around Christmas especially, so they opened it up to the public."

"That's so cool." Riley knew that the area was one of the biggest growers of cranberries, and the national company, Ocean Spray, was located nearby in Middleboro. There were lots of cranberry bogs on the Cape, too, but smaller ones. Sometimes they would flood over in the winter, and she and her sister used to go ice skating on them. She smiled at the memory.

When they pulled into the parking lot, it was almost four thirty and the place was absolutely packed.

They waited in line and Aidan bought tickets for all of

them that included a ride on the train and unlimited rides on the attractions. Luke wanted to ride the train first so that's what they did. They waited their turn, then climbed aboard and rode the old-fashioned steam train all around the many bogs on the property. As they rode the sun set and the sky grew dark. And the lights came on—so many festive lights all around them. It was really beautiful to see. The look on Luke's face was one of wonder. Riley felt it, too, that magical feeling that she'd always loved so much and generally only experienced around the holidays.

When the train ride ended, they headed over to the amusement rides and rode on most of them, except the Ferris wheel, which was being repaired. Riley's favorite was the bumper cars, which they did a second time, because Luke loved it, too. It was almost six thirty by then and Aidan asked if anyone was hungry.

"I noticed a hot dog stand, we could do that or find something else?" he asked.

"I want a hot dog!" Luke announced.

Riley laughed. "That actually sounds really good to me, too." Riley seldom ate them but once in a while, at a cookout or a baseball game, they hit the spot.

When they got closer to the stand, Luke asked if he could go get them.

Aidan pulled a couple of twenties out and handed them to Luke. "Here you go, buddy, we'll follow along to give you a hand when they're ready."

Riley and Aidan walked along slowly while Luke ran ahead to order the hot dogs.

"Are you having fun?" Aidan asked.

Riley smiled. "So much. Thanks for including me. I haven't been here in a million years."

Aidan laughed. "I can't really picture you here with Jack.

How are things going with him? Do you think you'll get engaged?"

"It has been almost two years. I think we're heading in that direction. We don't really talk about it, though, because a lot has to happen first. Jack is on the partner track and that won't happen for another year or two and then he'll still be working crazy hours for a while. Eventually it will slow down."

"Eventually. Are you sure you want to stick around that long? You must really love him."

Did she? Riley hadn't ever felt head over heels madly in love with Jack. But she liked him quite a lot. And so far it had worked for both of them that neither was in a rush to get married.

She just smiled and looked off into the distance where one of the trains was chugging along, sending swirls of steam into the cold air.

There was a long moment of silence before Aidan turned and faced her directly. "It's funny, I've only been in love twice, but both times it kind of slammed into me and I didn't want to wait. The first time she didn't feel the same way."

Riley felt a pang as she knew he was referring to her. She looked into his warm eyes, his handsome face, and couldn't help wondering for a moment what her life would have been like if she'd stayed with Aidan.

Aidan smiled and his eyes lit up. "But the second time, she was just as crazy about me and we got engaged six months after we started dating. When you know, you know."

"I suppose. But sometimes the timing just isn't right." Riley sighed. "It wasn't that I didn't love you, Aidan," she said softly. "I just wasn't ready to marry anyone and moving off-Cape was important to me. With Jack, the timing isn't right for us now but in a few years it may be." She realized as she said it that she was also trying to convince herself that she was making the right choice.

"Well, I'm glad things are going well for you and that you both seem to want the same things," Aidan said a little stiffly. It took Riley by surprise as he'd given no indication that he might still have feelings for her. A minute later, though, she told herself she'd imagined the vibe, as Aidan was laughing again as he passed her a hot dog and a bottled water. She added a little ketchup and mustard and they brought their food to a picnic table and sat. Luke had ordered a large box of fries for them to share as well.

As they ate, Riley watched Aidan and Luke laughing and her thoughts drifted again, imagining what her life would have been like if she'd married Aidan. They'd probably have a child about Luke's age. And Aidan was so good with Luke. It didn't surprise her at all that he was a devoted father. He'd always been kind and thoughtful. He'd been a great boyfriend. But he'd been ready to get married and she wasn't even thinking of marriage to anyone at that point. She didn't feel mature enough and selfishly, there were things she wanted to do first. And moving off-Cape and living in a big city was top on her list.

She had no regrets. She'd loved living in Manhattan and until recently, she'd loved her job, too. But she knew she would get another one. It was just a matter of time. What she was a little less sure of were her feelings for Jack. She'd been in love with the idea of a life with Jack. He was handsome and smart and they had fun together. But he was also busy and often unavailable as work always came first. And she hadn't minded so much.

But now that she'd been in Chatham and had been busy almost every day with her family or spending time with Aidan and Franny, she realized how much she liked being around people. And how lonely her life with Jack really was. She saw him once or twice a week, if that. She occasionally went out with friends after work, but most nights she stayed in, with Lily curled up in her lap. She'd grown used to that. But she was starting to wonder if it was enough.

Maybe she was just being overly sensitive because she wasn't working and had more time on her hands. Once she had a job and was working normal hours again, she'd probably fall right back into that routine and be fine with it. She was usually tired at the end of the day and didn't want to go out every night anyway. But maybe it would be nice to come home to someone? She and Jack hadn't talked about living together, and maybe they should. That might be a good next step, possibly.

"You look deep in thought," Aidan commented.

"Oh! Just thinking ahead to my job interviews this week," she lied. "I'm a little nervous." That part was true.

"I have no doubt you'll kill it. Just be yourself and tell them what you can do. They won't be able to resist." His eyes met hers and he smiled. She felt his warmth and his faith in her and it restored her confidence.

"Thanks, I hope so."

After they finished eating, Luke wanted to go on a few more rides. They finished up with a walk through the museum and the room with all the model trains. Luke was very enthused about that. "Dad, that is the coolest thing ever. I would love to have a train set like that."

"Might be tough in our room at the inn," Aidan joked. Luke's face fell and Aidan immediately clearly regretted the joke. "Once we get home, though, we'll have plenty of room and can look into that. Sound good?"

Luke grinned, happy again. "Awesome."

They finished up with a visit to Santa. Luke stood in line and sat on Santa's lap for a minute. He whispered something in Santa's ear and Santa nodded and looked quite serious. Luke was all smiles when he ran over to them.

"Did your talk with Santa go well?" Aidan asked.

"Really well. I can't tell you what I asked for, though. It's a secret between me and Santa."

Aidan smiled. "Okay, buddy, fair enough." He glanced at Riley. "Are we good to go?"

It was snowing lightly as they headed home. Luke fell asleep a half hour into the ride and Riley and Aidan talked softly the rest of the way. Their conversation was light. Aidan talked about the restoration at this house and how it was going.

"It looks like we might be back around the New Year, hopefully."

"It must be hard not being there. I mean, the inn is great but it's not home."

Aidan nodded. "No, but it's nice knowing people there. It's been good for both of us to be around friends during the holidays."

"It is nice. I haven't been around this many people in a while either. Usually it's just me and Lily and a few times a week, Jack," Riley said.

"Do you still love living in the city?" Aidan asked. She smiled at his tone, which clearly conveyed that he just couldn't imagine anyone loving it.

"There's a lot to love about it. It's so different from the Cape, much louder and busier. But it's home."

Aidan pulled into her mother's driveway and glanced at the back seat where Luke was sound asleep. "Please tell your mother I said hello. Looks like this guy is out cold. I should get him to bed." He smiled softly at Riley. "It was a great day. Good night."

"Good night, Aidan. Thanks again for today." Riley almost hated for the evening to end. She'd enjoyed Aidan's and Luke's company more than she'd expected. She got out of the car and watched as Aidan backed up and drove off. Once they were gone, she felt a rush of loneliness that was confusing. She turned toward her mother's house, where the cheerful glow of the Christmas tree glimmered through the living room window. It was warm and welcoming and Riley's spirits lifted as she stepped inside.

CHAPTER TWENTY-EIGHT

After breakfast on Monday, Franny went to her room, and called her sister's lawyer, Jess. After a brief hold, Jess came on the phone.

"Good morning, Franny, what can I do for you?"

"I just have a quick question. Who would you recommend locally if someone were in the market to buy a house?"

Jess didn't hesitate. "Lynnette Barker. She actually has an office two doors down from mine. Right next to the bookshop." Jess gave her Lynnette's number and Franny jotted it down.

"Fantastic. Thank you." She called Lynnette, who picked up immediately and said she'd be delighted to meet with Franny in an hour in her office. That didn't surprise Franny as she knew it was generally a slow time of year for real estate sales. But she also knew there were still things on the market and it might be a good time to buy because there were less people looking, especially around the holidays.

At a quarter to ten, she bundled up in her warm wool coat, cashmere hat, and mittens. She walked along Main Street, enjoying the warm sun on her face even though the air was decidedly cold. It was a sunny day, though, and no snow in the forecast. She walked along until she reached the real estate office and stepped inside. A very blond woman with big curls and a red-lipped wide smile stood and walked over to her.

"You must be Franny? I'm Lynnette. Come on in and get warm." Lynnette led her over to her desk, which was an antique pine, dark and shiny with lots of fancy moldings. It sat next to a gas fireplace and the flames glowed merrily. Lynnette gestured for Franny to sit in the leather chair next to the fire and she happily complied. The heat felt wonderful as she shook off her coat and removed her hat and mittens. Lynnette sat behind her desk and leaned forward.

"So, you're thinking you might want to buy a cottage in the area. What did you have in mind? Summer only or year round?"

"Year round, though I will probably mostly be here in the summer. But I want the option to come anytime. I don't need anything too big, two bedrooms is fine, and I don't need to be right on the ocean. I would like a view, though."

"Okay. What price range did you have in mind?"

Franny told her and wasn't surprised when Lynnette sat up taller in her chair. "Oh, well, that opens up a lot of possibilities." Franny knew her price range was wide, but she really was open. "I just don't want anything too big. I don't need a lot of room and I don't want to take care of it either."

Lynnette laughed. "I don't blame you a bit. Let's take a look at what we currently have available." She pulled up the listings on her laptop and showed Franny a few options. Most of them were much too big. And Franny started to feel disappointed. Since she'd made up her mind that she wanted to buy something, she was ready to do it now. It was frustrating to think there might not be anything for sale at the moment that could work.

"There is this new listing that came in last week. It's very small, though. It used to be a carriage house that went with a larger property. The owner subdivided it so it sits on its own acre. It is waterfront, though. So, the price is on the high side for the size of the property. It's really the land you're paying for." Franny wasn't hopeful as Lynnette pulled up the listing. She really wasn't keen on being on the water, but mostly because all of the waterfront homes she'd seen were so big. Still, she was a little curious to see what this one was like.

Lynnette turned the laptop around so Franny could see and she gasped a little. The house was adorable. It was only twelve hundred square feet, but it had a big wraparound farmer's porch that looked out over the ocean and the house was set high on a hill, so she didn't have to worry about flooding. As Lynnette flipped through the photos, Franny saw that the master bedroom was on the first floor and had an attached bathroom. The kitchen was cute and all white and opened into the living room, which was decorated with soft blue walls and had a fireplace that was painted white. The light colors made the space look very beachy and bigger. There was a guest bedroom on the second floor and a loft area that could be used as an office. In short, it looked too good to be true.

"I'd like to see it. Today if possible," Franny said.

"I think that can be arranged. Let me just call the listing broker. Her office is right down the street and I think there is a lockbox so it can be shown anytime. The owners are out of state."

Lynnette called the other Realtor and chatted for a few minutes, jotting something on a slip of paper. When she ended the call, she turned to Franny. "Good news. We can go anytime today. What works for you?"

Franny smiled. "How about now?"

Lynnette laughed. "Now works." She picked up the slip of

paper and explained that it had the lockbox code on it. Franny put her coat and hat back on and followed Lynnette to her silver Mercedes sedan, which was parked out back. Fifteen minutes later they pulled off Shore Road and into the driveway of the carriage house. Franny noticed that the main house was closer to the water and far enough away from her. She'd worried on the ride over that the two homes might be too close for her comfort but fortunately that wasn't the case.

Lynnette punched the code into the lockbox that hung on the front door handle. Once she had the key, she unlocked the door and they stepped inside. Franny felt an instant sense of calm and tranquility as she moved into the living room. And when she saw the view out the living room windows, she felt pure bliss. She could stare out that window for hours taking in the rolling waves on the very blue waters of the harbor. The windows were huge and went the full length of the wall, extending from a few inches above the floor to the ceiling. It almost gave the impression that the house itself was on the water.

They walked into the kitchen next and Franny liked that, too. The countertops were a marble-like quartz and the backsplash was all white subway tiles. The top cupboards were a creamy white and the bottom ones and the center island were a really pretty pale blue-gray. The color combination was striking. Franny liked to cook and the kitchen was small but laid out nicely. It had everything she needed.

The master bedroom was as lovely as the pictures and it also had water views from one side. It was a spacious yet cozy room and she knew she would sleep well there. They went upstairs and saw the guest bedroom, which was a little smaller but still very nice and the loft area would make a nice office area if she put a desk there. She had one that would fit perfectly.

They went downstairs and into the two-car garage, which

Franny was also happy with. Especially in the winter, she appreciated driving into a heated garage and not having to scrape car windows. There was a basement, too, and they went into it but Franny didn't get excited about basements. It was dry and had everything it needed to have so that was fine.

When they came back upstairs and walked back into the main house for a final look, Lynnette asked Franny what she thought of it.

Franny smiled. "How quickly do you think they would like to close?"

Lynnette's eyes widened. Franny knew she'd had no idea how serious Franny was until now.

"We can certainly find out. Would you like to make an offer today?"

"I would like that very much!"

They drove back to the office and Franny offered full asking price. It seemed like a fair price to her and she didn't want to play any games. She wanted that house. She wrote Lynnette a check for the deposit and signed the offer paperwork.

"I'll be in touch as soon as I have word. I don't think it will be long," Lynnette said.

Franny left and walked a few doors down to the bookshop. She was too excited to go back to the inn just yet. She knew she was going to be on pins and needles all day waiting for a response to the offer. And she didn't even know if they would hear today. Their offer was good until five o'clock the next day.

She strolled into the bookshop and there were a few people browsing the shelves. Alison, one of the owners, recognized her and came over to say hello.

"Hi, Franny. How are you on this cold day?"

"I'm good. Really good. Do you by any chance have *The Lioness of Boston*?" It was the book the book club was reading next.

And even though Franny wouldn't be there, she had thought the book sounded good.

"We do. I read that recently and it's very good." Alison walked over to one of the shelves and found the book. She pulled it out and handed it to Franny. "We had a delivery come in yesterday. There's a lot of new books on the front table that look good, too. If you need anything else," she suggested.

Franny smiled. "I'll take a look." She wandered back to the front tables and browsed a bit. Alison was right. Quite a few of them looked intriguing. She chose another and as she walked to the register, her phone rang. It was Lynnette.

"Franny, are you sitting down?" she said excitedly.

Franny chuckled. "No, I'm buying books."

"Well, I have the best news! We reached the owner and he accepted your offer. The house is yours!" Franny listened in a daze as Lynnette discussed the time frame and when they could finalize the sale. She mentioned a date two weeks away and asked Franny if that was too soon. Normally it took longer, but as Franny was paying cash that could speed up the process.

Franny felt a split second of nerves at how fast this was moving, but they quickly settled and a sense of joy took over. "Two weeks is fine. Thank you, Lynnette."

Alison was looking at her curiously as she ended the call. She'd already run up her two books. Franny handed her a credit card. She grinned and felt ridiculously happy.

"Good news?" Alison asked.

"The best. I just bought a house!"

Alison smiled wide and offered her congratulations. "That's wonderful news."

"It is. You might be seeing a lot more of me!"

Franny walked out of the bookshop with a smile on her face. She didn't just buy a house, she was already becoming a part of the community, again. If her sister was watching, she knew that she would be delighted. Though she'd lived in Albany for many years, Franny was a little surprised that she wasn't missing it, at all. It felt like her future was here, in Chatham.

CHAPTER TWENTY-NINE

"Franny sounded so excited at breakfast," Riley said. She was in the kitchen at home with her mother and they were making some appetizers. Her mother's friends, Jess, Alison, Donna, and Maddie were coming for a girls' night. Jess and Maddie were bringing an appetizer, too, and Alison was making her delicious gluten-free brownies.

"She did. I'm so happy for her. It seems like her sister's letters are working their magic," her mother said.

"It does. She said that it opened her eyes to all the wonderful memories she had here and made her want to spend more time in Chatham. This place does sort of grow on you, the more time you spend here." Riley could understand it. For years she'd only been back in Chatham for a few days or at the most a week during the summer. Too fast to really sink into it and experience living on the Cape. At first, it was because she was afraid she would miss it too much. And then it just became a habit.

"The house sounds perfect for her," her mother said.

"I can't wait to see it. She said she'll have us over once she's all set up. She needs to go shopping to furnish it," Riley said.

"Really? I'm surprised she's not moving stuff there from Albany."

"I don't think she's ready to give that house up yet," Riley said.

"Oh, right. Well, it will be fun for her to go shopping."

Riley put the final touches on her appetizer. It was a decadent garlic bread stuffed with artichokes, spinach, sour cream, and several cheeses. She'd just taken it out of the oven and sprinkled minced parsley on top before slicing it into small pieces.

Her mother checked on her sausage-stuffed mushrooms, which were still in the oven. She pulled them out and set them on the counter. They looked delicious.

Maddie was the first to arrive. She handed Riley a bottle of Hot to Trot, a red blend that was really good. She also had a bowl of caramelized onion dip and some cut veggies as well as potato chips. "Because veggies won't be enough, but if we have a few we won't feel as guilty about the chips." She set the bowl on the kitchen island and took the foil off the top.

Jess and Alison arrived together. They both brought wine, too, a bottle of Josh Cabernet and Bread & Butter Prosecco. "I've been on a Prosecco kick lately," Alison said as she set a pan of brownies on the counter.

Jess handed Riley's mother a charcuterie board that was covered with an assortment of cheese, prosciutto, salami, mini pickles, nuts, and crackers.

"This looks fantastic, thank you."

Donna was the last to arrive and rushed in, apologizing for running late.

"It has been a day," she said as she handed Riley a platter of cold cooked shrimp with cocktail sauce and lemon on the side. She also set a bottle of Prosecco on the counter and laughed when she saw the identical bottle of Bread & Butter. She glanced at Alison. "Great minds think alike, I see."

Riley opened the wines and poured a glass for everyone.

They stood around the island in the kitchen, eating everything and talking and laughing. Riley mostly sipped her wine and ate as she listened to the conversation. She'd worried about her mother from time to time, wondering if she was lonely, but it turned out she actually had a more active social life than Riley did. She didn't have a solid friend group like this in Manhattan. She had a few friends but no group of girlfriends that met up regularly like her mother's friends did.

"So, tell us all about Sean," Donna said after they'd been chatting for a while. "You like him and are going out again when?"

Her mother laughed. "We're going out tomorrow night. And I do like him, he's really easy company. And he's attractive, too!"

They all laughed in agreement. Jess asked Riley how her job search was going.

"I had a phone interview this afternoon, and it went well. They asked when I'd be available for an in-person and I let them know I have another interview there this Thursday. So, they set something up for that afternoon."

"Oh, good! Nice to have a few options. What kind of company is this one?" Donna asked.

"It's a law firm. It's actually where my boyfriend works. So I'm not so sure if that is a good idea or not. But I figured I would check it out at least. The job itself sounds pretty good."

"Hmm. That could be really good . . . or not, if things ever go south with the boyfriend," Jess said. Riley knew she was speaking from experience as she and her ex-husband, who was also a lawyer, used to work at the same law firm.

"I know. I'm more excited about the other role." She told them a little about the company.

"That sounds more similar to your last company possibly?" Alison said.

Riley nodded. "I think so. I guess I'll know for sure when I go in and meet the team."

"Well, good luck," Donna said. She looked thoughtful for a moment and then said, "You wouldn't be interested in any temporary work, like a project while you're home for the holidays?"

Riley was intrigued. "Possibly, what did you have in mind?"

"We had a new website done a year or so ago and it has a blog, but we've never put up any blog posts. Someone told me recently that we could be using that more strategically to drive traffic our way when people search on the internet."

Riley nodded. "That's exactly what I do. It's called content marketing. And we write blog posts around a specific topic that your potential customers might be interested in. So when they search online, your website will pop up."

"Would you be interested in helping us with that?" Donna asked.

"Sure. I'll be back Friday afternoon. I could start then and do some work over the weekend. You might want to have a lead magnet, too."

"What's that?" Donna asked.

"It's a short brochure with information that they can download. There's a process where it will move them onto your mailing list and then you can follow up a week or so after they get the reader magnet with an email asking if they'd like to discuss anything. It can work really well."

Donna looked very interested. "Let's do it. I can email you some information to get you started."

"Great. Thank you!" Riley was excited to have a project to work on. And the extra money would be nice, as well. The possibility of taking on freelance consulting work as a full-time gig had crossed her mind, but she'd instantly ruled it out. It seemed much riskier than a full-time job with a good salary and benefits. But she loved the idea of doing occasional projects on the side. Especially until she landed a new job.

"Maddie, how is the commuting going?" Donna asked.

Riley knew that Maddie and her husband, Richie, were splitting their time between Manhattan and Chatham. She'd accepted a big promotion to run the literary agency where she'd worked as an agent for years, but it required that she spent a big part of each month in the city.

"It was definitely an adjustment, but we're okay with it now. The job is great. It's a new challenge and I'm loving it. And we like being in the city. This month is a slow one in publishing, so I'm in Chatham through the New Year and we're closed completely the week between Christmas and New Year's Eve."

They ate their fill of the appetizers, had a bit more wine, and eventually tried the brownies.

"I know I say this every time we get together," Jess said. "But these brownies go really well with red wine."

Riley laughed. "They do actually."

Jess looked her way. "Your mom mentioned that your high school sweetheart and his son are staying at the inn. What's it like seeing him again?"

Riley smiled. "It's nice reconnecting. His son is really sweet. This time of year is still hard for both of them. It has been a few years, though, so I think it's getting better."

"So how are things going with your boyfriend?" Jess asked.

"Good. He was here over stroll weekend and met everyone."

"Oh. Well, that's that, then. I know Aidan and he's a really nice guy. He'll make someone a great boyfriend."

Riley smiled. "He definitely will." She wasn't sure she liked the idea of Aidan finding someone else. But that was silly. She had no right to feel that way. And she'd just told Jess that it was going well with Jack. It was a good thing that she'd be seeing him in a few days. They needed some time together.

CHAPTER THIRTY

Amy gave Riley a ride to the airport in Hyannis the next afternoon. The twins rode in the back seat and were sound
asleep ten minutes after they left Chatham.

"This is usually the time they go down, so it worked out
perfectly," Amy said.

"It gives us time to visit, too," Riley said. "I feel like I've
hardly seen you since I've been home." They talked by phone
every day or so, but still Riley had thought she'd see more of
her sister.

"You'll understand someday when you have kids. These
two keep me busy," Amy said.

Riley peeked into the back seat where the two girls were
sleeping peacefully. "They look so angelic," she said.

Amy laughed. "They are perfect children when they're
asleep. They're not so bad when they're awake. They're good
kids. Speaking of kids, how was your trip to Edaville?"

"It was fun. Luke loved it."

"I bet he did. He's adorable."

"He is," Riley agreed.

"And he still believes in Santa?" Amy asked.

Riley thought about that for a moment. "I'm not sure. He
sat on Santa's lap but he wouldn't tell us what he asked for.

Said it was a secret. I think he might know what is going on and is just playing along. I did that for a few years. I wasn't ready to give it up."

Amy grinned. "And at the same time you were searching the house high and low to see if you could find where Mom hid the presents."

Riley laughed. "I did. I didn't really want to see them, though. Just to check that they were somewhere in the house. That they existed."

"Has Jack mentioned marriage at all lately?"

"No. Not at all. We talked about it a year or so ago and we both agreed that neither of us is in a rush for that. He's focused on making partner and he's still going to be working crazy hours for a while after that. A few more years probably."

"Well, that's a long time to wait. You should talk to him about taking a step toward that, at least. You could move in with him?"

"Maybe. I'll think about it." Riley knew it was probably a good idea, if she was sure she wanted to marry Jack. But she wasn't completely sure that she did. And if she wasn't sure, then it didn't seem right to ask about living together.

When they reached the airport, Amy pulled up to the front door and leaned over to give Riley a quick hug. "Have a safe flight. Call me on Friday and I'll pick you up."

"Thanks, I will." Riley turned to say goodbye to the girls, too, but they were fast asleep. "See you on Friday."

Riley had a smooth flight back to LaGuardia and jumped in an Uber soon after she landed. She only had a carry-on bag so she didn't have to wait for luggage. It was still early, just a little before seven, but traffic was still heavy and it took over an hour to get to her apartment.

She unlocked her apartment door and stepped inside. It

seemed unusually quiet without Lily there. She was probably curled up on her mother's lap by now as the two of them watched TV. Riley smiled, picturing it. She tossed her bag in her bedroom and dialed Jack's number. She wondered if he was still working. He answered on the second ring.

"Hey there! Are you back in town?"

"Just got here. What are you up to?"

"I'm at the office still." He laughed. "What else is new? I'm here for at least another hour, maybe two. After that, I'm heading home, eating some leftover cold pizza, and falling into bed. Then I'll get up and do it again tomorrow. It might not be as late of a night, though. We could grab a drink and maybe a bite to eat when I finish up if you like?"

Riley smiled and her apartment suddenly felt less lonely. "I'd like that."

"Great. Oh, and good luck on your interviews tomorrow. We can have a drink to celebrate that, too."

"Thanks. I don't know if it will be a final interview, though."

"Oh, it will be. They know you have a final elsewhere tomorrow, so they moved quickly. They don't like to lose. I'll be shocked if you don't get an offer quickly."

"Really?" Riley was surprised by that. And she remembered something she'd forgotten to ask earlier. "Do you know why the position is open?"

Jack was quiet for a moment. "I'm not exactly sure. I think she went into a different industry."

"Oh, okay."

"Call me after your interview. I might be able to finish up early and we can head out from there."

"I will." Riley ended the call and went to make herself a peanut butter sandwich and a cup of tea. She needed to eat and get a good night's sleep.

CHAPTER THIRTY-ONE

Beth and Sean decided to go to a five o'clock movie and grab dinner afterward. When Sean picked her up he was apologetic. "I'd planned to take you to the Impudent Oyster. It's one of my favorite restaurants. But I totally forgot that they are closed on Wednesdays. I hope the Squire is okay?"

Beth didn't care where they went. "The Squire is always good." Sean drove and they found a parking spot right across the street from the movie theater, which was near the beginning of Main Street. If the weather had been nicer, Beth would have suggested walking there as well, but the walk in the winter cold and darkness would have been too much.

The theater wasn't very busy, so they had their pick of seats. Beth loved seeing movies at the Orpheum. It was a historic building that had been renovated and it was convenient that it was so close by. They decided to share a large buttered popcorn with a couple of waters and chose seats in the middle of the theater. Beth was excited to see this movie. It was a romantic comedy and the reviews so far were really good.

They both enjoyed it. The time flew by as they munched on their popcorn. They didn't make much of a dent in it, though, as the bucket was huge and Beth didn't want to ruin her appetite for dinner.

They walked to the Squire when the movie ended and it was busy for a quiet Wednesday in December, but there were still plenty of available tables. They took a quick look at the menu and both decided on cups of chowder. Sean went with steak tips and Beth chose grilled salmon.

As they ate, they caught each other up on what was new since they'd last seen each other.

"I saw the doctor and he likes my progress. I should be able to get the cast off on Monday and switch to a brace that I can wear during the day and take off at night." She smiled. "I won't miss the crutches. Though I am getting pretty good with them."

"You do fine. But that will be a relief, getting that thing off. I broke my leg once and hated wearing the cast. I especially hated the itching and not being able to scratch."

Beth laughed. "Yes, that's the worst." She took a bite of salmon. It was delicious, with a lemon butter sauce. "The house already seems quiet with Riley gone. It's nice having Lily around, though."

"Lily's her cat?"

Beth nodded. "Yeah, I've been thinking it's about time for me to adopt a new cat. I lost one a few months ago. I'd had him for over twenty years and it was heartbreaking to lose him."

"They become part of the family," Sean agreed. "You should get one. I have a dog, a golden retriever. Rusty's the best. He's young still, just four. So hopefully I'll have him for many years."

"Goldens are good dogs," Beth said. She could picture Sean with Rusty.

"You'll have to meet him soon. He'll like you."

Beth smiled. "I think goldens like everyone."

Sean laughed. "Rusty's smart, though. He never warmed to Marcy, the last woman I dated. I don't think she was much of a dog person or a cat person, now that I think of it. They can tell."

"They really can," Beth agreed.

"So, Riley has an interview in the city?" Sean asked.

Beth spread a bit of butter on a piece of bread and took a bite before answering. "She has two actually. One she's really excited about and the other is at her boyfriend's company, a law firm."

"What industry is the other company?"

"Some kind of software, educational, I think. Similar to her last company," Beth said.

"I would think she'd like that better. Software companies are usually sort of casual and laid back, right? Not like a law firm."

Beth agreed. "Riley said that exactly. She said Jack wears suits every day and works tons of overtime. Her job probably wouldn't require long hours, but it sounds a little stuffy compared to what she's used to. She did say the pay would be better, though."

Sean frowned. "That's never enough, though. Better to make less and love what you do and where you do it."

"I totally agree. I work longer hours with the inn, but it's my business and I love it. I've never been happier."

He smiled. "Same here. I actually used to have one of those corporate jobs for years when the girls were young. We lived in a suburb of Boston and I took the train into the city every day, wearing a suit and carrying a briefcase. I worked in finance and I pretty much hated everything about it. But the money was good. I wanted to quit long before I did, but my ex wouldn't let me. She said it wasn't fair to the girls."

Beth reached out and took his hand and squeezed it lightly. "That's awful."

"She was partly right. We had a mortgage and kids are not

inexpensive. I didn't have a plan for something else that would cover the bills. So I stayed put, for a while. But I started doing some woodworking on the side, as a hobby, and it slowly grew into a part-time income. When it matched the salary of the day job, I put my notice in. The ex still didn't like it. She preferred the prestige of saying her husband had a big job in finance, but she couldn't argue with the numbers."

"So you got to retire the suit. That must have been a happy day."

"It was. Not long after that, we divorced and I moved here. I figured I could do woodworking from anywhere and I'd always loved the Cape and loved to fish. When my father passed ten years ago, my mother sold her house there and followed me here. It's nice having some family nearby. And of course the girls used to love to spend a good part of the summers with me."

"It is nice to have family around. I'm grateful that Amy, Rob, and the girls are just ten minutes away. I don't love that Riley is in New York, but it's not so far. She still gets home a few times a year. I am sorry that she lost her job, but it has been a godsend having her here these past few weeks. I will miss her and Lily when they head home. I think that may be just around the corner."

Sean smiled. "Well, I'll make sure you're not too lonely when she goes. I look forward to spending more time with you, if you're up for that?"

Beth felt a rush of warmth as she looked into Sean's eyes. "I'd really like that."

"Good! So, I know it's only two days away, but I'd love to see you on Friday night if you can get out? With Christmas on Sunday, I'm sure you'll be tied up the rest of the weekend."

"Yes, let's do something on Friday. I will be busy the rest of the weekend. I can't believe it's already Christmas. I actually haven't been able to get out and shop at all as I haven't been driving. I've mostly been shopping online, which is fine. But I still need to get a few more things."

Sean grinned. "So, let's go Christmas shopping Friday night and then grab a bite somewhere after. We can drive into Hyannis and go to the mall. If you like Chinese food, I'm a big fan of Tiki Port, which is right by the mall."

Beth laughed. "You don't want to go shopping, do you? That actually does sound kind of fun. If you are serious, I will take you up on it."

"Absolutely. What time do you want to head out?"

Beth thought for a minute. "We have wine and cheese hour from five to six. Why don't you come for that and we can head out after."

"Perfect."

When they finished up, Sean once again insisted on paying the bill. Beth decided she was going to pay when he wasn't looking when they went for Chinese. She suspected that was the only way she'd get a chance to treat him, and since he was taking her shopping, he deserved it and she wanted to show her gratitude.

He walked her to her door when they got home. It was after nine by then and they both had to be up early the next day, so she didn't invite him in. But they did share a long and very sweet kiss at the door before she went inside. She was on cloud nine as she flopped on the living room sofa. Lily immediately hopped onto her lap and she petted her absentmindedly as she replayed their kiss in her mind. So far, there had been no red flags with Sean at all. He was easy to be around and she was falling fast.

CHAPTER THIRTY-TWO

Riley's first interview the next day was at eleven. The building was on the same street that she used to work on, just a few blocks down. She entered the lobby and a smiling receptionist welcomed her. Riley instantly liked the vibe. The walls in the reception area were a peachy pink and there were green plants everywhere and smooth jazz playing on the radio.

"I'll let the team know that you're here. Please have a seat, and help yourself to water or coffee."

Riley decided against either. She didn't want to risk a spill before her interview started and when she got nervous she sometimes was clumsy. She sat in a comfy chair and picked up a copy of *People* magazine and flipped through it. It was hard to focus on the celebrity gossip, though. She was nervous about this interview. The company seemed great and the job seemed right up her alley. She'd found that she often did better on interviews when she was less interested as it was easier to relax and be herself when she didn't care if she got the job. She cared about this one.

A few minutes later, a tall man with glasses walked into the lobby. He was casually dressed in a green button-down shirt and khaki pants. He looked around the lobby and since Riley was the only person there, he looked her way and smiled. "Riley Sanders?"

She stood. "Nice to meet you."

"Thanks for coming in. I'm Bill Westwood in human resources, we spoke on the phone." He led her into a conference room where she recognized the three people she'd had the videoconference with and a man Bill introduced as Alan Sherman, the CEO of the company. Riley was surprised that he was involved in the interview process, but it wasn't a very big company, just over a hundred people. He obviously liked to be hands-on with hiring, which actually impressed Riley. She smiled as Bill went around the room introducing everyone again. He pulled out a chair for her to sit and then left the room.

It was a little intimidating to be at a four-way interview, but they put her at ease quickly.

"I hope you don't mind that I joined the interview process," Alan began. "I started this company thirty years ago and I've met every employee before they started here. The people I've hired are a key reason for this company's success."

Riley nodded. Alan asked her about her past experience and what she'd liked most about the position. She smiled. That was an easy one to start with. She had loved that job and was happy to talk about what she enjoyed most.

"And what did you like least about it?" he asked.

Riley didn't hesitate. "The fact that we lost our jobs to AI technology."

They all laughed but Alan nodded sympathetically. "I'd probably be a little bitter about that, too," he admitted. "We do use some AI here, but not at the expense of anyone's jobs. We use it to enhance what we are already doing. I don't believe in replacing people with machines."

Riley relaxed a little and smiled. "That is reassuring," she said.

The other three she'd met with previously had a few more questions for her as well and after they finishing talking, Alan gave her a tour of the building. He pointed out the work area. "That's where the marketing team sits—where you might be." His eyes twinkled as she said it and Riley started to feel hopeful. The area was about half full and Alan explained that they had a flexible commuting policy.

"I don't mind if people work from home, as little or as much as they want. As long as the work gets done and everyone is happy, it's all good to me," he said.

That intrigued Riley. She'd never worked remotely much, unless she was traveling. Her last company preferred to have people on-site. She liked the idea of working from home a bit, especially on days when the weather was bad.

When they ended up back at the lobby, Alan said they would be in touch soon.

"Thank you for coming in. I enjoyed our talk," he said. "Are you close on anything else at the moment?" he asked casually.

Riley nodded. "I have another final interview later today. But your company is my top choice," she admitted. She thought it might help for them to know that. At least she hoped it would help. It was hard to know for sure.

"That's good to hear. Thank you, Riley. Hopefully we will talk soon."

Riley left the interview feeling pretty good about her chances. She'd liked everyone that she'd met with and the job sounded even better now that she had more insight into what they were working on. She'd been there for several hours and her stomach was grumbling a little. She had time for a quick lunch before she had to head over to Jack's law firm for her interview at three.

She decided to wait until she was closer to the law firm before stopping for lunch. She didn't want to risk getting there late. There was a Pret a Manger a block away from the law firm and she'd passed by several on her way over so by the time she walked into this one she knew exactly what she wanted. She got her usual—the blackened salmon and avocado bowl. It was light and she always felt good when she ate salmon.

She had a hot chai tea when she finished and sipped it as she checked messages and social media on her phone until it was time to head in for her interview. She felt much more relaxed for this interview as it wasn't her top choice. She was curious, though, about what the environment was like.

Riley walked into the building lobby and showed her license to the security guard. He checked his list of people that were expected for appointments that day and waved her on through. She took the elevator to the twenty-sixth floor and stepped into a plush lobby that had gleaming dark hardwood floors and beautiful oriental rugs under glass-topped coffee tables. Gorgeous artwork hung on the walls and there was chocolate-brown leather everywhere.

The receptionist was very polished and wore her brown hair tied back in an elegant French twist. Her makeup was perfect and her glasses were so fashionable that Riley wondered if they were just for show. She wore a lavender silk shirt and a black blazer that had the company's name embroidered on the pocket. She looked up when Riley approached the desk and gave her a polite half-smile.

"How may I help you?"

"I'm here for an interview. Riley Sanders."

The woman looked at a printed schedule and nodded. "Someone will be right with you. Please have a seat."

Riley did as instructed and sat in one of the leather chairs. Or rather she sank into it. The leather was so soft and buttery and comfortable. Two minutes later someone came to get her. She was a young woman, maybe in her early twenties, and she introduced herself as Taylor something from HR. Riley just nodded and murmured something about being happy to meet her.

Taylor led her down a long hallway to a big conference room where three people were sitting around an oval table. They all stood when Riley and Taylor entered the room. Taylor made the introductions. "Riley, this is Jim Stone, managing director, and you met Anne and Steve already." They'd been on the video call.

Riley nodded. "It's nice to meet you."

"Likewise," Jim said. "Thanks for coming in."

Riley sat down and the interview began. They asked a lot of the same questions she'd answered earlier and she answered them again with a smile. Even though she felt like she was repeating herself.

"So, Riley, what makes you want to work here?" Jim asked.

Riley hesitated. She supposed honesty would not be the best approach here. If she admitted that she really wasn't all that keen to work at a law firm they probably wouldn't appreciate that and think that she was wasting their time. So she tried to think of something positive to say.

"Well, the job description really lines up well with what I've done," she began.

"And I've never worked in a law firm, but I've always found it intriguing. My boyfriend is an attorney and he's always spoken so highly of the firm. He let me know about the opening and I decided to learn more."

Jim nodded. "Very good. And we all love Jack here." He looked around the room. "Does anyone have any more questions for Riley?" They'd been talking for well over an hour already. No one had any more questions.

Riley had already asked a few. She smiled and said, "I really appreciate the chance to learn more about this role and your company. Is there anything else that I can further explain?"

Jim glanced around the room and no one said anything. "I think we're good, Riley. We'll have a decision very soon. If we were to move forward, how quickly could you begin?" Riley thought for a moment. Her mother was going off her crutches on Monday and getting a leg brace that would make it easier to move around.

"I could probably start the Monday after Christmas. If you're open that week."

Jim laughed. "Oh, we're open! That's good to know you can start so quickly. You will hear from us very soon, Riley. Thanks again for coming in."

He left her in the lobby and she stepped outside and called Jack. He picked up immediately.

"How did it go?"

"I think it went okay."

"Good. Sit tight for a minute. I'll be right down. A bunch of us are heading out for drinks. We can go with them if you like or out to dinner, just the two of us. Your call."

It had been over a year since she'd gone out with Jack's colleagues after work. She was curious to meet them again and see if she could get more of a feel for the culture of the office.

"Drinks with your coworkers sounds fun. Let's do that."

Riley's fingers were crossed for the other job, but she didn't want to get her hopes up. If that one didn't work out, this could be an option. Right now, though, she didn't want to think about her job search. She was ready to relax and have a cocktail with Jack and his colleagues.

CHAPTER THIRTY-THREE

Riley waited just outside Jack's building and a few minutes later, he came through the doors followed by a half-dozen colleagues, four men and two women. One of the women, with long curly brown hair and big brown eyes, looked vaguely familiar. She didn't realize who she was until Jack introduced everyone and Brittany was last. Riley felt her eyes widen at the name. That was why she looked familiar. It was the girl on Facebook in the comments section. Brittany smiled and said hello and seemed happy to meet her.

As they walked over to the bar, Riley glanced at her a few times. Brittany was in her early to mid-twenties, slim and bubbly. She was smiling and laughing the entire time and Riley noticed that she touched Jack's arm when she spoke. To be fair, she did it to one of the other guys, too. Maybe that was just her way and it didn't mean anything.

Jack led the way into the nearby hotel bar. It was like an elegant pub with big leather chairs and dark polished wood. The bar itself was dark, the lighting dim and the windows were small and didn't let in much light. The bar wasn't crowded, which is why Jack said they liked it.

"We can almost always get space at the bar for our group," he said as they settled around the corner of the bar. The bartender came right over and took everyone's order. There were lots of martinis and whiskeys. Riley was the only one drinking wine. She didn't much care for vodka or whiskey. Once everyone had a drink, Jack raised his glass in a toast.

"Cheers to Riley. She might be joining us soon!"

Riley looked at him in surprise. "Did you already hear something?"

He smiled. "Just that you aced the first round. The in-person was really a formality. But I didn't tell you that in case it made you nervous. Better to keep your edge."

She was glad he hadn't said anything. That would have un-nerved her. She still wasn't at all sure about the law firm. But it didn't seem like the time to share that they were her second choice. They all seemed to really like it there.

Twenty minutes later, Brittany was standing next to her at the bar, trying to get the bartender's attention for another drink. He noticed her and headed over a moment later and she ordered another martini. While she waited for her drink, she finished the last few sips of the one she was holding. Riley had barely made a dent in her wine. If she drank vodka as fast as Brittany, she would be feeling miserable the next day.

"Have you been with the company long?" Riley asked.

Brittany smiled. "Just over a year. I joined right after grad-uating."

"How do you like being a lawyer?" Riley asked.

Brittany cracked up as if Riley had said something hilarious. "I'm not a lawyer. I'm a paralegal."

Oh. So that meant she was even younger. Maybe twenty-three or so. Just a baby. "Being a paralegal is okay. I get to do a lot of the same things the lawyers can do, but of course I can't go to court. I help with their research and documentation. I support Jack. He's great to work for." She glanced over at him, admiration shining in her eyes. But Jack wasn't paying attention. He was deep in conversation with the guy on his left.

Riley relaxed a little. Brittany was cute and a big flirt, but if she worked for Jack directly then she was very much off-limits. Not that she really ever felt like she had to worry about Jack that way. It was more Brittany's aggressive admiration that was concerning. Or had been. She wasn't worried about it anymore. She knew Jack would never do anything to possibly jeopardize his partnership.

They stayed for another two hours and Riley had a second glass of wine. She had fun, sort of. Jack's coworkers were friendly and fun. But every conversation circled back to work and they talked about cases and situations that Riley had no knowledge of. So she sipped her wine and people watched as the bar filled up with suits. It was a mix of attorneys and financial types. The traders had a certain air about them, a cockiness that swarmed around them. They were incredibly impressed with themselves and expected everyone else to be equally impressed. Riley found it tiresome.

"Lawyer?" The voice came from her left and when she glanced over she saw a suspected trader looking at her with a crooked grin and a gleam in his eye. His blond hair was a little too long and flopped over one eye.

"No. Unemployed at the moment, actually. What about you?"

He stood a bit taller and his chest puffed out. "I'm a trader at Bear Stearns."

Of course he was. She fought back a yawn. "That's great. Make any exciting trades today?"

She said it flippantly but he took it seriously. "Yeah, as a matter of fact. I made a killer trade. No one saw it coming. The best kind."

"So you love what you do, then?" she asked.

He grinned. "Well, truthfully, I'd rather be a surfer. But trading pays a whole lot better."

Riley took her last sip of wine and set her glass down. Jack saw it and walked over. "Do you want to get out of here, get a bite to eat?"

She nodded. "I'm ready."

Jack closed out his tab and they left. They went to a small Italian restaurant near Riley's apartment. It was still early, just a little after seven, and they had a relaxing dinner. Riley ordered eggplant parm and Jack went with his usual, a simple spaghetti and meatballs. Riley ordered a glass of red wine, but only drank half of it. She was just too full and too tired from the long day of interviews. Jack finished all of his food and the rest of her wine and ordered a tiramisu for them to split. She did manage to eat quite a bit of that.

Over dinner, Jack filled her in on everything going on at work, the different projects he was working on and he mentioned again that he was pretty certain that she would be getting an offer.

"They must be considering other candidates," Riley said.

Jack shrugged. "I think they talked to a few, but they weren't excited about anyone until they talked to you. I guess your background is a perfect fit. And of course I told them how wonderful you are."

Riley smiled. "Thank you. I think the interview this morning went well, too. I might get an offer from them as well."

Jack looked a little disappointed at first, but then he smiled. "Well, that's great and of course I'm not surprised. Did they tell you anything about the benefits at the law firm? Because they are pretty sweet." He went on to list them. "Five weeks of vacation, though no one actually takes the time, but you get the extra pay. Tuition reimbursement if you want to take any classes. They match on 401(k) immediately, up to six percent. And there's a pretty significant year-end bonus. It varies by position but I think roles like yours get at least twenty-five percent."

That was impressive. Riley had never worked anywhere that had bonuses higher than 10 percent. The starting salary was higher at the law firm, too, about twenty thousand dollars higher. That, combined with the bonus, put the total considerably above the software company.

But Riley still liked the software company and the role there the best. She also really liked the company's CEO. She hoped that they would make her an offer. More money was nice but ultimately she cared more about being happy in her job.

By the time the bill came, Jack was yawning, too. Riley had considered inviting him over to her apartment after dinner. But they were both so tired and she knew Jack had to be up and at work early in the morning. When the bill came, she reached for it but Jack was faster. "I've got it. You can get it when you're employed again."

She laughed. "Okay, deal." Jack rarely let her pay, which she appreciated, but she wished it was more equal. She'd feel better if she contributed more often.

"You ready to go? I'm going to jump in a cab. I have an early client meeting in the morning." He leaned over and kissed her. "Can't wait until you're back in town again. Call me as soon as you hear something."

"I will."

They walked outside and Jack walked with her to her building. He'd called for an Uber and it pulled up just as they reached Riley's building. He kissed her again and she watched as he climbed into his Uber. And then she went inside and up to her apartment. It was too quiet and empty without Lily there. Riley looked forward to seeing her and her mother and everyone else at the inn the next night. She had a flight at ten and Amy was picking her up. She'd be back in Chatham hopefully around noon. She was hoping to work on Donna's project for a few hours before heading over to the inn to get ready for the wine and cheese hour and the turndown service. She changed and climbed into bed and snuggled into the covers. Her last thought as she drifted off to sleep was that she couldn't wait to get home.

CHAPTER THIRTY-FOUR

The next morning, while Riley was in an Uber heading to the airport, her cell phone rang. She recognized the caller ID—it was Jack's law firm.

"Hello?"

"Riley? This is Jim Stone, managing director at Waters and Stone. We'd like to offer you the position discussed yesterday." He mentioned a salary that was ten thousand dollars higher than she'd expected. "And of course, there are our benefits." He ran through them all and finished with, "Lastly, you will be eligible for a year-end bonus of up to thirty percent of your salary."

Riley was speechless. The bonus was even better than Jack had mentioned. "We'll get this off to you in writing shortly. It will go out via overnight mail so you will have it tomorrow. I just wanted to confirm that you want us to send it to the Chatham address, unless you are staying in the city?"

"No, Chatham please. I'm on my way back there now."

"Very good. Congratulations, Riley! Take a look at the offer packet when it arrives and please get back to us early next week. If you let us know on Monday, we could arrange for the following Monday to be your start date."

"Thank you. I will look it over and call next week." Riley

hadn't expected to hear from them so soon. Even though she still preferred the other company, it was flattering to receive such a good offer.

She told her sister about it when she picked her up at the airport and she was impressed. "I didn't think those roles paid so well. That's a lot of money." Amy grinned. "Maybe working with your boyfriend isn't such a bad idea. Are you still thinking it's your second choice?"

Riley nodded. "It's a wonderful offer. I really like the other company better, though. But I don't have an offer from them yet." She felt pretty confident that she would hear from them soon.

And she did. Later that afternoon, just as she was finishing up writing a blog post for Donna's website, her cell phone rang. It was the other company.

"Riley, it's Alan Sherman. I just wanted to thank you again for meeting with us." Something in his tone seemed a little off and Riley started getting a panicky feeling.

"I wanted to call you personally to let you know how impressed we were with you. We were ready to put an offer together, in fact, but someone on our team raised their hand and expressed interest in the role. And she's a great employee. We talked about it and we feel like we need to give her a shot. I hope you understand. We'd love to keep you in mind if anything else opens up. Though I know the timing isn't ideal, as you mentioned you have another offer."

Riley's heart sank. Her disappointment was keen. She'd really wanted that job and it sounded like they'd wanted her, too. But she also appreciated that they wanted to consider their own people first. "I understand. This really was my top choice though, so I would appreciate if you would keep me in mind for future openings."

"I'll do that. Thank you for understanding, Riley."

Riley ended the call and her eyes were swimming with tears. She tried to force herself to look on the bright side. At least she still had a fantastic job offer. And maybe in a year or two, if something opened up at the other company, the timing might work better. She took a deep breath and sighed. She went in the bathroom and dabbed a cold washcloth on her eyes and added a bit of mascara and concealer. It was almost time to go to the inn and she was grateful that it would keep her busy and get her mind off losing her dream job.

When she came downstairs, her mother was sitting in the kitchen drinking a cup of tea. She looked up and instantly knew something was wrong.

"What happened?"

The concern in her mother's voice made Riley's eyes well up again. She took a deep breath. She was ordinarily not a crier. She forced the tears back down and then she told her mother about the call.

"Oh, honey, I'm sorry. I know you really wanted that job. You know what I say, though, I really do think everything happens for a reason. You weren't meant to get that job, not yet. Maybe something will open up there in the future."

Riley nodded. "They said that they'd like to keep me in mind for other things that may come up. I don't know if they really meant it, though. It could just be something they say."

Her mother shook her head. "They called you as soon as they knew and they told you they were prepared to make you an offer. It was considerate that they let you know so quickly so you could take the other job—if you want it. I think they meant it."

"I don't know what to do. I really wanted that job. It was flattering to get the other offer, but I never pictured myself working in a law firm. The money is really good, though. But Jack works there. I'm not sure that is a smart thing."

"Have you had any bites on anything else you've applied for?" her mother asked.

"No. Nothing at all. There really haven't been many jobs listed. Maybe more will open up after the holidays, but I can't keep the law firm waiting that long. I told them I'd give them an answer early next week." She sighed. "I really don't know what to do."

"Well, you don't have to decide this minute. Take the weekend to sleep on it and see how you feel on Monday."

Riley smiled and relaxed a little. Her mother was right. She didn't have to decide instantly. She could take the weekend and decide on Monday. She tried to look on the bright side. Maybe the law firm might not be so bad. It could even be interesting. And the money was really, really good. But would she be happy there? She decided to empty her mind and try not to think about it for the rest of the weekend.

CHAPTER THIRTY-FIVE

On their way to the inn, Riley and her mother stopped into the wine and cheese shop to stock up on both. An older man was behind the counter, with snow-white hair, blue eyes, and a big smile. The store was busy with holiday shoppers, but still he paused from ringing in a customer to welcome them to the store.

"Please look around and let me know if you'd like to try samples of anything. I have some smoked Gouda samples on the counter if you'd like to start with those."

They walked toward the counter and both took a sample. The cheese was creamy, sweet, and smoky at the same time. "We should get some of this," Riley said. She also picked out Manchego, which she knew Franny loved, and a sharp cheddar.

Her mother picked up a container of goat cheese smothered in honey and crushed almonds. "This looks interesting."

"Let's get that, too. It will be nice to have a sweeter option as well," Riley said.

They also bought a case of assorted bottles of wine. Some were for the inn and a few bottles of Prosecco and Cabernet were for Christmas Eve and Christmas Day. Riley's family had a custom of always having Prosecco on Christmas Eve when they mostly had fish dishes, and then a little red wine on Christmas Day with prime rib.

The man behind the counter nodded in approval when they gave him their selections to ring up.

"That Gouda was delicious," Riley said.

"That's a personal favorite of mine. The other is the honey goat cheese. I have a bit of a sweet tooth," he admitted. "We make that up here, adding the honey and crushed almonds to an excellent goat cheese."

"I'm looking forward to enjoying that one tonight," Riley's mother said.

"Thank you, and happy holidays!" he said cheerfully as he handed Riley's mother her receipt.

When they got back to the inn, Riley carried the case of wine into the kitchen and her mother managed to carry the bag of cheese as she slowly walked in on her crutches. She was able to do much more now than when Riley first arrived. Riley knew she was anxious to get her cast off and switch to the brace. She'd be able to move around much more easily then. And her mother had insisted that she'd be fine if Riley wanted to head back by the New Year. That gave her another full week to get used to the brace.

"If you want to go and do the turndown service, I'll get the cheeses all ready to go," her mother suggested.

"Sure thing." Riley paused for a moment. "Mom, how will you be able to manage the turndown service after I leave? You could stop it, I suppose."

Her mother shook her head. "I'll manage just fine. I'll be able to move around much better with the brace and that will only last a few weeks. The turndown service has been really popular, so I hate to stop. I think it's a selling point with the ads you have going."

Riley thought so, too. She'd put up a new blog post with pictures of the chocolates on the pillows and they'd quickly added several new bookings the same day the post went up.

She grabbed the bag of chocolates and headed off to the rooms. Half of them were occupied but they still wanted Riley to come in. She'd noticed that people seemed to get a kick out of watching her fluff the pillows and turn the comforters down and they especially liked seeing the little boxes of chocolate placed on the pillows. Franny was one of those people.

"Thanks so much, Riley. I do love those chocolates. I'll see you all downstairs shortly."

Riley expected Aidan and Luke to be in their rooms, but they didn't answer when she knocked. She waited a moment, then entered the room and did her thing. She wondered what they were up to. She hadn't seen either of them for almost a week, since they went to Edaville Railroad the prior Sunday.

Riley finished up and headed downstairs to the living room. It was only a few minutes past five but the living room was full. Just about all of their guests were there except for Aidan and Luke. Riley also noticed with interest that Sean was there, sipping a glass of Cabernet and chatting with Franny while her mother made the rounds. She always liked to chat with every guest that attended the wine and cheese hour, to make them feel welcome and included.

And her mother had always enjoyed learning more about the people that stayed at the inn. Riley did as well. It was fascinating to hear people's stories and learn where they lived. They came from all over. Most were from other areas of Massachusetts or New England, but occasionally they had visitors from other countries. She knew that they had a young couple from Germany staying through New Year's Eve but she hadn't had a chance to chat with them yet.

She poured herself a small glass of Cabernet and put a slice of Manchego and Gouda on her plate. While she was debating whether or not to try the honey goat cheese, a young couple walked over to take some cheese. As soon as she heard them talking she recognized the German accent and introduced herself and they did the same. Their names were Elsa and Henry and they lived just outside of Berlin.

"I hope you're enjoying your stay so far?" Riley asked them.

"Oh, we are," Elsa said.

"It's very peaceful here," Henry added. "We just lost Elsa's mother last month and we have no other family left in Germany, so we decided to travel."

"We thought it would be less sad than staying at home," Elsa said.

Riley nodded. "I'm so sorry for your loss. The holidays can be so hard sometimes."

Elsa smiled. "It has been hard. But we're glad we came. We're going to stay through the New Year and I'm hoping it will feel like a fresh start. A lovely way to ring in the New Year, as you say."

"I'm sure it will be. I don't know what your plans are for Christmas Day, but we are having a Christmas supper here that evening. It will just be a simple meal but we thought it might be fun and festive."

Elsa and Henry exchanged glances. Henry nodded and Elsa spoke. "We will come. That sounds wonderful, thank you. We weren't sure what we were actually going to do on Christmas Day. We thought we might head to a hotel for the midday meal possibly."

Riley smiled. "If you want a bit of a splurge, the Chatham Bars Inn has a grand Christmas buffet. It has everything you could imagine, all kinds of seafood, as well as carving stations and beef Wellington, and so many desserts. We went once and it was really something."

"Oh, that sounds marvelous," Elsa said and Henry agreed.

Out of the corner of her eye, Riley saw movement at the front door and turned to look. Aidan and Luke walked in carrying big bags. They'd been shopping. Luke ran over to Riley. "We just finished our Christmas shopping!"

Aidan reached them a moment later. "Just about all of it," he agreed. "We should go drop these bags off and we'll be back down in a moment."

Riley's mother made her way over and Riley introduced her to Elsa and Henry. Riley stepped away to mingle with the other guests.

"Did you try that goat cheese yet, Riley?" Franny asked as she scooped more of it onto her plate and added a few crackers.

"Not yet, is it good?"

"You have to try it, before it's all gone," Franny insisted.

So she did and it was very good. The sweet honey complimented the tangy, creamy goat cheese and the crunchy, savory almonds were the perfect topping. Riley immediately went back for a second serving.

As she popped it in her mouth, Aidan and Luke returned and came over to her.

"You have to try this goat cheese," Riley told them. "Luke, are you ready for a hot chocolate?"

"Yes."

"Yes, what?" Aidan said and Riley smiled.

"Yes, please, Riley. And thank you!" Luke said with enthusiasm.

Riley laughed. "You're very welcome. I'll be right back."

She went into the kitchen, and returned a moment later

with Luke's hot chocolate. They were still standing by the wine and cheese station. Aidan was sipping a glass of Cabernet.

"How were the stores? Were they packed?" Riley asked.

He nodded. "We went to the mall in Hyannis and it was a zoo. We got just about everything we were after, though. And I got all the info I needed for one last child-free trip. I have a babysitter lined up so I can run out for a few hours tomorrow afternoon." He spoke softly so Luke wouldn't overhear.

"I still have more shopping to do, too," Riley said. "And lots of wrapping."

Aidan made a face. "That's the worst part. We went to one of those stands in the middle of the mall and had everything wrapped. The money goes to charity and it's worth it not to have to do that. Especially here. All that stuff—tape, paper, tags, is all at home. I didn't want to clutter our room here with it."

"I don't blame you. Speaking of Christmas, Mom and I are having a holiday supper on Christmas night here at the inn. Very casual, some kind of soup probably and something sweet. We thought it might be fun to watch more Christmas movies and have a meal together."

Aidan's eyes softened. "That's really nice of you both. We'll happily be there. Luke doesn't care about a fancy meal. I figured we'd have our usual breakfast here and that maybe we'd catch a movie in the afternoon. We love to go to the movies on the holidays. I remember the first time we went, I thought we'd be the only ones there, but the theater was packed. I guess lots of people like to get out on holidays."

"They do," Riley agreed. "I used to work at the movie theater when I was in high school. Thanksgiving night was always super busy. After eating such a huge meal maybe people want to get out and move around."

Aidan nodded. "I think a lot of people are alone on the holidays, too, so it is something to do."

Franny walked over and caught the last bit of their conversation. "My husband and I used to always go to the movies on Christmas Day. It was a fun treat and we always looked forward to it."

Aidan smiled. "Would you like to join us, Franny? Luke and I are going to an afternoon matinee right up the street."

Franny looked pleased with the invitation. "I just might do that. Thank you, dear."

Riley hadn't had a chance to say hello to Sean yet and smiled as he walked over. "Mom says you two are going Christmas shopping tonight?"

His eyes twinkled. "That's the plan, yeah. We both have a few more things to pick up. How did your interviews go?"

Riley filled him in on where she was at. "I'm grateful for the one offer. I'm just not sure it's the right job."

"It's good to be sure. Nothing worse than getting stuck in a job or a company that you don't like," Sean said.

Riley nodded. "I know. There are pros and cons. I really need to weigh everything and decide. I'm trying not to think about it until after Christmas."

Sean raised his eyebrow. "Excuse my bluntness, but the fact that you don't want to think about it should tell you something."

"He's right," Aidan agreed. "If you're not excited about this job, let it go and wait for the right one to come along."

"Well, that's the problem. What if the right one never comes along? I haven't gotten any other interviews and there are very few new openings."

"There's bound to be more after the New Year, don't you think?" Aidan said.

"Maybe. I don't know for sure. The money is really good for this job. It would be hard to turn it down without something else to go to."

Sean looked thoughtful. "Your mother mentioned that you're doing a side project for her friend Donna for her law firm's website. If you have any more free time while you're here, I could use some help with my website, too. It's pretty basic. Maybe you could add a few blog posts and whatever else you think I should have?"

"Really? I will have time next week. I'll be finishing up Donna's project Monday. I could start on Tuesday."

"That works. Why don't you give me a call Tuesday morning and we can talk about it."

"Thanks, Sean. I will do that." Her mother walked up at that point and Riley filled her in on the conversation. "I'm going to do a project for Sean next week, similar to what I'm working on for Donna."

Her mother looked pleased to hear it. "That's wonderful news, honey. Maybe you can build up a little consulting practice. Sean told me that's how he changed careers into woodworking. It started as a side gig."

"And thankfully it grew. I do not miss wearing a suit." He looked miserable at the thought of it and they all laughed. Riley couldn't picture him in a suit. He was more of an outdoorsy, rugged kind of guy, more comfortable in faded jeans and flannel work shirts. That was another change Riley was in for. The dress was more formal at the law firm. Most of what she owned was business casual. She might need to pick up a few more dress shirts and pants. The thought of shopping for work clothes did not excite her. She had enough to get by for the first week, but after that she would need to pick up a few things. She didn't want to think about that, though. She still hadn't made a decision on whether or not to take the job.

"What are you up to tonight?" Aidan asked as he reached for another slice of cheddar.

Riley grinned. "Wrapping. I always wait till the last minute. But I can't put it off any longer. What about you?"

"I think Luke and I are going to have an early night."

"Do you and Luke have plans tomorrow night? My mother has family and friends over Christmas Eve, kind of like an open house. You're both welcome to come by."

Aidan smiled. "We'd love to come."

"Great, we'll be heading over there after the wine and cheese hour tomorrow," Riley said.

"Perfect. I'll probably see you at breakfast tomorrow," Aidan said. Riley laughed as she saw Luke cram two pieces of cheddar in his mouth. Aidan looked embarrassed.

"He does like cheese. I need to talk to him about his manners."

"I love his enthusiasm," Riley said.

"I do, too, most of the time. I'm going to see if I can drag his enthusiasm upstairs now so we can get out of your hair." It was a few minutes past six and everyone except for her mother and Sean had left the living room. Aidan went to get Luke and they said their goodbyes.

"Mom, I can get this cleaned up. You guys should go and have fun."

Her mother hesitated. "Are you sure, honey? I don't want to leave you with everything."

"It won't take me long and I'm in no hurry. I'll see you later at home."

"Thanks, Riley. Talk to you on Tuesday," Sean said.

Riley quickly put everything away and headed home. She heated up a mug of leftover soup and curled up on the sofa with Lily by her side. She had a mountain of wrapping to do, but no energy to do it. It had been a long day. She could go to bed early and deal with the wrapping early tomorrow morning.

The soup was not satisfying, but the pint of Ben & Jerry's Cherry Garcia she found in the freezer was. She polished it off as she watched the classic movie *When Harry Met Sally*... She never tired of it. And when the movie ended, she and Lily went to bed and she dreamed that she was in a store filled with hundreds of navy suits and none of them fit.

CHAPTER THIRTY-SIX

Beth had a great time shopping in Hyannis with Sean. They went to Macy's at the Cape Cod Mall where Sean helped her to pick out a pretty pink cashmere cardigan for Riley and she helped him choose sweaters for his two girls. She also helped him decide on a gold bracelet for his mother. They each found a few other gifts as well and when they were done, Sean led Beth to the gift-wrapping station in the middle of the mall.

She laughed but happily had them wrap all her gifts, too. "I've always done this myself, but it's one less thing to worry about."

"It's so worth it," he agreed.

When they were done with their shopping, they went across the street to the Tiki Port Chinese restaurant and split a few dishes. Beth hadn't been there in ages and it was still as good as she remembered. She dunked a chicken finger in some duck sauce and wondered why she didn't get Chinese food more often. It was such a treat when she did.

"So, you're heading off-Cape tomorrow afternoon?" Beth asked. Sean had mentioned that he was going to stay with one of his daughters for the holiday.

"Yeah, my mother and I will probably head up there mid-day. One sister is hosting tomorrow night and the other is do-ing Christmas Day. I'll be home late Sunday night if we don't stay over and come back Monday. That's still up in the air."

Beth had a great time again with Sean. It was just so easy with him. It almost seemed too good to be true. She didn't want to get her hopes up too soon, but she was enjoying spend-ing time with him. And she hoped it would continue.

When Sean excused himself to use the restroom, Beth flagged their server and gave him her credit card to pay the bill. He brought it over for her signature as Sean was sitting back down.

"What did you do?" he asked and seemed shocked that she'd paid the bill.

"I told you I wanted to treat. It was my pleasure." She echoed the phrase he often said, and she meant it. It felt good to do something nice for him.

He smiled and gave her hand a squeeze. "Thank you. You know the whole time I dated Marcy she never once even of-fered to pay."

They headed back to Chatham and when they reached Beth's house, Sean grabbed her bags and carried them to the door.

"Do you want to come inside for a bit?" Beth asked.

"Sure. I'll carry these in for you. I have something I want to give you, as well."

They went inside and Beth saw that the TV was off and that Riley had gone up to bed.

"Would you like a coffee or a tea?" Beth asked.

He smiled. "No. I can't stay long. I just wanted to give you a little something. And wish you a Merry Christmas." He reached in his pocket and pulled out a small, gift-wrapped rectangular box. He handed it to Beth. She opened it carefully and sighed when she saw what it was—a delicate charm bracelet with a little inn and a bookcase. It looked similar to the one he'd just built. It was adorable.

"Sean, I love it. Thank you!" She leaned in and gave him a kiss. He pulled her closer and held her. The kiss went on for a bit, until Beth pulled back.

"I have something for you, too. It's just something small that made me think of you." She pulled the gift-wrapped book out of her tote bag and handed it to Sean.

He looked happily surprised as he carefully unwrapped the gift and then turned it over to see the cover and read the title aloud. "*Beautiful Woodworking.*" He flipped it open and looked at a few pages. "This is awesome. It will look great on my coffee table and maybe I'll get some good ideas from it."

Beth had ordered the coffee table book from Amazon and wrapped it earlier that day. She didn't think she'd see Sean again before Christmas so she'd stuck it into her tote bag.

He pulled her in again for a thank-you kiss and it went on and on. Finally, they ended the kiss and just stared into each other's eyes for a long moment. "I'll call you next week. Have a very Merry Christmas, Beth."

"You, too."

She walked him to the door and they kissed again before he headed to his truck and drove off. She watched him go and felt like she missed him already.

CHAPTER THIRTY-SEVEN

Riley was in a better mood the next morning. Jack had called to wish her a Merry Christmas and to invite her to a black-tie New Year's Eve party that one of his friends, a senior partner at the law firm, was having in his penthouse apartment. "We'll do gifts then, before we go. Since we won't see each other until then. And we'll be celebrating, I think? I heard the good news. Though I'm a little surprised you didn't call to tell me yourself."

Riley felt a twinge of guilt. She'd thought of calling him, but hesitated because she didn't want him to assume she was taking the job. "I'm sorry, Jack. They called right before I left for the airport and yesterday was nonstop. They did make an offer. And I heard from the other company as well."

She paused for a moment and he jumped in, "Oh, so that's it then, you're taking the other job and didn't want to tell me?"

"Not at all. They actually called to let me know that I didn't get it. They are going with an internal candidate."

"Oh! So, you'll be accepting the law firm job. It's really a great opportunity, Riley."

"I know it is. I just need the weekend to digest it. I told them I'd let them know early next week."

"Well, of course you'll take it. It's a no-brainer. You don't have anything else pending, do you?" Jack sounded so sure that this was the job for her. There was no doubt in his mind.

"No. Nothing else." Riley wished she was as enthusiastic as Jack about working at the law firm.

"Well, I'm excited for you. Call me next week once you've called them and officially accepted. And we'll plan to ring in the New Year and celebrate."

Riley shook her head. Jack was so determined but she knew he meant well. The New Year's Eve party did sound fun.

"Thanks, Jack. I'll call you next week as soon as I talk to them."

"Great, and tell your mom I said Merry Christmas, too."

"I will." Riley ended the call and turned to her mother, who had just walked into the kitchen. "Jack wishes you a Merry Christmas."

Her mother smiled. "That's nice of him. What is he doing for the holidays?"

"His parents live in Hartford. He'll be heading there. He invited me to a New Year's Eve party—black tie."

"That sounds fun. Fancy. Do you have anything to wear?"

"No. I'll have to go shopping. You know, I had the funniest dream the other night. I was trying on suits for the new job and nothing fit. Hundreds of suits. I kept trying them on one after another."

Her mother gave her a long look. "Well, hopefully you'll have better luck with the dress."

CHAPTER THIRTY-EIGHT

After breakfast on Christmas Eve day, Franny went back to her room. The day stretched before her and she thought about how she wanted to spend it. She glanced at the small desk by the window, and the one remaining letter that lay there, unopened. She was going to open it the next day on Sunday. But something compelled her to reach for the envelope. One day wouldn't make that much of a difference. And she felt restless and wanted something to do.

She carefully slid the flap open and withdrew the heavy notepaper with her sister's wobbly but elegant handwriting.

Dearest Franny,

This is my last note to you and I do hope I have saved the best for last. You are probably wondering why I wanted you to stay and to visit all these places. I wanted you to remember and to open your mind to possibilities. You've always loved the Cape and I know you loved Albany and your married life, too.

It is my hope that during your month here after my passing, that you might find yourself falling in love again with the Cape—with Chatham. I only ever want to see you happy, Franny. And that is why I saved the most important information until the last letter. I could have told you up front, but I wanted to better prepare you to be fully open for whatever magic might happen when you open this door.

Franny wondered what on earth her sister was going on about.

I only discovered this wonderful surprise when I read an article in the Chatham paper. I wanted to go in person to see for myself, but I was too weak. So, I want you to go, Fanny. Go to the new wine and cheese shop on Main Street and ask to see the owner. And remember, Franny, I will always love you and want the very best for you.
    Love,
    Ella

Franny had been to the wine and cheese shop several times now and the only person she'd seen in the shop was the lovely woman behind the counter who was so helpful. Was she the owner? And why would her sister want Franny to introduce herself? It was an intriguing mystery. Franny had been planning to go there today anyway. She wanted to pick up some more cheese and had a few ideas for gifts, too.

Her curiosity was aroused and Franny did not want to wait any longer. She decided to head over to the shop immediately. She bundled up with her heavy wool coat, hat, and gloves and set out down Main Street. The shop opened at ten and even though it was only a few minutes past, there was already a small crowd inside. Like before, the same woman was behind the counter, dishing out samples and ringing people up.

Franny walked around and gathered up everything that she wanted and got in line. When it was her turn, the woman smiled, recognizing Franny.

"Good morning! It's so nice to see you again. Is there anything else I can help you with?"

Franny shook her head and placed her items on the counter. She handed over her credit card and when the woman handed it back with the charge slip, Franny cleared her throat. "I do have a quick question. I'm just curious, are you the owner of this shop?"

The woman laughed. "No, I just work here."

"Is the owner in by any chance?"

"Sure. Hold on, he's out back unloading a shipment. I'll go get him." Franny took her bag of cheese and moved to the side, to get out of the way. The woman stepped into the back of the store and returned a moment later with a man about Franny's age, with a head of thick white hair and eyes that were so familiar. And when he saw her, he stopped short and smiled and Franny's heart jumped. It was Joe. Her Joe from so many years ago.

"Franny? Is it really you? I thought you moved away years ago?"

"I did. But I came back for my sister's funeral. She passed recently."

He nodded. "I saw that in the paper, but not until about a week later. I wanted to offer my condolences, but I didn't know how to reach you. I didn't think that you might still be in Chatham. Franny, I am so very sorry for your loss."

"Thank you. I thought you were gone, too, that you lived on the West Coast."

"I did, for many years. But my wife passed about five years ago and I grieved for several years. This year, I decided it was time to move home. I always wanted to come back to the Cape. I watched for the right opportunity and when this shop came available it seemed like a sign. We opened just six months ago." Joe seemed like he was in shock, that it wasn't really her. And he still had that same smile when he looked at her, like there was no one else for him. Of course Franny knew that was just her memory playing tricks on her. It had been much too long for Joe to still have feelings for her.

"I've been in the shop several times. And I told Beth about it. She's the woman that owns the inn I am staying at. Her daughter loves it here, too. I'm so proud of you, Joe. I can't believe you're here."

He grinned. "How long have you been here, Franny? How long are you staying?"

"I've been here for a little over a month. I was due to head home after the New Year, but I went and bought a house! I close in a week, so maybe I'll stay a little longer. I bought it so I'd have the option to come whenever I want. I was thinking it would probably be for the summers. But I'm really not in a rush to leave." That was an understatement. Chatham and the people here were beginning to feel like her true home.

He smiled and it reached his eyes and sent the most adorable laugh lines dancing across his face. "Well, you don't know how glad I am to hear that. Franny, we have so much to catch each other up on. When can we meet? I'm leaving tonight as soon as the shop closes to head to my son's house. He still lives in California. I'll be back Monday night. Are you available Tuesday evening? I'd like to have you over for a home-cooked dinner."

Franny's heart beat faster. "Oh, I'd love that. I didn't know you could cook?"

He laughed. "I've picked up a few skills over the years. I'm actually a very good cook and I would love to make you my favorite dish." He jotted his address down on a piece of paper and handed it to her. Then he came out from behind the counter and pulled her in for a big bear hug. "I couldn't let you leave without a hug. It's just so wonderful seeing you, Franny. You're just as beautiful as I remember. You haven't changed a bit."

Franny felt herself melt as Joe's warmth wrapped around her. "You look just the same, too, Joe. As handsome as ever." And it was true. His hair wasn't dark brown anymore but his eyes and smile were exactly the same. "Merry Christmas, Joe."

"Merry Christmas, Franny. See you soon."

Franny walked out of the cheese shop in a bit of a daze. The magic and wonder of Christmas was all around her and her sister had given her the best present of all. Franny couldn't wait to see Joe on Tuesday.

CHAPTER THIRTY-NINE

Later that morning, Riley helped her mother cook for the Christmas Eve gathering. She also put together a French toast casserole they could heat and serve in the morning with powdered sugar, fresh berries, and maple syrup.

They'd run into Franny at the inn after she'd returned from the cheese shop, and they'd heard her story. On their way home they'd stopped at the fish market and picked up several pounds of freshly shucked lobster meat that they'd called and ordered in advance. That would be the last thing that her mother put in the oven as it was the fastest and easiest main dish. She just mixed melted butter with crushed Ritz crackers and some chopped parsley then added the lobster and baked it in a casserole dish until it was heated through. Sometimes she drizzled a little sherry over the top, but it was just as good without it.

They'd also picked up a big platter of cocktail shrimp. The fish market made the best cooked shrimp. They were always nice and plump and the cocktail sauce had just the right amount of spiciness. Riley put together the scallops wrapped in bacon, trimming the side muscle off each scallop and wrapping each one in a few inches of lightly cooked bacon, so that when they heated them in the oven, the bacon would crisp up while the scallops cooked.

Her mother was seasoning a tenderloin with salt, pepper, and a bit of crushed rosemary and olive oil. Riley knew it would be delicious and soon the kitchen would smell incredible.

"I'll put it in the oven when we get back from the wine and cheese hour. It can cook while we enjoy the appetizers and relax." Her mother smiled and Riley noticed that she seemed happier than usual, and more relaxed.

"That sounds good. Oh, by the way I invited Aidan and Luke to join us," Riley said.

Her mother looked pleased to hear it. "Perfect. I invited Franny, too. I hated the thought of her sitting alone in her room."

"I'm glad she's coming. I loved her story about the last letter. It's so romantic that Joe at the cheese shop is her first love." Both Riley and her mother had grown fond of Fanny.

"I'm thrilled for her, too. And to think she's already bought a house. I have a feeling she'll be spending a lot more time in Chatham," her mother said with a twinkle in her eye.

Riley agreed totally. "Her sister's letters worked their magic. I bet she's watching from above and loving it."

Riley looked around the kitchen and went through a mental list of what else they needed. Her sister, Amy, was bringing a charcuterie platter and an apple pie. That left slicing and seasoning the mini potatoes. They'd decided to roast those ahead so they could just be reheated as well. And roasted asparagus, which could be cooked at the last minute, but Riley could prep them by seasoning and wrapping them in tin foil packets that could be tossed in the oven when they were ready.

She opened a cupboard and saw a box of soup mix. "I could make a French onion dip? And cut some fresh vegetables for it."

"That's not a bad idea, though I'm sure most people will go for the potato chips," her mother said.

Riley laughed and got out the sour cream. The afternoon flew and by the time they left for the inn, everything was just about ready. All they would need to do was put a few pans in the oven when they returned.

Her mother had picked up some Italian cookies from a local bakery and set those out by the cheese and crackers to make it a little more festive for Christmas Eve.

The living room filled up quickly, but most people didn't stay long. They had a few bites of cheese or a cookie with their wine and headed off to dinner. Her mother encouraged everyone to take some cookies for later, and most of them did.

Riley noticed a few minutes after Aidan and Luke joined them that there were two stockings hung by the fireplace.

"I hope you don't mind," Aidan said. "Luke wanted to hang his stocking and we don't have a fireplace in our room. He was worried that Santa wouldn't find him."

"Of course we don't mind." Riley's mother had overheard. Luke was out of earshot—he was investigating the cookies—so she leaned in and spoke softly. "You're welcome to put his presents under the tree, so he can open them there in the morning."

Aidan looked grateful. "Thank you. We'll be up early so we won't be in anyone's way."

"We're not at all worried about that," Riley said. "It's Christmas, after all. It will be nice to see the tree with presents under it."

At six, they quickly cleaned up and headed home. They'd told everyone to come around six thirty. By the time they got home it was a quarter past and her mother put the tenderloin in the oven to begin roasting.

Amy, Rob, and the kids arrived at six thirty sharp. Aidan,

Luke, and Franny came a few minutes later. Riley had made a big bowl of bubbly holiday punch with Prosecco, vodka, cranberry juice, and a splash of Grand Marnier, which gave it a lovely hint of orange and just about everyone wanted to try it.

Donna, Jess, Alison, Maddie, and their partners stopped in as well. Jess's daughter, Caitlin, from the coffee shop, and her boyfriend, Jason, also came with Alison's daughter, Julia, and her boyfriend, Tim. Julia's long brown hair had turquoise tips, which somehow worked. She had it pulled back, which highlighted her earrings, which were gorgeous. They were pieces of hammered gold that looked like a wave and moved as she spoke. Riley guessed that she'd made them in her jewelry shop, as her bracelet matched.

Riley knew Caitlin from going into the coffee shop, and she knew of Julia, as they'd gone to the same school in Chatham, but Julia had been a year behind. Riley hadn't really kept in touch with any of her old high school friends. And she knew that most of them had moved off-Cape.

It was nice to chat with Caitlin outside of the coffee shop and to get to know Julia a bit. Riley learned that her boyfriend, Tim, played in a band occasionally on the weekends and that they would be playing at the Chatham Squire in a few weeks.

"You should come," Julia said.

"I'd love to. I may be back in New York by then, though."

"Well, keep it in mind if you happen to be here."

"I've heard them play," Aidan said. "They are really good. It's been a few years since I've seen them, though."

Aidan knew Julia and Tim and they all chatted about people they knew. Caitlin had moved to Chatham from Charleston. Riley asked her if she missed living in a bigger city.

"I thought that I would. When I first came here it was just going to be for the summer. My mom and I stayed with my grandmother and we were both dealing with breakups. It was just supposed to be a relaxing couple of months. I went back to Charleston for a party at the end of the summer and I was surprised by how much I didn't miss it there. It's a great city, but I'm much happier here. I really like the small town and close-knit community."

When the food was ready, Riley helped her mother put it all out on the counter and they set it up buffet style so everyone could help themselves. The tenderloin was sliced and her mother had made a quick red wine sauce on the side. It was all delicious. Everyone sat wherever they could find a seat. Her mother had extra chairs in the kitchen and living room. It was very casual. Riley sat with Aidan and Luke on the living room sofa. They balanced their plates on their laps.

"I got some good news today," Aidan said. "The work on the house will be done by the end of next week. So we'll be home by the New Year."

"Oh, that's great news," Riley said.

"It will be nice to sleep in my own bed again. Not that the beds aren't comfortable at the inn—they are."

Riley laughed. "I know. It's just not the same. I'm sure Luke will be happy to get home."

Luke looked up from his plate, which was only half-eaten. "Can I get some pie, now?"

"A few more bites, buddy," Aidan said.

When they were finished, they all got small slices of apple pie. Riley had made sure to save room because her sister's apple pies were so good. She always thought of the holidays when she took a bite of her pie. Amy made them for Thanksgiving and Christmas.

"What's it like where you live, Riley?" Luke asked.

"I live in New York City. It's huge and loud and busy. I live in a tall building with lots of apartments. Lily and I live there."

"Who's Lily?" Luke asked. At the sound of her name, Lily

darted out of the corner where she'd been hiding and hopped up next to Riley on the sofa. Riley reached out and petted her. She seemed a little nervous to have a houseful of people.

"This is Lily. She's not used to being around so many people."

"Can I pat her?" Luke stood quickly and Lily tensed beside Riley.

"Yes, but move very slowly so you don't scare her. And put your hand near her, let her go to you."

Luke did and Lily sniffed his hand, then rubbed her head against it.

"She likes me!" He petted her a few more times before she tired of it and walked off, flicking her tail as she retreated to the corner of the room.

Luke yawned and Aidan checked the time. It was almost nine. People were starting to leave. "We should probably head out," Aidan said. "Big day tomorrow." He pulled Riley in for a hug. "Thanks for having us. Merry Christmas."

"Merry Christmas. See you both in the morning." Riley walked them to the door. Before long they'd said goodbye to their last guest and it was time to clean up and head to bed.

"That went well, I think," Riley said, once everything was cleaned up and put away.

Her mother looked tired, but also happy. "It was a wonderful night. And I am so ready for bed. See you in the morning, honey."

"'Night, mom. Merry Christmas," Riley said as they walked up to bed. It had been a fun, festive night. And tomorrow would be more of the same, hopefully.

CHAPTER FORTY

Christmas morning, Riley and her mother headed to the inn a bit earlier than usual. Riley wanted to cook the French toast casserole at the inn so it would be warm from the oven. They also wanted to get there before Luke opened his presents as they had a few more to add under the tree. Riley and her mother had picked up a few small gifts for Franny, Aidan, and Luke.

They got there just in time. Riley had just put the casserole in the oven when she heard footsteps followed by Luke's excited voice.

"Santa came! He found me."

Aidan was right behind him, looking amused. "Of course he did."

Franny came down a moment later and helped herself to a coffee, then joined everyone else in the living room. She had a little basket with her with several small bags inside it and handed one bag to everyone. They all looked the same, except Luke's was a bit bigger.

"Oh, Franny, you didn't have to get us anything," Riley said.

"We picked up something for you, too." Her mother handed Franny a similar-looking bag. They were all red bags tied with a curly silver ribbon.

Riley laughed when she recognized it. "We gave Joe lots of business!" She and her mother had made up a bag filled with Franny's favorite cheeses: the Manchego, Saint-André, and the honey goat cheese. They added a box of crackers, too.

"Oh, thank you both. I'll enjoy some of this today," Franny said.

Riley and her mother opened their bags from Franny and they were both the same, a box of pecan turtles and raspberry truffles. "Thanks so much, Franny," Riley and her mother said at the same time.

Luke opened his bag from Fanny and it was a huge milk chocolate Santa. "This is awesome! Thanks, Franny." He jumped up and gave her a hug and she looked thrilled. Aidan looked in his bag and saw the same chocolates that Riley and her mother had received. He thanked her as well and they turned their attention back to Luke, who was about to open his big gift.

"Do you have any idea what that is?" Riley asked him.

Luke grinned. "I think so. I told Santa what I wanted." He ripped open the package and screamed with happiness. It was an electric toy railroad set, complete with several trains and a track.

"Can I set it up now, Dad?"

"Why don't you open your other gifts first and then we'll figure it out."

When Luke opened the gift from Riley and her mother he screamed again and ran over to hug them both. "How did you know I wanted this one? I didn't tell anyone, not even Dad."

Riley laughed. "It was a lucky guess. I saw how much you liked the railroad when we went to Edaville." Aidan had also told her that he was getting Luke the train set.

"He can set that up here in the living room if he wants to. It could go around the tree. That might be fun to watch," Riley's mother suggested.

"Are you sure?" Aidan asked.

"Yes, I think that will look really cool," Riley added.

"Around the tree it is, then." Aidan picked up three small gifts from under the tree and handed one each to Riley, her mother, and Franny. "I got you all a little something, too."

Franny opened her gift and held the pretty buttercream candle up. It was in a shimmery glass holder. "Thank you, Aidan, this is really lovely."

Her mother received a similar candle and thanked him. Riley reached into her bag, expecting a candle but instead pulled out a copy of Hannah McIntosh's newest book, a Christmas rom-com. Riley was touched.

"Thank you. I love her books. How did you know?"

He smiled. "Lucky guess. I was in the store poking around and saw it on the new releases table and it sounded like something you'd like. I know how much you used to love watching *When Harry Met Sally* . . . and all those holiday romantic comedies."

"Thank you. I'd been meaning to pick this one up, and just hadn't had a chance yet."

Aidan looked at Luke, who'd opened all his gifts by now and was anxious to set up his new train set.

"Hey, buddy, let's clear this stuff up and bring everything upstairs except the trains. We'll eat some breakfast and then get your railroad set up."

By the time Riley and her mother were done serving breakfast and ready to head home before going to Amy's house for brunch, Luke and Aidan had the railroad all set up. It looked really cute as it circled around the Christmas tree. Luke was totally mesmerized by it. Aidan gave them a wave as they headed out.

"Thanks again. We'll see you all later tonight."

When they got home, Riley's mother filled her slow cooker with the leftover potatoes and tenderloin from the night before as well as carrots and celery, beef broth, and a sprig of rosemary.

"This should work for soup for supper tonight at the inn," her mother said as she put the lid on the pot and checked the settings. Once that was set, Riley made them both fresh cups of coffee and they took them into the living room to relax for a while, before heading to Amy's for brunch.

They sipped their coffee, nibbled on some leftover coffee cake, and exchanged their gifts. And laughed. They'd both given each other similar things, books that they thought the other would like and that they'd probably lend to each other when they finished and several sweaters. Riley loved the pink cashmere cardigan that her mother had found for her.

"I haven't had one of these since high school. Thanks so much."

"I remember how much you loved it. And they never go out of style," her mother said.

Her mother loved all her gifts, especially the charcoal-gray fisherman-knit sweater that Riley had been so excited about when she stumbled onto it in a local gift shop. Her mother always commented on how much she liked Riley's fisherman-knit sweater, yet she didn't have one of her own.

A few hours later, just after one, they headed off to her sister's house with a bag of gifts for everyone, some cheese and crackers, and a bottle of Cabernet to go with the prime rib that Amy was cooking.

When they walked into her sister's house, Riley was hit

with the smell of roasting beef and the sweet scent of pow-dered sugar. There were stacks of wafer-thin pizzelle cookies on the counter.

"The girls helped me make them and we just dusted them with sugar a few minutes ago," Amy said.

"We had to wait for them to cool," Bethany said as she ran over and gave them both hugs. Emily was right behind her. They'd already opened their gifts from Santa and there were piles of toys and children's clothing under the tree. Riley put their gifts under the tree and then joined her mother and Amy in the kitchen.

"What can I do to help?" Riley asked.

"Not a thing. Everything is done now. The prime rib just needs a few more minutes. I just finished mashing the pota-toes. The broccoli is in the microwave. Oh, I know. You could open the wine and pour us all a glass. And let's open some presents."

Riley found four wineglasses and poured a half glass for all of them. They went into the other room and exchanged presents. Riley loved watching the girls open their gifts, they got so excited over the littlest things. She and her mother got them toys and books mostly. They knew Amy had plenty of clothes for them. More sweaters and books were exchanged with Amy and Rob.

When the prime rib was ready, they ate in Amy's elegant dining room.

"You're really going back to the inn for another meal to-night?" Amy asked.

"It's just soup," Riley's mother said. "It's simmering away in the Crock-Pot. It's no work at all. I just hate to think of people being alone in an inn on Christmas. It seems like the least we can do. Some of them have become friends. Plus we've known Aidan and Luke for years."

"Aidan and Luke. It was like a blast from the past seeing him at the tree lighting. He still looks the same. And his son looks just like him." She looked at Riley. "What is that like for you? The two of you were always together in high school. And you looked pretty close last night." She smiled. "You almost looked like a family sitting there together on the sofa. Are there still any sparks there?"

Riley took a sip of wine. She'd always loved being around Aidan and it had been really nice catching up and spending time with him while she was in Chatham. It made an uncertain time a little easier. And there most definitely were sparks, but she didn't feel comfortable saying it out loud.

So she smiled and avoided answering directly. "It has been great seeing him and Luke. I am still with Jack, though," she reminded everyone. "We're going to a New Year's Eve party in Manhattan."

"Oh!" Did she imagine it or did Amy look disappointed to hear that she was going back to Manhattan and to Jack? "That sounds fun. I guess that means you're probably taking the job?"

Riley sighed. Just the mention of the job and moving back to Manhattan seemed to put a damper on things. But it was almost time to make a decision.

"I haven't officially decided. But it probably would be the smart thing to do. It's a good job, and the salary is higher than what I had." Riley just wished she was more excited about it.

"Well, as long as you think you'll be happy there, that's the main thing," Amy said. It was clear though, from her tone and expression that she had doubts that mirrored Riley's own.

Riley sighed and took a bite of prime rib. It was cooked perfectly pink in the middle. Would that job make her happy? She was still unsure about working at the same company as Jack. That didn't seem as smart. But he was all for it. Every time she thought about going back to the city and accepting that position she felt tense. But she chalked it up to nerves. Changing jobs was stressful. And you never knew if it was the right job until you were actually in it. She supposed there was only one way to determine if it was the right move for her.

Riley and her mother headed back to the inn with the big pot of beef stew. Earlier at her sister's house, when she was full from their meal and the cookies after, she didn't think she would be hungry again. But it was hours later now and the stew smelled pretty amazing. When they got to the inn, Riley put a package of dinner rolls in the oven and her mother plugged the Crock-Pot into an outlet in the dining room to keep the stew warm.

Soon after they arrived, the others gathered in the living room and Riley's mother invited everyone into the dining room. Riley took the hot rolls out of the oven and put them in a basket. She'd already set the butter out earlier. Everyone helped themselves and talked about how they'd spent their day.

"We loved the brunch at the Chatham Bars Inn," Elsa said.

"There was so much food," Henry added. "We went early and we made several trips up to the buffet. And then we came home and needed a nap!"

"We went to the movies," Luke said. "We saw the new Marvel movie and it was awesome."

"It was pretty good," Aidan agreed. "And the theater was packed. We went early to make sure we got good seats."

"It was much better than I expected. All those special effects. I can see why people love those movies," Frannie said.

"We had a nice time at my sister's house. She's a good cook and the girls were so cute," Riley said.

Everyone agreed that the beef stew was excellent. Both

Aidan and Henry went back for second helpings. When they finished, everyone brought their bowls into the kitchen and Riley quickly rinsed and put them in the dishwasher. They all gathered in the living room and Riley's mother set out a stack of the pizzelle cookies that the girls had made with Amy. Amy had insisted on sending them home with a big box of them because the recipe made so many and she knew they could use them tonight.

The cookies were one of Riley's favorites. They were delicate and faintly tasted of anise and sugar and reminded her of a very thin waffle. They were light as air so it was impossible to just have one.

They decided to watch the classic Christmas movie *It's a Wonderful Life*. Riley sat on the big sofa with Aidan and Luke. Elsa and Henry took the love seat and Riley's mother and Franny both sat in the comfy club chairs. They took a break halfway through the movie and Riley went to make Luke and Henry a hot chocolate. Everyone else was too full. Aidan came with her, to help.

While Riley stirred the mix into the hot water, Aidan surprised her. He took her hand and looked her in the eye.

"Riley, I just wanted to say, these past few weeks, seeing you again, well, it's been wonderful. It took me back and it made me realize that I still think we could work. I still feel that spark, and I wonder if you do, too?"

Riley slowed her spoon. She hadn't expected Aidan to say anything like that. It had crossed her mind more than once that he was still as attractive as ever and he was so easy to be around. She enjoyed spending time with him and with Luke. But she was with Jack. And about to join his company. She didn't say anything and Aidan cleared his throat.

"I know the timing might not be the best. I know you're with Jack. I don't know him but if you're happy with him, I don't want to get in the way of that. I just had to tell you how I'm feeling. Before you decide to go back to Manhattan."

Riley nodded. "I am still with Jack, and we are happy. And I still have a home in Manhattan. It's been wonderful spending time with you and with Luke. I'm just not sure the timing is right, again. I'm sorry, Aidan." The last thing she wanted to do was to hurt him again, so she didn't want to start something that she couldn't finish. That wouldn't be fair to Jack either.

He smiled sadly. "I figured as much. Can't blame a guy for trying."

They headed back into the living room with the hot chocolate and watched the rest of the movie. By the time it ended, everyone was yawning and they all said good night. Aidan gave her a hug before she left and she squeezed him tight, inhaling his familiar fragrance. "Merry Christmas, Aidan."

CHAPTER FORTY-ONE

Riley called the law firm Monday morning and accepted the position. She let Jack know that night and he was excited for her.

"You're going to love it here. It's a great firm. Good people. I'll get us an extra-good bottle of champagne to celebrate on New Year's Eve."

His enthusiasm was contagious and lifted some of the doubt she'd been struggling with. Especially since her conversation with Aidan the night before. But she felt that she had to do the responsible thing and at least give the position a shot.

Riley found her mother in the kitchen, sipping coffee and reading emails. She told her she'd accepted the role and Beth was quiet for a moment, then nodded.

"That would be a difficult opportunity to pass up." She smiled at Riley reassuringly. "And if doesn't work out, you can always find something else."

Riley relaxed a bit. Her mother was right. And there was always the possibility that she might love the job.

Later that day she went with her mother to the doctor and Beth was able to swap the cast for a brace. Her mother found that much easier to deal with, especially since she knew it was just for a few more weeks.

Riley finished up Donna's project on Monday afternoon and started on Sean's the day after. She called him in the morning and asked him a bunch of questions about his business. He followed up with an email with more details and also the kinds of projects he enjoyed working on the most. Riley spent the next two days mapping out a content marketing strategy for his website and writing blog posts and marketing materials that would hopefully result in people finding him when they searched on the internet.

It kept her busy until Friday when she was planning to head home to Manhattan, with Lily. She was actually looking forward to getting back, going shopping, going to the New Year's Eve party and then to work the following week. Maybe once she was settled and everything was back to normal, she'd stop thinking about Aidan and Luke so much.

Joe called Franny first thing Tuesday morning and confirmed that she would come to his house for dinner that evening.

"I'm looking forward to it. What can I bring?"

"I don't need a thing. Just you," he said.

She laughed. "I'm not coming empty-handed. Do you like red wine or would white be better?"

He thought for a moment. "For what I'm making a creamy Chardonnay would be nice, I think. But if you prefer red, that would be fine, too."

"Chardonnay it is. I'll see you tonight."

Franny dressed carefully that evening. She wore her best rose-pink sweater. She'd always thought it brought out the pink in her cheeks. She paired it with a long, slim, black wool skirt and a string of pearls. For a final touch she added a splash of the perfume she'd been wearing since high school, Chanel. She wondered if Joe would remember it.

She left the inn and drove to Joe's house. She had done a dry run the day before so she knew that it would take her about eighteen minutes to get there. Joe lived in a modest house with a big yard on a cul-de-sac. She could see when she drove by in the afternoon that it looked like he had a garden in the backyard. Joe had always loved gardening.

She pulled into his driveway right on time and shivered a bit as she walked to the front door. But it was from nerves, not the cold. This felt big, that they'd found each other again after so many years. And she wasn't sure what it meant. She was excited to find out, though. She was just thrilled to have Joe back in her life, however that would be.

She knocked on the door and he opened it wide a moment later. Joe was wearing a big white apron over his baby-blue sweater. He had always looked good in blue, but now it really popped against his white hair. He pulled her in for a hug.

"I'm so excited to see you. I woke up Christmas Day and I wondered at first if seeing you in the shop was just a dream. Was my Franny really coming to dinner? I'm so glad you're here. Let me take your coat."

Franny stepped inside, shrugged her coat off, and handed it to him, along with her hat and mittens and then she followed him into the kitchen. Something delicious-smelling was bubbling away on the stove.

"It's my version of coq au vin—chicken stew made with white wine. That's why I thought Chardonnay might be good."

Franny handed him the bottle. She'd kept it in her mini-refrigerator so it was nice and cold. Joe opened it and poured them both a glass. He had a small bowl of salted nuts and some cheese and crackers on a slate tray.

"Let's go in the other room and sit for a bit before dinner." He carried his wine and the cheese tray into his living room, which had a big window. Although it was getting dark, she could still see that it overlooked a pond and beyond that, she guessed that there might be a glimpse of the harbor.

"I can see the ocean a little," Joe confirmed. "I like the pond view, too. It's relaxing and there are often people fishing or on small boats. Or even paddleboarding. That's gotten popular on the ponds now that there are so many sharks in the ocean."

They sipped their wine and chatted for over an hour before they decided to eat. There was just so much to talk about and they continued the conversation over dinner. Franny felt like she could talk to Joe all night and in some ways it was like the years disappeared in an instant. They'd always connected that way. There was never a lull in conversation and often the conversation moved so fast that they rushed to get the words out. And more than once they finished each other's sentences and laughed.

Franny told him all about her marriage. "We met in college and it was love right away for us both. We felt very lucky and we had a long and mostly very happy marriage. I helped him with the business and we both enjoyed that. We never had kids. It just never happened for us. We were disappointed at first but we lived busy lives. We went out often and we traveled quite a bit. It has been ten years now for me. I still miss him. But I'm used to being alone now and I really don't mind it."

"I didn't think that I minded it either. My story is similar. I had a good marriage. We had a lot of love and respect for each other. And we were blessed with one child, a boy. He's married, but they don't have kids yet. She's a nice girl. I've been telling them how beautiful it is here and I'm hopeful that if they spend more time here maybe I can at least get them to consider the East Coast. I would love to see them more often."

"Have they been out here yet?" Franny asked.

"Not yet. They promised to spend their vacation here in July. I'm going to take some time off then as well. I have some great people that can cover for me in the shop. I'm looking forward to playing tourist and showing them all around Chatham. If you're in town then, I'd love for you to meet them." He looked at her hopefully and Franny felt her heart melt.

"I'd love to meet them and I'm planning to spend the summer here. Honestly, now that I've bought my house, I'm not in any hurry to head back to Albany. Maybe I'll stay a little longer."

His eyes lit up. "I don't dare to hope, but I would love if you extended your stay." He reached out and took her hand. "Now that we've found each other again, I just want to spend more time with you. I feel like we have so much more to catch up on. And I've always just liked being around you, Franny. You know that. That hasn't changed."

Franny squeezed his hand gently. "I feel the same way. I still can't believe that my sister read that article and brought us together again. It just feels . . ."

"Meant to be," Joe said and they both smiled at each other.

Franny didn't want the night to end, but by ten they were both fighting yawns and she reluctantly said she should go.

Joe walked her to the door and looked deeply into her eyes. "Franny, it may be a little bold to say, but I want us to be more than friends. Now that we've reconnected, I don't want to waste a minute. How do you feel?"

Franny smiled and felt sheer happiness and joy. "I feel the same way."

She saw the same emotions reflected in his eyes as well as a bit of relief. He smiled wide before pulling her into his arms and giving her a sweet kiss that she felt all the way to her toes. She sighed happily when the kiss finally ended.

"Good night, Franny. I'll call you tomorrow and we'll make a plan to meet again—very soon."

CHAPTER FORTY-TWO

Wednesday evening around five, Beth had just opened the refrigerator and was staring at the contents, hoping to be inspired about what to make for dinner. Riley was at the kitchen table tapping away on her laptop as she worked on Sean's project. Her cell phone rang and she saw that it was Donna. She closed the refrigerator door and answered the call.

"What are you up to?" Donna asked.

"I was just thinking about what to make for dinner."

"Good, I caught you in time then. Hubby is out of town this week and I've had a day—want to meet me at the Squire for a quiet drink and a bite? Bring Riley if she's around, too."

Beth turned to Riley, "Do you want to come with me to grab dinner at the Squire with Donna?"

Riley closed the laptop. "Sure. I'm ready to go."

"We'll see you there in fifteen minutes," Beth said.

The Squire was busy for a Wednesday night. The week between Christmas and New Year's Eve tended to be somewhat busy in general as quite a few people had the week off and schools were closed. Donna was waiting for them at the bar and there were two open seats, one on each side of her with glasses of water in front of them.

"I told the bartender you'd be right in, so he was okay with saving the seats for a few minutes," Donna said.

The bartender came right over and Beth and Riley both ordered a glass of wine—Cabernet for Riley and Pinot Grigio for Beth. Donna was drinking a hot and spicy martini, straight up with a blue cheese–stuffed olive floating in it. She fished the olive out and popped it in her mouth.

"That looks intriguing," Riley said. "How spicy is it?"

Donna laughed and pushed the glass toward her. "Try it. Take a sip."

Riley did and Beth laughed at the expression on her face. She didn't think Riley would be ordering that drink.

"It's actually pretty good, but a little too spicy for me to have more than a sip."

"Well, your timing was perfect, because I had no idea what to make for dinner. I really wasn't in the mood to cook," Beth admitted.

They decided to share a few appetizers instead of full meals and ordered loaded chicken nachos, coconut shrimp with a raspberry sauce, and barbeque chicken wings. It didn't take long for their food and as they waited, Donna made them laugh with details of her day.

"I swear you can't make this stuff up. Some of the things clients say to me or do, it's insane. Especially when they are getting a divorce. It makes me wonder how these people ever got married in the first place."

After they finished eating, they ordered another round of drinks and by then the bar was crowded and all the seats were filled.

"When are you seeing Sean again?" Donna asked.

"He's having me over for dinner tomorrow night and he mentioned something about New Year's Eve, but we don't have any definite plans yet," Beth said.

"It sounds like things are going well then?" Donna said.

"I think so. I really like him," Beth admitted. It was still going so well that she didn't quite trust it and was waiting for a red flag to pop up, but so far her relationship with Sean had just been so easy.

Donna turned her attention to Riley for a minute. "I meant to tell you earlier that your blog posts seem to be working. We've had a few new potential clients call this week that said they found us by searching on the web."

"Oh, that's great!" Riley said.

"She's doing something similar for Sean's website," Beth said proudly.

An attractive blond woman with an enviable figure and what Beth assumed had to be a spray tan came up next to her at the bar and tried to get the bartender's attention. She was standing with a friend who was searching the bar looking for empty seats, but there were none.

"I'm pretty sure that woman standing next to you is Sean's ex—Marcy," Donna whispered just loudly enough that only Beth and Riley could hear. They all stopped talking for a moment when they heard her say Sean's name.

Beth wasn't entirely sure but she also thought that Marcy glanced her way first. But that probably didn't mean anything. She was sure Marcy had no idea who she was.

"Yeah, so I saw him Christmas night," Marcy said. "It was great seeing him again. He did say he's been dating someone but it's not serious. And we know he's not going to get serious with anyone. I told him I miss him and that I'm really okay just taking things slow and hanging out now and then."

"And he's okay with that?" The other woman sounded surprised.

"Well, he didn't say no." Marcy laughed. "I didn't really give him a chance to say anything!" They got their drinks and walked off but not before Marcy shot another look Beth's way and this time there was no question that she knew who Beth was. Beth felt sick to her stomach. Had Sean really seen Marcy on Christmas night? She hadn't heard from him until the next day when he suggested dinner at his house on Thursday.

"Mom, I think she's full of it," Riley said.

"I would talk to Sean. You don't want to get in much deeper if he really is open to seeing her again. But I think I'm with Riley. She knew who you were and maybe was just trying to scare you off," Donna said, then added, "but you never know. Talk to him."

Beth felt miserable at the thought that Sean might want to revisit his relationship with Marcy. Her mind started spinning. Surely Marcy wouldn't make up that she'd seen him on Christmas? So if that was true—what else was true? Maybe they missed each other. Maybe now that he'd spent time with Beth, he realized that Marcy was the one that he really wanted. The thought made her eyes water.

It was the red flag she'd been dreading. She knew things were too good to be true. Now she had to talk to Sean and she dreaded that, too—especially if Marcy was telling the truth. Where did that leave her? She was not going to continue dating Sean if he thought he could also see Marcy. That didn't work for her at all. But Sean did say he wasn't keen on getting married again or getting too serious too soon. She'd thought they were on the same page. But maybe they were reading a very different book.

CHAPTER FORTY-THREE

Beth was a nervous wreck as she got ready for her date with Sean. She was meeting him at his house. She was finally able to drive again, now that she had the brace instead of the cast, and she steeled herself for the conversation she knew she had to have with him. She was torn between wanting to see Sean and dreading the conversation over dinner that might not go the way she hoped.

She brought a bottle of wine with her, a Daou Cabernet as he'd said he was serving steak. When she arrived at his house, he had the door open wide before she even reached it.

"I heard your car in the driveway," he said as he pulled her in for a welcome kiss. She pulled away quickly, though, and handed him the bottle of wine. "This is one of my favorites."

He took it and glanced at the label. "Thanks. Looks great. Come on in."

She followed him inside and was struck by how cozy and yet how masculine his house was at the same time. It was a rustic contemporary with wood beams and a cathedral ceiling. Hardwood floors with a living room that opened into the kitchen area with a beautiful island in the middle.

"Did you make that?" Beth asked. It was shaped like an L,

with a raised counter made of two different kinds of polished wood. It was the first thing she noticed when she entered the room. He looked pleased that she mentioned it.

"I did. I came up with the design myself and it worked better than expected." He set the wine on the island counter and fished around in a drawer for an opener. While he opened the wine, Beth looked around the room and took in the chocolate-brown leather sofas, and the potbellied stove in the fireplace that heated the room. She could feel the heat it generated from where she stood in the kitchen.

Sean poured two glasses of the wine and handed her one.

"What are you making?" There was a sauté pan on the stove with something simmering in it.

Sean walked over and gave the sauce a stir. "It's a red wine and shallot sauce for the filets. I browned them in butter first in this pan, then moved them to the oven to finish cooking. They have a blue cheese panko crust and they should be almost ready."

Beth was impressed. "That's pretty fancy. I pictured you as more of a throw the steaks on the grill kind of guy."

He laughed. "I am that, mostly. But I like to cook and I have perfected a few dishes that are winners. This is one of them."

Beth's thoughts immediately went to Marcy. Did he ever make this dish for her? She didn't ask. Didn't want to know. But she suddenly felt a little less hungry.

Sean checked the steaks. "They still have a few minutes. Want to relax by the fire for a bit before we eat?"

"Sure."

He led her to one of the leather couches, the one facing the stove, and clicked on some music. It was a classic Marvin Gaye tune. It would have put Beth in the mood for romance if she hadn't overheard the conversation with Marcy. Was this what Sean did? Cook a fabulous meal, turn on smooth music, and have the night end in the bedroom? She told herself she was being silly. This was a normal progression in dating. It didn't have to mean Sean was sleeping around. But she did need to find out what was going on with Marcy. She took a deep breath but just couldn't get up the courage to have the conversation yet. Maybe over dinner.

But when they sat down to eat, everything was so delicious and Sean was so charming that she relaxed again and just enjoyed herself. She didn't want to ruin the evening. Not yet.

Sean had picked up a cheesecake for dessert with a cherry sauce. Beth was full but she couldn't ever pass up cheesecake and cherry topping was her favorite. She remembered mentioning that to him at one point and was touched that he remembered. Or maybe it was just the way he preferred it, too.

She helped him clean up in the kitchen, passing him the dirty dishes before he rinsed and stacked them in the dishwasher. When they were done he topped off her wine and his and they settled on the sofa again. Beth felt her stomach clench. She couldn't put off the conversation much longer.

"You're quiet tonight. Is everything okay?" Sean asked.

"It's fine, I'm just a little tired," Beth lied. The words had come out automatically. She took a sip of her wine and braced herself to ask Sean about Marcy. But she just couldn't find the words.

Sean smiled at her and set his wine down. "Come here." He leaned toward her, wrapped his arms around her, and pulled her in for a kiss. As soon as her lips touched his she pulled back. She just couldn't do it until they talked.

"Something is wrong," Sean said.

"It's just that I have a few questions," Beth began.

"You can ask me anything. Shoot," Sean encouraged her.

"Did you see Marcy Christmas night?"

She could see in his eyes that her words had shocked him and he didn't deny it. He nodded.

"I did. She stopped by. It was unexpected and it was late. I didn't get home until after nine and it was almost nine thirty when she showed up and knocked on my door. I wasn't exactly thrilled by it." He frowned. "How did you know that?"

"I was out with Donna and Riley last night at the Squire. Marcy was there, too, and stood right next to me when she ordered from the bar. It was crowded. I am pretty sure that she meant for me to overhear her."

"What else did she say?" Sean looked frustrated and annoyed.

"She implied that she was going to see you again. That she told you she was fine with not being serious and that you said things weren't serious with us." She cringed at the last part of that. She knew they weren't serious yet, but Beth wanted to be and she thought that Sean did, too.

Sean sighed heavily. "She did say that. But I made it clear I had no intention of seeing her again. I also said that we weren't serious yet . . . but that I hoped that we would be. I think she only relayed part of the conversation."

Beth nodded. She wanted to believe him but she was still concerned that Marcy had gone to see him at all. And that he hadn't told her. She supposed he didn't need to tell her, but it still made her nervous.

"Okay. It was a little unsettling to hear that. Especially that she'd seen you on Christmas. I didn't know what to think."

Sean took her hand. "I'm sorry she did that to you. This is the kind of reaction she was hoping for. But Beth, even if things don't work out with us, and I hope that they do, please know that I will never date Marcy again. She is not a threat to our relationship."

Beth took a sip of wine. She wanted to believe him and she

felt that he was telling the truth. But she'd been lied to before and she just needed a little time to process this and she told him that.

"I do believe you. But I think I need to head home now and just digest all this. It's a lot," she said.

He looked concerned. "Beth, please don't give up on us. Let me take you out on New Year's Eve like we planned. Let's make it a special night."

Beth suddenly felt exhausted and anxious to go home and crawl into bed.

She put her wineglass down and stood. "I'll let you know. Thank you for dinner tonight."

Sean walked her to the door and he didn't try to kiss her. He just pulled her into a tight hug and gently kissed her forehead. "Sweet dreams, Beth. I'll talk to you soon."

CHAPTER FORTY-FOUR

Riley left for New York after breakfast service at the inn on Friday. She ate spinach and artichoke quiche with Franny and her mother and it was bittersweet to say goodbye to both of them. She was so happy for Franny, who was smitten with Joe. They'd seen each other almost every day that week and Franny was excited about their plans for New Year's Eve.

"We have dinner reservations, early ones, at the Impudent Oyster. That's Joe's favorite restaurant in Chatham and it's mine, too. And then we're going back to his house for coffee and dessert and to watch the ball fall at midnight."

"That sounds so fun, Franny." Riley turned to her mother. "What are you and Sean doing? You still have plans, right?" Riley knew her mother had been upset by what she'd overheard Marcy say and that Sean had tried to ease her worries. Riley liked Sean and she'd enjoyed doing some work for him. Her mother had been very quiet since she'd seen him the night before and just said she had to really think about everything. She seemed somewhat calmer today, though. And she smiled at the question.

"Yes, I'm going to go out with him. I'm not exactly sure where, but he said something about going somewhere for dinner and to hear some live music."

"That sounds great," Riley said. She was relieved that her mother was going to go and hopefully would have a wonderful time.

"I close on my house next Friday, can you believe it?" Franny said.

"I can't wait to see it," Riley said. "I'll come home in a few weeks or so and I'd love to visit then."

"Absolutely. I'll have you both over. I'd love to cook for you for a change," Franny said.

Riley already looked forward to it. It was funny, she'd been gone for so many years and it wasn't until she'd come back and spent several weeks in Chatham that it started to really feel like home again. She found herself feeling sad to go. She chalked it up to the coziness of the holiday season and being around so many people. That's what she'd enjoyed the most. Especially spending time with her mother and with Aidan and Luke and Franny. She was going to miss them all. Her apartment in Manhattan seemed so far away and very empty. Though she would have Lily, of course. And she was certain once she was back there, she'd settle right in and love it again. She was sure of it.

She rented a car, packed up all her things and Lily, and arrived back in Manhattan late that afternoon. Once she was unpacked, the evening stretched before her. She knew that Jack wasn't around. They'd talked earlier in the week and he'd let her know that he had a big card game with his guy friends Friday night. It was an annual thing, always the night before New Year's Eve.

Riley had no food in her apartment and didn't feel like going out. It was a cold night and it had started sleeting as she drove into the city. She ordered a pizza and when it came she ate on the sofa, with Lily by her side. She flipped through the channels and nothing grabbed her attention. Then she remembered the book that Aidan had given her—the Hannah McIntosh Christmas story.

She read a few pages and was hooked immediately. It was a story of best friends that reconnected over the holidays and it suited Riley's mood perfectly. She read until her eyes grew heavy and she finally crawled into bed a little after eleven.

She woke early the next day and after feeding Lily, she made a shopping list and went to the grocery store and stocked up on everything as her refrigerator was empty. When she finished she ate a quick turkey sandwich and headed back out again, this time on a mission to find a dress to wear that night. Jack had said the party was black tie, which meant a full-length formal gown.

Riley went to several shops and nothing she tried on seemed quite right. Finally, she wandered into an upscale consignment shop, mostly to take a break from shopping. She didn't expect that she would find anything there but the shop was right next to the one she'd just left so she'd decided to poke around. And she was surprised to find several intriguing dresses. Still, one never knew until you actually tried a dress on. She'd found several that seemed promising until she saw them in the dressing room mirror.

But one of the dresses in the consignment shop, a black slip-dress style with satin spaghetti straps and an airy chiffon fabric that hugged her curves in a flattering way fit perfectly and made her feel beautiful. Best part—it was half the price of the other dresses she'd tried on. She paid for the dress and headed home.

Jack had said that the party they were going to was near Riley's apartment, so he was planning to come by and then they would walk over. Jack whistled when he saw her and pulled her in for a hug and kiss. "You look fantastic."

Jack looked very handsome too, and she told him so. He was wearing a black tux with a crisp white shirt and black tie. His hair was slicked back with a bit of gel and it glistened in the light. She'd noticed that most of the guys in his office styled their hair similarly. Jack confessed that for some of them it was a way to hide stray grays.

"We can be a little vain about that, too," he admitted. He didn't have many gray hairs yet, but there were a few that popped up here and there. He hated it and yanked them viciously with tweezers when he spotted them. The gel was insurance for any others that might attempt to show themselves.

"Are you ready to go? Eric's place is right around the corner," he said.

He led the way and they walked a block to Eric's building and went to the top floor, the penthouse.

"Wait until you see his place. It's sick. He paid ten million for it and he could probably get almost twice that now."

Riley couldn't even imagine.

They checked in with security in the building lobby and were waved ahead to the special elevator that went to the top floor. When they stepped out they were welcomed by a server holding a silver platter with flutes of champagne. They each took one and made their way into the living room. Riley looked around as they walked, taking it all in.

There were soaring ceilings with skylights that probably let in tons of light. The floors were sleek white Carrara marble and the same marble continued into the kitchen and onto the island and countertops. It was beautiful, although it also felt somewhat cold to Riley. There was no clutter, nothing on the countertops. It looked like the kitchen was never used. Jack told her that the caterers operated out of a second, smaller kitchen that was out of sight, tucked away in a different area of the sprawling custom-built apartment.

"Eric has a full-time chef. Neither he nor his wife cook, but they like having a beautiful kitchen. It's all for show," Jack said.

Servers glided by with appetizers on platters: plump shrimp, crab cakes, mini beef Wellingtons. And there was a vodka and caviar bar where people were gathered, and were pouring vodka down an ice chute to chill it on the way to a crystal shot glass. They drank the cold vodka after swallowing a bite of caviar spread on blini—little pancakes, topped with sour cream and onion.

"The caviar is outstanding. Definitely try it, but I'd limit yourself to one of the vodka shots. Those things can sneak up on you." Jack grinned and Riley sensed he was speaking from experience.

"I think I'll stick to champagne or wine." Riley wasn't much of a vodka drinker. And she'd never cared for caviar.

Jack loved it, though. He headed over, said hello to the guys gathered around the vodka bar, and introduced Riley to everyone that she didn't already know. He ate a little caviar and washed it down with iced vodka.

There was no actual sit-down dinner, which Riley was kind of glad about. It was already close to eight so she didn't want a heavy meal. There was plenty of food, though, and all of it was delicious. Jack also introduced her to the wives and girlfriends of his coworkers and though she had a hard time remembering all of their names, they were friendly and welcoming. Which was good because she kept losing track of Jack as he wandered off to talk to his colleagues. He knew everyone there and was having a fabulous time. After about an hour or so, though, Riley's feet were beginning to hurt in the high heels that she'd dragged out of her closet and that she didn't wear often enough. She could feel herself getting blisters on the back of her heel.

There was a band in a corner of a very large room that was

almost like a ballroom. Jack said it was just used for parties. The music was good and the dance floor was crowded but Jack wasn't much of a dancer. He kept disappearing and joining groups of his guy coworkers while Riley wandered around. She didn't really know anyone there but the other women were good about including her and she noticed that their husbands or boyfriends were all with Jack, too.

"What do they talk about, do you suppose?" Riley asked at one point when she'd glanced over and saw the men leaning forward, listening intently to one of the senior partners.

"Work. It's always work. They are obsessed." Blair, a woman about Riley's age who'd been married for about a year spoke matter-of-factly.

"Do your husbands all work extremely long hours?" Riley asked.

They all nodded. Even one of the older women, Dana, whose husband was a partner. She must have seen Riley's look of surprise, because she added, "I thought it would stop or at least slow down once he made partner, but we're three years in and nothing has changed. I don't see my husband often at all."

One of the other women grinned. "But working those long hours does have some benefits. I'm able to be a stay-at-home mother and have a nanny so I can meet up with friends for lunch or dinner or shopping anytime. It's really not so bad."

Riley looked around the room. If she stayed with Jack, this would be her future. It was a somewhat depressing thought.

Jack circled around a few times to chat with her before being drawn back to his circle of colleagues again. It was all men, so Riley didn't feel comfortable intruding and stayed chatting with the women. Jack found her again a little before midnight and they danced the last song before the ball dropped. A large-screen television showed the countdown as the ball dropped in Times Square. Everyone cheered when it was officially the

New Year and Jack pulled her in for a quick kiss. It was over in an instant and Riley felt somewhat deflated—by the kiss, by the night . . . and by the future that lay ahead. She'd thought there was a light at the end of the tunnel—that Jack's workload would slow after a few more years. But now that looked doubtful.

She was exhausted and more than ready to go home. And she assumed they would leave once the ball dropped. But Jack didn't seem to be in any hurry.

"Isn't this party great? Eric said the band will play for two more hours. He's making it worth their while. And then they'll be putting out breakfast for everyone."

"Jack, I'm ready to go. If you want to stay that's fine. I'll just talk to you tomorrow." Riley really didn't care at this point if he stayed or not, she just wanted to go home and crawl into bed.

He looked torn for a moment. "You sure you don't want to stay?"

She nodded. "I'm sure."

Jack glanced back at his group of friends that were gathered in a circle. There was a burst of laughter and high-fiving all around. He flashed her his most charming grin, the one he used when he wanted to win her over. "Okay. I am going to stay then. I'll call you tomorrow."

CHAPTER FORTY-FIVE

Beth found herself missing Riley as she did the chocolate turndown service on New Year's Eve before starting the wine and cheese hour. She started a little earlier than usual to make sure she got all the rooms done before five. The inn was completely full thanks to the holiday weekend and Riley's marketing efforts.

In addition to the usual red and white wine options, Beth added a bubbly choice—Prosecco—in honor of the holiday. She hoped that Riley was having fun. Her daughter had called earlier to wish her a happy New Year and to text her a photo of the dress she'd found. It was lovely and Riley had gotten such a good deal on it. Beth was happy for her. She just hoped that the event and Jack were worthy of the dress.

She smiled when she saw Aidan and Luke enter the room. They'd had another delay on their house, one last thing that needed to happen before they could move home. But Aidan had said they were working over the weekend to make sure they could move home on New Year's Day. She knew they were ready.

"Hi, Luke, hot chocolate for you?" she asked.

"Yes, please," he said and then ran over to the tree to check on his trains.

Beth disappeared to make his hot chocolate and returned a few minutes later. Aidan was sipping a glass of Merlot and slicing a piece of cheese. Luke came running when he saw the marshmallows bobbing on his mug of hot chocolate.

"Have you heard from Riley? Is she doing anything fun tonight?" Aidan asked casually.

Beth sensed there was more than casual interest there. "She's going to a fancy party tonight. Someone that Jack works with. And then she starts her new job on Tuesday."

Aidan frowned but forced a smile a moment later. "That's great," he said flatly.

"What are you and Luke up to?" Beth asked.

His smile this time was genuine. "We've been having a blast today going to different First Night activities. We did the bubble wrap stomp, went to Candy Land, and Luke had his face painted—though he washed it off as soon as we got home. And we went to a special display at the Railroad Museum. That was his favorite. We're in for the night now."

"Oh, that sounds like a fun day. Chatham does such a great job with the First Night activities." They paused for a moment at the sound of fireworks. Luke raced to the window to look out.

"That must be the fireworks over Veterans Field," Beth said. "I think I read that they were going off at five thirty."

Franny walked over and poured herself a small glass of red wine. "I am so impressed with all of the different artists and musicians that come to Chatham for First Night. Joe had to work today in the shop and it was very busy, so I kept myself occupied by checking out a few of the artists. I listened to a wonderful jazz quartet and a blues band this afternoon. And I think after Joe and I have dinner, we might go listen to a woman, Natalia Bonfini, who plays a combination of jazz and blues."

"I think I've heard of her," Beth said.

"What are you and Sean doing?" Franny asked.

"He should be here shortly. We're heading into Hyannis to go to his favorite Italian restaurant, Alberto's Ristorante. On the way back, I think we're going to hear one of his favorite local bands here in Chatham. I don't remember where he said they're playing but it's nearby."

"They're playing at St. Martin's Lodge. They play the blues," Sean said. He'd walked up behind Beth.

She turned and smiled. "That's it."

Aidan nodded. "I love blues music. I think I saw that listed. I've heard them play before and they are very good."

It was almost six and everyone started to clear out. Beth wished them all a happy New Year then quickly cleaned up.

Sean drove and made easy conversation. Beth had left their last discussion with mixed feelings. But after she slept, she woke feeling calm. She trusted Sean and realized she didn't have any solid reason not to trust him.

Beth knew that she had trust issues after the way her marriage ended. But she also knew that she needed to risk getting hurt again. There were never guarantees that came with love. So, she'd decided to put her worries aside and just try to live in the moment and see where things went.

Alberto's was an Italian restaurant that had been on Main Street in Hyannis for as long as Beth could remember. They had a reservation and even though the restaurant was crowded, they were seated right away. Their dinner was wonderful. They ordered a nice bottle of red wine, an Amarone that their server recommended, and it was so smooth and delicious. And it paired well with their meals. Beth got the gnocchi with tomato sauce and a meatball. Sean got the veal osso buco.

Halfway through the meal, after Sean topped off her wine-glass, he held her gaze for a moment. So far it had been such an enjoyable night.

"Are you having a good time?" he asked gently.

She nodded. "I am."

"Good, because I really am falling for you, Beth. I hope that you're feeling better about things with us."

She took a sip of her wine and smiled. "I was upset after I left your house the other night. I reacted that way because of my marriage—I've had trust issues since then. But I slept on it and when I woke I just let those worries fall away. It was just my fear getting in the way. You haven't given me any reason to worry." She grinned. "And hopefully you won't."

He reached across the table and took her hand. "Beth, you're the only one that I think about. There's no one else. And I can't imagine that there will be. I just want to spend more time with you."

"I want that, too." Beth's heart felt full.

When they left the restaurant, Sean pulled her into his arms before they got into the car. "I wanted to do this at dinner, but it probably would have been frowned upon," he said. He kissed her passionately and she kissed him back with just as much feeling. Finally they pulled apart and Sean brushed a few stray snowflakes off her face. "Happy New Year, Beth."

"Happy New Year!" As they climbed into the car and rode back to Chatham, Beth felt blissfully happy. Her world seemed happier and more complete now that she was spending time with Sean. She looked forward to the coming year and seeing where it would take them. She didn't feel any fear, just a calm sense of excitement for what her next chapter would bring.

CHAPTER FORTY-SIX

Jack called New Year's Day around eleven and invited Riley to go to brunch with him.

"I'm starving and thought we could go to one of those places that has a big brunch buffet. What do you say? I can pick you up in twenty minutes?" He was full of energy and assumed she would want to go. But she didn't. Riley was still a bit annoyed with Jack.

"I just ate breakfast. I think I'm going to relax and putter around here. I need to do laundry and figure out what I'm going to wear on Tuesday." She paused for a moment then couldn't resist asking, "What time did you stay at Eric's until?"

Jack laughed. "I think it was almost three by the time I rolled out of there. They brought tons of food out around two, French toast, omelets, hash browns. And pizza and burgers if you didn't want breakfast stuff. Speaking of breakfast, I'm going to go find some food. Don't worry about Tuesday. I'm sure whatever you decide to wear will be fine. I'll see you at work." Jack ended the call and Riley just shook her head. She had no regrets about leaving when she did. It was disappointing, though, that Jack was happy to stay behind, on New Year's Eve, instead of leaving with her. She realized that she had some thinking to do about this relationship and what she wanted out of it.

She threw a load of laundry in and did some cleaning around the apartment. Her neighbor Phoebe came over later that afternoon and they decided to share a pizza and catch up. Riley filled her in on the highlights of her time in Chatham and the party the night before. Phoebe was quiet as she listened. And she didn't say anything until Riley specifically asked what she thought of Jack staying when she left at midnight.

"I wouldn't have liked it," Phoebe said. "If you'd been spending a lot of time with him, then maybe not as big of a deal. But it wasn't just any night, and you had barely seen him over the past month or so. You would think he'd want to spend time with you."

Riley nodded. "He called to see if I wanted to go to brunch this morning. But I wasn't in the mood."

"Has he always been like this?" Phoebe asked.

Riley thought for a moment. "He was more attentive when we first started going out. I think he was trying to impress me then. He sent flowers, we went to fancy restaurants. We still do that but there are weeks where I hardly see him at all. And I'm starting to see that it will only get worse, not better, when he makes partner."

"It seems exhausting. All those hours he works. Not a good work-life balance," Phoebe said.

Riley laughed. "That's an understatement." Her phone pinged with a text message and she smiled when she saw it was from Aidan. *Just wanted to wish you a happy New Year and good luck for Tuesday.*

She texted back, *Thanks! Same to you and Luke!*

"You're smiling. Was that Jack?" Phoebe asked.

"No. That was Aidan. He just wanted to wish me a happy New Year and good luck on the new job."

Heather had a funny look on her face, but said nothing.

"What is it?" Riley asked.

"Well, just that you didn't smile like that even once when you were talking about Jack. It's kind of interesting."

"Aidan is an old friend. We used to date in high school, and it was great to spend time with him and his son, Luke. But Aidan knows about Jack. He met him actually."

"Just saying. Aidan sounds like a great guy."

"He is."

They changed the subject and watched TV for a while before Phoebe left. Riley thought about what Phoebe had said and she couldn't help but compare Jack and Aidan. And she'd thought about both Aidan and Luke since she'd come home. She missed them and she wondered what Aidan had done for New Year's Eve. She guessed that he probably spent it with Luke. He was a great guy and it would just be a matter of time before he found someone. She also remembered what he'd said in Chatham, how if the timing was different he'd love to try again.

Riley felt restless as she drifted off to sleep. She couldn't help but wonder if she was making a huge mistake by starting this new job. But she'd already accepted it and she didn't want to make Jack look bad by pulling out at the last minute. Plus, she had nothing else lined up. She'd been looking at the online listings for the past few weeks and there was really nothing else out there.

So she would start the job and she'd see where it went. Maybe it would help her and Jack's relationship as they might see each other more often. Though she had her doubts about that, too. She had a lot to think about.

On Monday, while reading a book online, Riley got an email from a friend of Donna's in Chatham. Morgan owned a mortgage company and said that Donna had told her about the content marketing work that Riley and done and she wondered if Riley might be interested in working on a project for her company. She left her number and said she was available that day if Riley was around, or they could talk later that week.

Riley welcomed the offer to talk as she had the entire day free. They spoke for about a half hour on the phone, agreed to the terms of the project, and Riley dove into the assignment. She spent the rest of the day and well into the evening working on creating blog content and a lead magnet short ebook as a giveaway in exchange for an email address. This would help her client build an email list of potential leads for mortgages.

She finished two-thirds of the work that day and intended to finish the rest in the evenings after work that week. It got the wheels turning and Riley wondered if she might be able to drum up even more of this kind of consulting work if she made some efforts on her own. She decided to hold off and see how things went at the job first. She wanted to really give it a fair chance.

For the first day at the new job, Riley wore her best navy suit and put on a string of pearls. She'd never felt so corporate before. When she arrived at the law offices, she had to fill out a stack of paperwork with human resources and then was directed to the marketing department. Everyone was friendly but busy and focused on their own work. Riley was shown to her cubicle. Only the lawyers at the firm had private offices. Riley didn't care about that, though. She was used to an open environment and preferred it. With marketing especially it usually helped when they could hear each other and easily communicate and collaborate. The other departments she'd worked in had always been high energy, chaotic at times, and often loud. And she'd loved it.

Here you could hear a pin drop. But maybe they were just tired after the long weekend and settling in to their workweek.

It took Riley a while to get access to her computer. Most of her morning was spent waiting for IT to configure her laptop so she could access email and the company network. It was a long, very quiet morning. But finally, a little before noon, she was up and running.

She'd brought a sandwich for lunch as she didn't know what people usually did at the law firm, if they actually took a lunch break or not. At most of the places she'd worked people rarely took a set lunch break, they usually ate at their desks and continued to work unless they were going for a rare lunch out. Riley had never minded that, preferred it even as she'd rather get more work done and leave a little after five.

So she wasn't surprised to see that no one in the marketing department took an actual lunch break. Most either brought something or ran out and then brought it back and ate at their desk. Riley filled a water bottle in the kitchen and unwrapped her peanut butter sandwich at her desk and read through her emails. She had quite a few already. Her boss had sent a bunch of files to bring her up to speed on what they were working on and she had plenty of work to keep her busy.

She dove in and began working and the afternoon went by quickly. Before she knew it her watch dinged that it was five o'clock and time for her to get up and move around. It did that every hour and it was a good thing, otherwise she could get so into her work that she'd spend hours glued to her computer, which wasn't good.

She got up and filled her water bottle again and noticed that everyone was still hard at work. She thought that HR had mentioned the hours of the company were generally nine to five. But she also knew that Jack went in earlier and always stayed later. She was curious what time people in her department arrived. She'd spent about an hour with HR in the morning, so when she'd reached the department of course everyone was in by then.

She continued working, not wanting to be the first person to leave. Her stomach started rumbling when six o'clock rolled around and there was still no movement. It wasn't until six thirty that the first person got up to leave. Another followed ten minutes later and Riley packed up and left as well. She wondered if they were maybe just working under some tight deadlines. That must be it. Surely they didn't work that late all the time?

When she got home, she fed Lily, and then dived into her side project for Morgan's mortgage company until her eyes grew heavy. Jack had called around eight to ask how her first day had gone and she'd said it was fine. She did have a question for him, though.

"Do you have any idea how late the people in marketing usually work?" She'd assumed they worked normal hours because they weren't billable, like the attorneys.

"I really don't know. I'm sure they just work as late as they need to, to get the work done. Like we all do. The rest of this week is going to be all late nights. But I'm just working in the morning on Saturday. Do you want to try and grab dinner around seven?"

"Sure." Riley was almost done with her side project and should be able to finish it up the following night—assuming she left earlier than she had today.

The next night, when everyone was still there at six, Riley was done with her project and didn't want to stay a minute longer. She shut her laptop down, stood up, and glanced around the room. Everyone was still at their desks. A few looked up and seemed surprised to see her heading out. But she didn't care. She was done for the day and she had work to do at home.

She finished her project later that evening and emailed it off to Morgan. And it's a good thing because when she came in the next day her boss asked her to come to his office.

"I see you finished the project I gave you." He smiled. "Now that I have a better understanding of what you can handle, I'm ready to assign you to a few more projects. These have some tight deadlines, but I'm sure you'll manage. If you check your email, you'll see that everything is there. Let me know if you have any questions."

When Riley went back to her desk and checked her email she felt a sense of dread when she saw the amount of work he'd just sent her way. It would be fine, if the deadlines were reasonable. But they were not. She'd need to work late the rest of the week to have a chance of getting it all done on time. And now she understood why everyone stayed late and why the room was so quiet. No one had time to talk as there was work to be done.

She didn't leave work until almost eight and she still wasn't the last to leave. She was tired and hungry when she walked into her apartment and Lily wasn't too happy about the situation either. Her mother called as she was feeding Lily. Riley answered the call and grabbed herself a banana for dinner.

"Hi, honey, how's the new job going?"

Riley almost started crying but she didn't have the energy. "It's pretty awful," she admitted. Since she'd been home it just felt so empty in her apartment and the new job left her feeling even lonelier.

"I'm sorry, honey." Her mother already knew about her disappointing New Year's Eve. They'd talked the next day. Riley was thrilled for her mother that she'd had such a great night with Sean. She told her about the project that Donna had referred to her.

"I can hear the excitement in your voice when you talk

about that. Do you think you might be able to get more projects like that if you tried?"

"I was actually wondering the same thing. It's tempting," Riley admitted.

"And what will you do about Jack?" her mother asked gently. "I just want you to be happy, Riley."

"I know and I appreciate it. I have some decisions to make. I actually miss working at the inn. And I miss everyone in Chatham." Riley never thought she'd say that. There was one particular person she missed the most, but she didn't want to talk about that with her mother just yet.

"You know you're always welcome here, honey. You and Lily. I miss you both. Aidan asked what you were doing for New Year's. I forgot to tell you that the other day."

"He did? Did he say what he and Luke did?"

"They did some of the First Night stuff during the day and stayed in that night. They moved back home on Monday. And Franny closes on her house this Friday, so she'll be moving out soon, once she gets it furnished. It's going to be quiet around here."

"Well, I'll plan to at least come for a visit soon. I want to see Franny's place and I told her I'd come and see it."

"Good. Sleep well, honey. You have a lot to think about."

Riley slept horribly that night. She tossed and turned, and woke up at four and couldn't get back to sleep. She decided to head into the office early and see if she could make a dent in the pile of work she'd been given. She didn't want to be there until eight o'clock or later every night.

She arrived at the office a little after six and expected to be the first one in the office but was surprised to see her boss there already, as well as one other person. He looked up and smiled his approval as she walked in. Riley dove into her work and didn't take a real break until almost two. Her stomach was screaming by then so she unwrapped her tuna sandwich and went to the kitchen to fill her water bottle. She stopped short when she saw Brittany and Jack by the coffee machine smiling at each other. Brittany was lightly touching his arm while he laughed at something she'd said. They both looked up when they saw her and Jack turned his big smile her way.

"Hey there, how's your day going?" he asked.

"Very busy," she said shortly. The sight of the two of them had irritated her. There was clearly an attraction there—even if Jack didn't realize it just yet. Brittany clearly adored him and probably worked the same insane hours so she wouldn't mind that he did. Riley was feeling very over it all. She filled her water and went back to her desk. She noticed they also went back to their department a moment later. She turned her attention back to her work and focused on getting it done.

She stayed until eight again because she wanted to get as much done as possible and unlike Jack, she had no intention of going into the office on a Saturday.

Riley slept better that night and when she woke she felt calm and at peace now that she'd made two big decisions.

The next day she and Jack went to the Italian place that they liked. They had a nice dinner and Jack talked nonstop about the cases he was working on and also mentioned more than once what a great help Brittany was.

Riley waited until the tiramisu landed in front of them before she said what she needed to say.

"Jack, what we have isn't working for me anymore. I think you're a great guy but I don't think we want the same things. I thought I could deal with the hours that you work if I knew it wasn't going to last, but I don't see it changing anytime soon. Work isn't enough for me. I want to spend more time with the people that are important to me."

She paused to let her words sink in. Jack looked shocked at first but then he finally just nodded.

"I get it Riley, I do. I'm sorry that this didn't work out. I think you're amazing. But you're right—my hours aren't going to change anytime soon."

She paused for a moment then said, "I think you should date Brittany. She clearly adores you and you're around each other all the time."

He looked taken aback at the suggestion. "Brittany? I couldn't do that. She works for me. That would be frowned on," he protested.

"It was just a thought. Maybe she could support someone else?"

Jack ignored what she'd said, and asked, "Are you sure about this?"

She nodded. "I am. I think it's for the best."

He sighed heavily. "All right. I'm not happy about it, but I understand." His eyes clouded. "What about the job? How is that working out?"

"It's not a good fit for me. I'm sorry if it reflects badly on you if I leave but I never wanted to work these kinds of hours. They didn't make it clear in the interviews that it was expected."

"That's fine. They'll understand, especially when word gets out that we broke up. What will you do though? Maybe you should stay until you line something else up."

She shook her head. "No, I think it's best if I leave ASAP. I'll give notice, of course."

Jack chuckled. "They'll have you leave the same day. They never have people stay once they give notice. Most law firms are the same way."

Riley was surprised but also relieved. She didn't want to work there for two more weeks.

Jack walked her out and gave her a sad goodbye hug. "Goodbye, Riley. Be well."

"Thanks, Jack. Same to you."

They walked in different directions and she couldn't help thinking it was the most civilized breakup she'd ever had. She sensed that Jack was disappointed but ultimately knew that Riley was right. If theirs had been a great love, things would have been different between them. Work was his passion and would be for the coming years. Riley needed more of a balance. And since she'd been back in the city, her life here felt so empty compared to the warmth she'd known in Chatham over the holidays.

She gave notice first thing Monday morning and her boss was surprised and dismayed. "Are you sure? You've done wonderful work for us so far."

But Riley told him she was sure. "It just isn't the right cultural fit. I didn't realize the expectation for the long hours."

He nodded. "I assumed that you worked similar hours since you came from a software company. I thought all start-ups were like that."

Riley shook her head. "No, they actually had a great work-life balance there."

"Okay, well, our policy here is once you give notice, we escort you out of the building."

It was Riley's turn to be surprised. "You don't want me to finish out the day even?"

"No. I'll notify HR and they'll send someone right up."

Twenty minutes later, Riley stepped outside. It was a quarter past eight and the whole day stretched before her. And she knew exactly what she wanted to do.

She booked a rental car on her phone, stopped by her apartment, and packed two big suitcases. Two hours later, she and Lily were on their way to Chatham. She called her mother on the way and she was excited. "I'll get your room ready for you. Drive safely." Riley felt just as excited. She couldn't wait to get to Chatham and settle in.

Lily meowed loudly from her cat carrier next to Riley in the front of the car. At the next stoplight, she reached her hand inside and scratched under her chin to calm her. "Just a few more hours, Lily, and then we'll be home for good."

CHAPTER FORTY-SEVEN

Riley's emotions were all over the map as she drove home to Chatham. They swung from euphoria that she was heading home and starting a new venture to excitement at the possibility of growing her own little business. That was immediately followed by uncertainty and fear of failure. And then the tears that she'd been too exhausted to shed earlier came fast and furious as she wept for the end of a relationship that at one point she'd thought would eventually lead to marriage.

She felt in her gut, though, that she was on the right path. Even in her sadness and uncertainty, she felt lighter and happier. She tried to focus on those feelings and to let the others go. But that was easier said than done. She couldn't just turn the sadness off like a water faucet. But by the time she reached Chatham, she thought she'd cried most of the sadness out. She was starting to feel excited about seeing everyone again, especially Aidan.

Until she stepped inside her mother's home, holding Lily's cat carrier, and her eyes welled up again. Her mother pulled her in for a hug and murmured soothing words as Riley's tears spilled. She sniffled finally and smiled through the tears. "I thought I'd done all my crying in the car."

Her mother handed her a box of tissues. "Get it all out, honey. It's normal to be sad. It's been a tough week for you. Lots of change." She brushed Riley's hair off her face. "I'm so glad you're here, though. How about a cup of cinnamon tea?"

Riley nodded. Tea sounded perfect. She fed Lily while her mother made the tea and then they settled in the living room and chatted for over an hour, until it was time for her mother to head to the inn. Riley offered to go and help but her mother insisted that she stay and rest.

"You can help tomorrow at breakfast if you like. You've had a long day and an even longer week. You need your rest. I'll see you in a few hours, and we'll have a nice relaxing evening. Sound good?"

"Sounds perfect."

When her mother left for the inn, Riley picked up her laptop and after another crying jag, she finally felt like maybe she was all cried out. She decided to focus on the future and starting her consulting practice. She came up with a simple name for her business—Content Consulting—and she updated her LinkedIn profile. She didn't even put the law firm job on there as she hadn't been there a full week. Instead she listed the name of her new company and what she intended to offer for services. She listed the scope of the three projects she'd done so far and encouraged people to email her for more information. Riley knew how powerful LinkedIn could be as she'd been contacted many times over the years by recruiters hoping to entice her to interview with their clients.

She started on a website next. She wasn't a developer but she knew enough to put up a basic site on WordPress and to get a domain to link it to. And all the things she did for clients to market their businesses online, she did for her own website. She set up a blog and planned to post a series of blog posts focusing on marketing a small business and how content marketing could help. And she would ask Donna, Sean, and Morgan for testimonials she could post on her site as well as give examples of the kind of work she did for them. She was excited to apply her marketing strategies to her own enterprise and generate some new business.

By the time her mother came home, Riley was in much better spirits and had the beginnings of a website up. She could finish it over the next day or two and was excited to get started on her new business.

Her mother opened a bottle of Chardonnay and they toasted to her new venture. Her mother heated up some leftover pasta and they watched a Hallmark Christmas movie, which suited Riley's mood perfectly. She slept like a rock that night and woke feeling rested and ready to head to the inn for breakfast service.

When Franny came into the dining room she looked delighted to see Riley. Riley gave her a big hug. She was thrilled to see Franny as well. Over breakfast she told them how the closing went.

"It's all mine now! I can't believe it. I went shopping last week and found a sofa and dining room set that I love at Boston Interiors. It's being delivered next week. Beds are being delivered today, so I'm heading over there from here to wait. The cable and internet are being hooked up this afternoon. Everything else I bought online from Pottery Barn and Williams Sonoma. By next weekend, I should be all settled in."

"That's great, Franny!" Riley was happy for her. "I can't wait to see it."

"Well, you're invited to Sunday supper at my place two

weeks from now. Both of you." Franny looked at her mother, who nodded.

"We'd love to come," Riley confirmed for both of them.

When Riley returned home, she dove into working on her site again, but around lunchtime, she took a break and texted Aidan. She didn't want to wait any longer.

I'm back in town. Are you around tonight? Would love to see you.

His reply came back ten minutes later. *Just confirmed a sitter for five thirty. Where shall I meet you?*

Come to the inn. I'll be helping with the wine and cheese hour.

Perfect. Can't wait to see you.

Riley felt all warm and fuzzy as she read Aidan's last text. Her mother knew instantly who she was texting.

"Is that Aidan?"

Riley nodded. "He got a sitter and is going to come by the inn."

Her mother smiled. "And you won't be staying to help me clean up. I've got it this time."

CHAPTER FORTY-EIGHT

Riley helped her mother with the turndown service. With the two of them doing it, it didn't take long at all. She sliced up wedges of brie cheese and a nutty cheddar, and put out a dish of the honey-smothered goat cheese. Her mother offered that one all the time now as it was so popular. Riley opened several bottles of wine while her mother brought out a tray of glasses. Riley handed her mother a glass of Pinot Grigio and poured some Cabernet for herself.

Guests started streaming in and every time someone entered the room, Riley's eyes darted in that direction, hoping it was Aidan. Finally at a quarter to six, the front door opened and she saw him come in. As soon as he saw her, Aidan grinned and walked over. He pulled her in for a hug and held her tight. She handed him a glass of Cabernet and they walked to a corner of the room for some privacy.

"So, you're back," Aidan said. "For how long?" He held her gaze intently as he asked the question.

She smiled. "Indefinitely. I think I'm done with New York. The job didn't work out. I gave my notice yesterday morning and they escorted me out of the building. I ended things with Jack. His lifestyle wasn't a fit. I thought I didn't mind him working so much, but after being here for a month and around people all the time—especially seeing you again and meeting Luke—well, it just felt lonely and empty in my apartment." She paused for a moment. "I realized that what I wanted—the life I wanted—wasn't there," she said softly.

And she saw a mix of emotions reflected in Aidan's eyes. Relief followed by something else that took her breath away—love. And she felt it, too. She saw a lifetime of happiness with Aidan—friendship, kindness, happiness, and a true love.

Aidan looked around the room, took a sip of his wine, and then set it down. "Do you have to stay or could we leave now?"

Riley smiled. "I don't have to stay." She brought their glasses into the kitchen, said goodbye to her mother, and stepped outside with Aidan. He pulled her into his arms and kissed her and she melted. It had been so many years since she'd kissed Aidan and it felt like coming home. This was where she was meant to be.

Aidan pulled back and looked into her eyes and she saw wonder and a little uncertainty.

"Is this for real? You're back here for good? And you want to be with me?"

She grinned. "Yes, to all of the above. Losing my job turned out to be a blessing. Spending time here, seeing you again, and getting to know Luke. I missed you all so much when I went back to Manhattan. And I realized that Jack and I weren't right for each other."

"What will you do for work? Just help your mother or try to find a job here?" Aidan still seemed a little worried that she might change her mind.

She shook her head. "I'll work with her at the inn, but I'm also starting a consulting business." She told him about the work she'd done and the website she was building. He looked impressed and relieved to hear she had a plan.

"That sounds great. I can spread the word, too. I know

people that could use some marketing help possibly." He pulled her in for another kiss and it was a more passionate one this time and she responded in kind.

"Should we go grab some dinner? Where would you like to go?"

Riley smiled. "I don't care where we go—as long as I'm with you."

EPILOGUE

Riley checked her email on her laptop at the kitchen table while her mother put the finishing touches on a cake she was making to bring to Franny's house. It was Sunday and they were heading there for supper to see her new house for the first time. Aidan and Luke were meeting them there. Riley smiled thinking of them. Since she'd seen Aidan at the wine and cheese hour, they'd pretty much been inseparable. She'd seen him almost every day and they were taking things slow out of respect for Luke, but both knew this was it for both of them and Riley had never been happier.

Her little business was off to a good start, as well. Sean, Donna, and Morgan happily provided testimonials for her to use on her website and they'd also referred her to people they knew. Aidan had, too, and so she'd picked up a few new clients. The website had brought two in, as well, so she was busier than she'd expected to be at this point.

An email caught her eye in her inbox. It was from Alan Sherman, the CEO of the educational software company. She was curious to see what he wanted. She clicked open the email.

Riley, I hope all is well. I noticed you updated your LinkedIn profile and it looks like you've started up a consulting business. That's why I am reaching out. We are getting ready to launch

two new products and could use some additional marketing help.
Would love the chance to work together if this interests you?

He went on to describe the scope of the work and it was a big project that would provide her with steady work for several months.

Riley couldn't contain her excitement. She immediately replied back that she'd love to discuss the project and suggested a few times early in the week to chat. Her mother raised her eyebrows when Riley stopped typing and looked up. She explained about the new development and her mother looked pleased.

"Everything really does happen for a reason, honey. Now you have the chance to work with that company on your own terms."

"I know. I'm so glad I left the law firm job!" She had no regrets, other than she still had a few months left on her apartment lease. She'd let her landlord know, though, and he didn't think he would have a hard time renting it sooner. Good apartments were always in demand. So that meant she'd have to go back soon and move all her stuff out. She planned to sell her big stuff, like her sofa and bed. She didn't need any of it anymore. Her mother had said she could stay as long as she liked, but she and Aidan had talked about her moving in with him in a few months, once they got engaged. It was fast, but they were sure about their feelings and their history went back so much further.

When the cake was ready and safely packed into a big plastic container, Riley and her mother headed out to Franny's. Sean was meeting them there, too. He pulled up right behind them and Riley smiled at the look on Sean's face when he saw her mother. The two of them were so smitten with each other. That was another reason why Riley wanted to move in with Aidan sooner. She wanted to give her mother more privacy.

She knew that the two of them didn't have any plans to get

engaged or live together. Her mother had said that they were both used to living on their own and neither was ready for that big of a change. But they were together all the time and she'd never seen her mother so happy.

Aidan and Luke were already there. Franny's Joe was busy in the kitchen. He had a big pot of something simmering on the stove. Riley didn't know what it was but the smell was intoxicating. Sean's mother was already there, too. She and Franny had become fast friends.

Franny came to the door and welcomed them in. She took the cake from her mother and brought it to the kitchen. "Thank you so much, Beth. It looks amazing."

Now that everyone was there Franny gave them the grand tour. She'd chosen a seafoam-green sofa with cream-colored accent pillows for the living room. There were pretty watercolor paintings on the wall and the feeling overall was both beachy and elegant.

"I'm hosting the book club here next week," Franny said happily. She ended the tour in the kitchen, where Riley admired the white cabinets, subway tile backsplash, and the unusual blue-gray shade of the island.

"Joe loves the kitchen, as you can see," Franny said.

He looked up from his simmering pot, dipped a spoon in, and held it out for Franny to taste. She swooned. "That's delicious, Joe!"

He looked pleased but uncertain. "It doesn't need anything else, more salt or pepper?"

She shook her head. "It's perfect." She smiled and addressed everyone in the room. "Joe makes the best Bolognese sauce I have ever had."

Joe beamed happily behind her.

They ate at Franny's new dining table, which was to the right of the living room and also overlooked the ocean. The view that day was stunning as it was slightly foggy and the waves were a bit more intense than usual. They were topped with whitecaps while the misty fog swirled just above the water. In the distance, Riley could faintly hear the soothing sound of the waves crashing against the shore.

They sipped wine, and enjoyed Joe's Bolognese pasta. Franny was so right about it being the best. They all laughed and talked for hours, lingering over dessert and coffee. It was a perfect evening and Riley's heart felt full as she looked around the table and saw all these people that were so important to her—who all felt like family.

Aidan met her gaze and reached over and squeezed her hand. "Happy?" he whispered softly and she nodded.

"So happy."

She loved all of these people, especially Aidan, and wanted nothing more than a lifetime filled with days like this. For the first time ever, she was sure about her future and where she wanted to be. She leaned over and whispered in Aidan's ear, "Do you have any idea how much I love you?"

His eyes lit up and he smiled. "I think I do, and you know I feel the same way."

She did. She had no doubts about Aidan or Luke or their future as a family.

She lifted her glass in a toast and looked at Franny. "Thanks for having us here in your beautiful new home. I think we all wish you a lifetime of happiness and many more suppers like this one."

They all tapped their glasses together and said "cheers" at the same time. Riley glanced out the window and by the glow of the outside lamp, saw flurries of fat snowflakes dancing in the air. She sighed with happiness as Aidan gave her hand a squeeze and met her eyes with a warm smile. It was so good to be home.

ACKNOWLEDGMENTS

As always, thank you to my family—my sister, Jane, and nieces Taylor and Nicole, for reading early. Thank you to Cindy Tahse, for your friendship and support and story advice. Thank you to my wonderful agent, Christina Hogrebe, for all of your wisdom and support. A huge thank-you to my editor, Alexandra Sehulster, for sharing my excitement for this book and for the best suggestions to make it better. Also, thank you to the rights team at JRA—Sabrina Prestia, Maria Napolitano, Tori Clayton, Allison Hufford, and Jack McIntyre. And, to the team at St. Martin's Griffin, thank you all so much for everything that you do—Cassidy Graham, Marissa Sangiacomo, Alyssa Gammello, Brant Janeway, Kejana Ayala, Anne Marie Tallberg, Lisa Davis, Danielle Fiorella, and Meryl Levavi.

ABOUT THE AUTHOR

Alison Thompson Photography

Pamela Kelley is a *USA Today* and *Wall Street Journal* best-selling author of women's fiction, family sagas, and suspense. Readers often describe her books as feel-good reads with people you'd want as friends. She lives in a historic seaside town near Cape Cod. She has always been an avid reader of women's fiction, romance, mysteries, thrillers, and cookbooks. There's also a good chance you might get hungry when you read her books, as she is a foodie and occasionally shares a recipe or two.

Read more by
PAMELA KELLEY

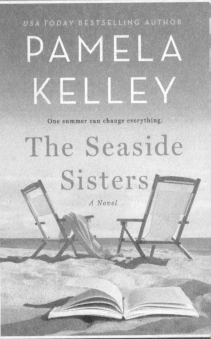

"Anyone who's ever felt the promise of
a fresh start will fall in love with Kelley."
—MARY KAY ANDREWS,
bestselling author

ST. MARTIN'S GRIFFIN